I0788156

WAXING CRESCENT

CHILDREN OF THE MOON
BOOK TWO

SERENITY RAYNE

CONTENT WARNING

Content warnings are an important element to any novel. I don't ever want to harm a reader. So for this reason, I will list the warnings here.

- Horrible monsters
- Biting and blood exchange
- Temporary death of a harem member
- Violence outside of harem
- Unchecked Alpha / Luna powers
- Blood and gore
- Ends on a cliffhanger
- Book 2 of 6

This is a paranormal why choose romance with poly elements. It's a journey of self-discovery and personal growth.

There are many situations included that are intended for MATURE audiences (18+)

Throughout this book, there are references/ instances that may trigger some individuals such as:

Difficult relationships inside the bond. Stubborn cantankerous dragons, temporary death of a harem member, emotional damage, biting, marking, mating, submission. Dealing with the discovery of dead parents. BDSM elements.

Through out the book I have linked MAPS as well as a CREATURE GUIDE in this book so you can follow along.

Author Ramblings:

Dear Readers,

It's been a hell of a ride since I started back in 2019. As I continue on my author journey, it's been a path of growth and constant learning. I feel in the last year my craft has grown from the savage and aggressive in your face FMC's to the ones that have depth and problems like the rest of us. As silly as it sounds, I call them more realistic fantasy female main characters. I feel like my girls have become more relatable over time and their worlds are more immersive than before.

It's been a hot minute since I can honestly say that I know what peace feels like. Feray lets me explore a FMC that starts from the bottom and works her way up. She's the hopeless romantic I used to be, and hope one day to be again. Her mates each have qualities I if I could squish them into one person, I'd be the happiest human ever.

Through everything I could always count on Cass my emotional support muppet and Felicia. Both always know just what to say to help get my head back on straight. I want to thank my two new beta's Becky (Kyogre) and Katherine (Pikachu). Thank you for your valuable input in the story. Can't forget the dynamic duo of Ammo and Remi, whose inappropriate antics made me laugh when I needed it most.

They say that authors leave a little piece of themselves on the page and it's true. Feray is the part of me I miss the most. The innocent romantic that sees the good in everyone. She is in love with the idea of being in love.

Feray has helped me to pick up the pieces of who I once was. Who knows, maybe one day soon I'll allow myself to love again.

Through out the book I have linked MAPS as well as a CREATURE GUIDE in this book so you can follow along.

There is always a light at the end of the tunnel if you put the work in.

Blessed be.

Serenity

READERS NOTES:

This is the second book in a new universe. There will be six books in this series with an expansion of the universe in the future after Children of the Moon concludes.

This is a why choose romance with poly elements, meaning that everyone can love each other however feels right as long as all parties consent to it. This is a slow/ med burn novel heavy on plot and major world building.

You will watch how Feray and the guys work through everything together. Each of them knows what they bring to the table and work as a team. With that being said communication becomes a topic of conversation in the poly group at a point in the story. Communication and consent are huge corner stones in a poly relationship.

Through out the book I have linked MAPS as well as a CREATURE GUIDE in this book so you can follow along.

For signed books please go to. Signed Books

If you find this book anywhere other than on a major retailers site, please email me at serenityrayneauthor@gmail.com with the link to the site.

"'Tis better to have loved and lost than never to have loved at all."
Lord Alfred Tennyson

PREVIOUSLY ON NEW MOON RISING

Feray-

My life was perfect...

I have parents that love me, and a protective sister that I love more than life itself. My parents went out, and they died in an auto accident. Fiadh took control of our situation shortly after. My long standing fear of the outside world grew exponentially. The police didn't seem to do their job and we suspect there's a coverup in progress.

We had to fight for everything we had. Some nights barely eating just to keep a roof over our heads. A savior in the form of a grumpy satyr named Philly gave us a job and a home. For the first time in a long time, we were safe. We learned how to work the bar and serve the patrons. I felt safer behind the bar, so Fi took the floor. I was in my element mixing drinks and watching the tips roll in.

School wasn't easy for me. I couldn't grasp magic if someone dropped it in my hand. I excelled in the academics like math, science, and other quantitative subjects. The magical subjects, I was barely passing. I don't like feeling like I'm failing.

Then the Ascension came, and it all made sense. My world shifted on its axis as my hands became paws. I am a wolf, not a witch. Everything I thought I knew had been a lie. Powerless, mateless and now ... truly an orphan. The hits keep coming when we go home and find it on fire. Everything we've known for the last few years is burning. Our friend was scorched and was being sent to the hospital. What's left of our effects either burned to ash or barely survived.

Because of the kindness of a stranger; we were given hope and a direction. Fi takes charge and I just follow along having my mental breakdown. I'm not a witch, I may not even be related to Fi. Over the course of a few days we find a home and a job and dare I a light at the end of the tunnel.

Mating baskets at our cottage gives me hope that I have a mate. Fi is suspicious, yet supportive through the whole thing. My mate Torben opened my eyes to a world I should have been a part of for the last of twenty-plus years. He taught me to shift and to hunt. He showed me all the things I should have known all along.

One by one, different mates make themselves known. It becomes apparent we are not what we seem. Fi obviously has magic, wild and unbridled, like she is. For the first time in forever, we search for our own answers around Briarvale.

Hints of where I may belong surface and my stomach tightens. All paths point west, then north. Fi's clues point her to an entirely different realm to start with. As a family, we put our plans together and prepare to embark on the journey of a lifetime. This is my first journey without Fi and it feels daunting. But with Torben, Khal, Easton, and Diaval at my side, I know I'm safe. I'm just scared of what we may find.

You are all caught up and prepared to embark on the next leg of the journey with me!

PROLOGUE- FERAY

As the first light of dawn creeps over the horizon, the world transforms into a tapestry of enchantment. It is a crisp fall morning in mid-September, a time when the realms of nature and fantasy converge in a breathtaking display of beauty. The air is cool and invigorating, carrying with it a promise of adventures yet to come. I stand on the porch, taking in all the changes that are happening around me. I'm going to miss this place.

The trees, resplendent in their ancient glory, stand tall and proud, their branches swaying in a graceful dance. Leaves of every imaginable hue adorn the trees, a testament to the magic coursing through their veins. The leaves change as if each one is a painter's brush dipped in the palette of the gods. The emerald greens of summer surrender to the fiery reds, the sun-kissed oranges, and the golden yellows of autumn. *The seasons' changes seem to be parallel to my own.*

With a gentle breeze, the leaves take flight, descending in a graceful spiral. Each leaf is a miniature work of art, adorned with intricate patterns that whisper secrets of the world beyond. Some leaves glow with an ethereal luminescence, while others shimmer with iridescent hues that defy description. They dance and twirl in the air, creating a symphony of colors, as if the very essence of the forest has decided to celebrate the start of our journey. The changing of the season marks the beginning of our journey. *I've never left home before. If I'm honest with myself, I'm scared.*

Not only did the scenery change, but there was also a noticeable shift in temperature. The cool breeze bears a touch of magic, as it brushes against my skin. The wind carries a sense of anticipation, as if the very earth is preparing for the shift in seasons. The chill in the air is no longer merely a reminder of winter's approach; it is a reminder of the journey that lies before me. I get to follow in the footsteps of my ancestors. The journey to the north won't be without its issues, but with my mates by my side, I'm sure we'll be alright. It's almost as if we are playing a gigantic game of where's Waldo, except in this case Waldo represents my parents and my past.

Animals of our woods stir from their slumber, sensing the shift in the seasons. Elusive creatures emerge from hidden groves, their fur, and feathers mirroring the colors of the falling leaves.

In this moment, the line between reality and fantasy blur. It is a time when one can believe in the impossible, when the ordinary world gives way to the extraordinary. Stepping into the crisp fall morning in mid-September is like entering a gateway to another world, where nature and magic coexist in a dance of pure enchantment. Every falling leaf serves as a gentle reminder that the fantastical is just as tangible as the familiar. Living in the woods for the change of the seasons is a far different experience than living over Philly's bar. Sighing, I stare out at the woods I have called home since the fire at Philly's, and I know deep in my heart I'm going to miss it.

Torben and Tiernan left early this morning to make sure the last of the preparations for their businesses was complete. I can only assume that's where the twins and the ancients are as well. Revelin has his ass parked at the edge of the woods, looking to be in deep meditation.

Fiadh is sleeping in this morning. She and the guys were up late last night getting the last little things in order while I spent time with Torben's sleuth. Mostly snuggled in close with his mom, venting my anxiety over the trip. His mother held me and ran her fingers through my hair, trying to settle my nerves over being separated from my sister for the first time ever.

Stepping back inside the cabin, I draw in a deep breath, then look around as if seeing the place for the first time. The early morning sun gently filters through the curtains, casting a warm, golden glow into the cozy kitchen. To my surprise, I find Tiernan at the stove, preparing breakfast. He must have concluded his business faster than expected. The air is filled with the inviting aroma of fresh coffee and a tantalizing mix of breakfast foods. It is a scene that promises a delightful start to the day.

The coffee machine gurgles, its rich earthy scent filling the air as it brews a fresh pot of dark roast coffee. The bubbling and hissing of the hot water mixing with the coffee grounds adds a comforting rhythm to the morning.

Our wooden table is adorned with a checkered tablecloth and is set for breakfast. Plates and utensils are neatly arranged, waiting to be used. The smell of buttery croissants and crispy bacon waft through the air, tempting anyone nearby to indulge in a hearty meal.

The sizzle of eggs in a hot skillet adds a harmonious note to the breakfast symphony. As the eggs cook, their aroma mingles with the savory fragrance of sauteed mushrooms and onions. It is a medley of scents that promises a flavorful morning feast.

"Welcome home Tiernan." I step around the island and press my cheek to his in greeting. A soft purr escapes his lips, and he chuckles.

"Thanks, it feels weird that today is the last morning we'll be having breakfast here for a while." His words hit hard in my heart as my thoughts about separating from my sister spiral.

"Yeah." I walk away to curl up in my favorite chair and watch him cook. "I've never been apart from Fiadh. I'm scared." As I admit to being afraid, Revelin walks in and shakes his head.

"Fluffy, whatever this Luna gift is of yours can definitely keep you safe. You have powerful mates to protect you that won't leave your side." He flashes his cocky rockstar smile at me and I roll my eyes.

Pausing, I hold a finger up and then point to my ear, then down the hallway. Revelin nods and we silently decide to shelve this conversation for later. The slap of Fiadh's feet hitting the floor prompts me to move and grab the last of her energy tonics from the fridge and set them with a glass of ice on the counter. Tiernan plates food as his phone goes off. "Torben is on his way back and the others should be here within the hour to load the car and for everyone to leave."

He doesn't look up to see how the thought of leaving affects me. A soft whine escapes my lips, and I feel my wolf bristle under the surface. Even though she knows we need to go, she's reluctant. Fiadh finally emerges and looks like she's ready to kick ass and take names as she heads to the counter to grab her caffeine of choice.

"Where's everyone else?" She hazards a glance around the room, then finally looks at me and her expression falls.

"Oh Fer…" She closes the distance between us, and I let go of the heartache I was feeling and let several tears escape. "It's not going to be forever…" she says softly near my ear as she strokes my hair.

"I know, it's…" Drawing in a deep breath, I try to steady my quivering bottom lip. "We've never been apart for more than a night." Fiadh pulls back and forces a smile.

"We both have journeys we need to complete. You need to find out why your fur is almost white. And I need to know why I have multiple branches of magic and glow like a snapped glow stick at a rave." She laughs a little at her own expense and I smile slightly. "What if you're wolven royalty and can put Prince fancy pants in his place?" She tilts her head to the side, and she finally gets me to laugh.

"That would be funny."

"No, it wouldn't." Revelin chimes in as he waves a breakfast roll in our direction.

"No, what wouldn't?" Torben says as he opens the door, returning home from handling his final preparations. With him, Easton, Diaval, and Dezi enter the house behind him. The three ancients take their time looking around the interior before heading to the nook in the corner.

"If my sister ends up being wolven royalty and outranks Revelin." Fiadh snarks. The fae in question sticks his tongue out at Fiadh behind her back.

Rolling my eyes, I move to hug Torben and settle down, feeling all my stress melt away in his embrace. "Looks like we're just missing the twins."

"You mean the twins with the twins…" Fiadh says as she kills off her first energy tonic before going for the second one.

"Do I even want to know, little wolf?" Torben rumbles, looking down at me.

Standing up on my tiptoes, I whisper in his ear that the twins have two penises a piece. His eyebrows shoot up and he cocks his head off to the side. "That explains why he was so hesitant about mating with you."

"Nuh uh, big guy, those two are poisonous. That's why…" Fiadh helpfully supplies as she smiles and touches her bite mark.

Torben double blinks, looking down at me, then over at my sister. He shakes his head and walks over to the counter, leaving me looking at the gathered ancients.

"You have a basilisk, a wyrm black dragon and a phoenix in your family group, Bubbles." Dezi reaches out and takes my hand in his. It's odd for him since he normally doesn't do physical contact with me. "You are safer now than you have ever been in your life, especially with your Kodiak mate. Listen to Diaval's wisdom. Follow Easton's directions, he's lived a thousand lives. And don't contain the Basilisk's rage, he's damn near indestructible." Dezi offers his sage advice and leaves me speechless.

My eyes flitter over to Diaval and he's adjusting his tie, showing how uncomfortable he is. Easton is openly staring at me. Fingers snapping drags me out of my happy bubble to look over at my sister. "We have to figure out how we are going to keep in touch between the realms. We already know cell service sucks balls." Fiadh cracks open her second energy drink and knocks half of it back.

Diaval mutters under his breath about roasted Fae being outlawed as he passes me, heading towards the food. Fi's question prompts me to look over at Revelin again. His eyes gleam mischievously and then he snaps his fingers and a small pixie pops into existence. She flutters close to Revelin's ear, and he laughs. "Oh no, you're going to watch over Fluffy." He waves his hand over in my direction and she flitters in front of me.

She's about six inches tall and has liberty spikes in a myriad of colors on the top of her head. She's in head-to-toe leather and I smile at her. "Hi, I'm Feray." I raise my hand palm up and offer her a place to land.

"Thoughtful this one is, I like. I'm Rowenna. Or Ro. Not row row your boat." She turns and glares at Revelin, and he winces.

I try to cover my mouth and hide the laughter from her firing back at the prince. "So, I'm guessing she can just pop up wherever you are and pass messages?" I tilt my head and look down at Ro and she nods, looking at me, agreeing with my statement.

"More or less, that is correct. I can summon her and send her back to you at will," Revelin says as he types away on his phone. "Stupid organizers ... it's plus four..." He yells at his phone as he dials whoever sent him the message and steps outside.

"What's got Prince picky pants in a tizzy?" Khol and Khal enter just after Revelin steps outside. We can clearly hear him yelling at someone about the type of lights for the tour.

"Tour shit," Fi offers before looking over at the twins. "Make sure to take pictures of everything so we don't forget anything." Khol mutters, *yes boss* before heading to the hidden room.

Khal stops over by me and kisses me softly. "Go spend time with your sister before we leave." He looks down at the Pixie and she leaps up onto my shoulder and hides under my hair. "Hitchhiker?" He tilts his head looking at where the pixie went to hide.

"She's how we're going to keep in touch between the realms in case the phones stop working. This is Ro. Ro, this is my mate Khal." I attempt to do introductions. Out of the corner of my eye, I see her small hand stick out of my hair and wave at Khal.

"Pleasure's all mine." He whispers, then kisses my cheek. "I better go help Khol before he has a fit. I'll grab the scrolls and books we need for the trip." Nodding, I watch him go before I sit next to my sister.

Ro comes out of hiding and jumps onto the table. "Call me when you need me." With a wave of her little hand, she poofs out of existence.

Shaking my head, I really look at Fi now. The way her brows are pinched in the center shows the stress she's trying to hide. "Rev and I went over where he thinks the items I need are in the faerie. His tour comes within several miles of where we need to go." Fi explains their route using a piece of paper and a pencil that Tiernan supplies her with.

Sighing, I pull my phone out and show her the map program and the route to Blackmoor. "According to the Sphinx, I have relatives in Blackmoor. They may know where my parents are. So, we're going to head there first and hope for the best." Biting my bottom lip, I study the serious face my sister is making.

"Seems like a solid plan." She nods and smiles. "The only part about this entire adventure is that I can't be there to keep you safe." Her eyes betray her. There's fear and concern behind her gaze.

Before she can utter another word, Tiernan comes up behind her and presses his chest against her back. "Knuckles, she has two mates that can wield fire, one that can poison or turn beings to stone and the fourth has the strength of at least ten men. His people are known for being berserkers in battle. Don't underestimate the Kodiak. He may be all peace and snuggles with Fer, but don't let that fool you. He will kill to protect what's his."

Glancing over behind Tiernan, I see Torben freeze and nod, agreeing with his statement. My giant teddy bear would raze the earth for me, and I know it. Khal already said he would turn the world to stone if it meant keeping me safe.

"Just remember Fer, the hidden wolf clans are hidden for a reason. They won't take kindly to strangers entering their territory. You may have to shift and fight." He glances over his shoulder at Torben. "We've already talked. Torben is going to start your fight training on the road. That should put Knuckles' mind at ease so that you will know how to defend yourself in your fur." He pats Fi on the shoulder and goes to the pile of bags and starts carrying some outside.

The three ancients are gathered in the corner, whispers of their plans to barter for information along the way drifts to me. "This is it, huh?" The twins come out with items from our hidden room and move through the house to go outside to finish packing for the trip. Fear, anxiety, and excitement are at war within me. I'm afraid and anxious to be separated from my sister for this long. Hell, we do not know how long this quest will take us.

"Yeah, I get to wrangle this bunch." She motions to her mates and a small smile creeps across her lips. She doesn't act like it, but she loves them in her own way. Maybe not Dezi yet, but the mosquito is slowly wearing her down.

My gaze falls on Khal and Torben, and my heart is ready to explode with how much I love them already. Feeling eyes upon me, I see Easton glancing up from time to time, watching me. My hand absently drifts up and touches the amulet that holds his feather. It's warm to the touch and glows when it's in contact with my skin. He's said in his own way that he knows he's mine. He has a few societal hang ups he needs to work through.

"Give him time, little wolf." Torben stops next to me and whispers in my ear before kissing my cheek. He offers me a gentle smile and I nod, looking at him. Torben winks as he walks off, carrying the last of our bags out to the car.

Fi leans in and hugs me briefly and smiles, looking at me. "He's good to you. They both are." She motions to Khal, who's packing my favorite snacks.

"Yeah, for once, things actually went well for us. Your mates are great, too." I laugh to myself, Out of my sister's mates. I'm closest to her snow leopard mate, Tiernan.

"Yeah, the cat and dog are always scheming together. What happened to cats hating dogs?" Fi yells, trying not to laugh.

Arching a brow, I look shocked at my sister. "You want me to hate your mates? That doesn't make any sense Princess Craft Herpes..." At the mention of her glitter explosions, Fi chases me around the island. I'm barely jogging and she's giving it her all. *Shifter stamina for the win.* Finally, the time I've dreaded is upon us when Revelin motions for us to head outside. Instead of stopping, I run past him and out into the yard.

In the corner of the yard blocking the trail I would normally take to the field Tiernan and I hunt in is a portal. Not just any portal, the one my sister is going to walk through. The twinkling of the portal is a captivating and mesmerizing phenomenon that beckons travelers from our world to the mystical and enchanting Fae realm. Its ethereal qualities and enchanting allure are nothing short of extraordinary. The portal's surface is a radiant tapestry of light and luminescence. Upon closer examination, I realize that it's not just a singular glow but an intricate mosaic of countless tiny, shimmering lights. These lights are reminiscent of fireflies on a warm summer night, yet they possess an other-worldly quality, twinkling with a sense of purpose. Some blink like stars, while others flow and weave in mesmerizing patterns, creating an ever-shifting kaleidoscope of colors that defies description.

"Wow..." I stare, amazed at what I'm seeing, and soon my sister grips my hand, staring right along with me. Glancing over at her, I chuckle. "Your personal rave is more intense than this." Fi slaps my arm and I see reality sink in.

"Fer it's time..." Her normally strong voice wavers as she squeezes my hand harder.

I pull Fi to me, hugging her tightly to me and bury my nose in her hair to memorize her scent. "I'm gonna miss you." Sniffling, I tremble in her arms as she reluctantly pulls away.

"We will find a way to be together for the holidays. Or some prince will be sleeping alone." She glares over her shoulder at Revelin.

"Holidays are on the list..." Revelin types furiously on his phone and then smiles. I can almost bet that he just added reminders for the holidays so we can try to make it.

Tiernan and Khol step through the portal, followed by Dezi. Revelin is standing at the entrance waiting for Fi as the guys pull me back towards the blacked out armored car that is apparently Khal's. I'm fighting the tears that want to fall as I watch my sister reach out and take Revelin's hand. "Be safe, Fluffy ... Remember, I am only a Pixie away." Revelin smiles as he looks at Fi.

"I love you Fer!"

"Love you more!" No sooner are the words out of my mouth Revelin pulls my sister into the Faerie and with a snap his fingers shuts the portal.

I stand there stunned for several moments before Torben wraps his arms around me and guides me to the car. Once inside, Khal is in the driver's seat with Diaval up front with him. Easton is in the back seat and as soon as Torben slides in, he pulls me into his lap. His bear rumbles to me, trying to soothe my frayed nerves.

Khal starts the car, and we head down the long driveway. The rustic dirt road winds through the serene forest, departing from the comfort of our forest home. The path is lined with towering trees, their leaves forming a natural canopy overhead. Sunlight filters through the leaves, dappling the road with specks of gold. The earth is covered in a carpet of fallen leaves and twigs as we embark on our journey. *Blackmoor, here we come.*

CHAPTER 1

FERAY

I WATCH MY HOME GRADUALLY FADE AWAY IN THE REARVIEW MIRROR. The familiar sights and sounds of my little slice of heaven become smaller and more distant with each passing moment. The engine hums softly, and the road stretches out before us, leading into the heart of an old growth forest.

The forest surrounds us with towering trees, their branches forming a natural canopy overhead. Sunlight filters through the leaves, casting dappled shadows on the road ahead. The air is filled with the earthy scent of moss and the sweet fragrance of wildflowers. Birds sing their melodic tunes, creating a soothing symphony that accompanies us on our journey.

As we drive deeper into the forest, the ancient trees stand like silent sentinels, their gnarled roots, and massive trunks a testament to the passage of time. The road winds its way through the forest, curving gently and revealing glimpses of hidden streams and clearings. Watching the cabin I've come to call home fade into the distance is bittersweet. But it also marks the beginning of a journey into my past, one that I have no clue where it will lead us.

It's hard to say good-bye to Fi and the log cabin we've come to call home.

When I can finally pull my eyes away from watching where we have come from, I look at the puzzle before me. The doctor and the banker, two ancient shifters that are my mates. Easton is a phoenix and who knows how long he's lived. Every time he resurrects, he becomes young again. That could be a blessing and a curse all the same. At least that's what the one book I had from school said. So far, half of what the books have told us is true, the other half fiction. Socially, the book said they are mostly loners and mate for life like wolves. There's no notation if there's any polyamory in their society. From what I can piece together, it doesn't happen with their people.

That brings me to Diaval. He puzzles me more than Easton does. Easton at least came out and said he needs time. Diaval the grumpy dragon hasn't said squat to me about what I am to him. He gave me a coin that scares the shit out of any that see it in my possession. Khal told me he noticed Diaval had packed the mug that I gave him, so it must mean something to him. The book said that dragons live in flights and once upon a time the females outnumbered the males. Now, like with most shifters, it's the males that outnumber the females.

I remain snuggled in Torben's arms. He runs his fingers through my hair as I look at Easton since he's in the back seat with us. Just as we get out of the forest and on the open road, Diaval huffs. "Easton, you better drive. Her anxiety is driving my dragon insane." Khal's tongue flicks out, and he nods and pulls over.

The guys switch positions, and Khal pulls my feet into his lap and starts massaging my arches. He kneads and strokes my feet, targeting various pressure points. The sensation is a delightful mix of gentle pressure and soothing strokes. I can feel the tension in my feet slowly melting away as his fingers work their magic.

Khal uses his thumbs to apply targeted pressure on specific points, and I feel a subtle sense of relief and balance spreading through my body. Time seems to slow down during a foot massage, and I become acutely aware of the sensations in my feet. The warmth, the pressure, and the skilled touch all combine to create a sense of comfort and tranquility. Any stress or tension that I was carrying with me gradually fades away.

"Fi will be fine. She's well-guarded and her mates will keep her safe." Khal's tone is warm and inviting. It soothes the rough edges of my soul. His eyes hold a softness only meant for me as he allows a gentle smile to grace his lips. The way he's looking at me, I know something is bothering him. He suddenly pulls out his phone and glances at it for a moment.

Then I realize, he's worried too. He's separated from his twin, and who knows if that's ever happened before? "Khol is fine too, you know." I offer as I press my forehead against Torben's neck. I extend a hand out to him and he grips it and nods slowly. My deadly basilisk is a big softie under it all.

"Heh, yeah. Just like you and Fi. Khol and I haven't really been separated from each other for long. Maybe a day or two at most." He shrugs his shoulders and I know admitting to his own anxiety has made me feel better. He releases my hand and returns to massaging my arches.

There's a clearing of a throat from the front seat and I lift my head up to look at who's about to speak. "A very long time ago, white wolves were very common in Briarvale. They used to migrate to the south into the warmer climates to give birth then head north for the winter following the big game animals they love to hunt." Diaval's voice resonates with a deep, seductive allure that seems to wrap itself around every word he utters. As he speaks, his words flow like molten silk, each syllable carrying a rich, velvety texture that sends shivers down my spine. There is a certain confidence in his voice. His words are measured and deliberate, each one chosen with care to maximize their impact. It is rare to hear him say more than a short sentence. I sit up to pay better attention.

"We used to migrate? Why would we migrate? That almost doesn't make sense. How do you know?" Sliding off Torben's lap, I move to sit in the center seat and lean forward so I can get closer to Diaval, drawn to him like a moth to a flame. "Did you get to witness the migrations?" Other than Easton, I don't think anyone knows Diaval's true age, only that because of a slip of the tongue we know he's a wyrm dragon. An ancient among ancients when it comes to dragons.

Diaval and Easton look at each other, and then it's Easton that answers. "Everything is relative. We've lived many lives over the eons. Time is not a valid quantifier." He looks at me in the rearview mirror and I sit back and stare into his eyes. Flames seem to flicker in his iris for a moment then vanish just as fast as they appeared.

"Long ago, before we settled into villages and towns, we lived as our animals more than our human forms. In a way, it was better. Our animals don't have the hang ups that society has placed on us when it comes to taking mates." Easton says and lets out a sigh. He's at war with himself over the pull of the mate bond between us. I get it. He was raised to believe he would have his mate all to himself. Here I am with four mates, three more than he was expecting.

"Let's get back on course, shall we?" Diaval saves Easton from the question that was on the tip of my tongue. "The wolves segregated themselves based on build and coat color. The timber wolves took to the dense forests and the grassy plains because they would blend in better." He turns slightly in his seat, giving me a little more than just his side profile. "The wolves whose coats are more black or dark gray took over the shadow mount. Or, as it's referred to now, as the base of the mountains and the caverns within."

I reach down and pull out the book on the area and look at the map for the region we live in. "White wolves are able to endure the cold better than any other subspecies of wolf. White wolves are otherwise known as arctic wolves and have far more layers to their fur than the others. Witches used to hunt the arctic wolves for their fur, thinking that is why they can endure the cold." Diaval laughs as he shakes his head. "Only the pure white females would be Luna's, leaders of their kind, blessed with gifts from Gaia herself to calm and control the masses." He arches a brow at me, and it makes sense why I was able to get everyone to settle down.

"But it didn't work on you and Easton."

"You noticed that, huh?" Diaval's deep chuckles sends a shiver of anticipation through me.

"Well, yeah everyone else sat down and you two just stared at me."

"It won't work on Mythics. Your true power lies with the pack. The more members in your pack, the stronger the Luna. The stronger the Luna, the stronger the gifts." Diaval stops talking for a moment and looks over at Easton.

"We have a long trip ahead of us. There are several towns that we will pass through on our way to Blackmoor." Easton motions to Diaval and he pulls a different map out and passes it back to us.

Scooting back, I take the map with me and look at it closely. To the far north there's snow as far as the eye can see. Before the tundra there're jagged mountains with a Mordor style spire sticking up in the middle.

"That's where my people come from." Khal points to the horizon and what looks more like mountains of death than a place to enjoy growing up.

"It doesn't look like a fun place to visit." I wince, saying my thoughts out loud.

"Definitely not. Unfortunately, there's only one way to get to the route we need, and that's passing through Norburg. Norburg is a town of thugs and venomous inhabitants." Khal says and looks up at Easton. "If we don't have to stop, let's not. It wouldn't be safe for Feray." The way Khal says that makes a whine escape my lips and Easton's eyes whip up to look at me in the rearview.

"Noted, we'll pass through and nothing more unless we need fuel." Diaval says and then looks back at us. "Have you seen the ocean, Feray?"

"What difference does that make?" I tilt my head to the side, puzzled by his question.

"Just answer the question and don't be as infuriating as your sister." Diaval's tone turns to a rich honey, and I feel like I'm falling under a spell bewitched by him.

"I've never left Briarvale." I draw in an exaggerated breath and look down at my hands as I play with the hem of my shirt. "Fi said it wasn't safe. We've always suspected our parents' deaths weren't an accident. So, I've never been much of anywhere." Biting my bottom lip, I turn to fidget with a fuzzy on Torben's shirt to distract myself.

"Then it's settled. We'll cut through Norburg and head towards Vasserdell. It's a village on the coast. I want you to see the ocean." How Diaval said that with such finality it almost made me nervous. But in another sense, it's made the butterflies in my stomach flitter around. He wants to take me to the ocean for the first time.

"Do you have questions about the packs Feray?" Diaval turns back to look forward as he asks the question.

"If I am a natural born Luna, is there anyone that I bow to?" Not being raised in a pack has its disadvantages.

"The other wolves will try to force their dominance on you. Now, your human side is soft and gentle. But your wolf, she will not tolerate someone less than herself trying to dominate her. If it's a challenge of wills, let her take the wheel and do what is needed." Diaval's statement makes me sit up and turn to look at Torben.

"What he means is your wolf knows what is needed to keep you safe. So, when she fights you for control, let her have it. Just like with my bear, if the situation gets dangerous, I give myself over to him." Torben presses a kiss to my forehead.

"So, if she doesn't like something, or someone is trying to force us to do something, let her have control?" I tilt my head, looking at Torben, then to the review mirror to look into Easton's eyes.

"For the most part, yes," Diaval answers. "Within reason, of course." He turns in his seat to look at me and I watch his eyes become his dragon's for the briefest of moments.

I nod at him, then snuggle back against Torben. I'm so used to Fi handling all the trouble that I'm not sure if I can do it. Then again, she started some of the trouble sometimes. There's a mix of excitement and trepidation boiling within me. I'm an emotional paradox at the moment. As much as I want to know who I am, I'm afraid of being away from Fi.

Pulling my arms close to my body, I press my forehead against Torben's neck, using his beard to help hide me. Diaval was smart, putting my two bonded mates back here with me. Their presence soothes me, yet knowing the mythics in the car are also mine is a comfort in itself. They will burn the earth to ash to protect me. At least that's what my wolf tells me.

CHAPTER 2

TORBEN

My sweet little mate is a ball of anxiety and fear, and I can't fix it. After she asked her questions, she curled back up into a ball, using me as a pillow. *I don't mind it.* But I know being away from Fi is going to have repercussions we can't anticipate. Her breathing slows, and I feel her mouth pop open as her hand slides down my chest to rest at my hip. My little wolf has stressed herself out enough that she's fallen asleep.

"Is she okay?" Khal whispers as he stops massaging her feet.

Easton's eyes keep jumping from the road and up to the rearview. "Yes, and no. They have hammered the fear of what's out there into her for so long that leaving her territory is terrifying for her." Banding my arm tighter around her, I listen to her breathing. It's still slow and steady. Her body has become pliant in my arms. Thankfully, she can rest for a while in peace, knowing I will protect her with everything that I am.

"I don't know what was worse for her. The way the witches treated them from what I was told, or the fear of not knowing who killed Fi's parents." Khal mentions as he types on his phone absently.

"Neither is good," Easton states, and I hear how the steering wheel creaks under the pressure of his grip.

"Precisely, throw in she only recently has been able to access her wolf. It's a recipe for disaster." Diaval says as he looks back at our sleeping mate. "Damn witches sticking their noses where it doesn't belong. She would have been better off if she was raised with her own kind."

"Do you understand what you are saying? We may never have met our mate if that happened." I whisper yell at Diaval.

"I understand that. Unlike you, I am blessed with long years." Diaval shuts up at that moment and turns back to face the road.

"The elephant in the room is why did they hide a bound wolf in a witch family?" Easton offers as he glances up at the rearview mirror. Murmurs of agreement echo softly within the car. None of us can begin to comprehend why that was done.

"We should probably find a place to rest for tonight. There's an inn just outside of Norburg. It looks like it's named the Claw and Fang Inn." I'm holding the map with my free hand while the other holds Feray securely to my chest.

"I wouldn't suggest that one. It's owned by my people, and if we are trying to remain under the radar, we should skip it." Khal keeps texting someone and I'm becoming more curious the longer it goes on.

"I agree, there's a dragon owned inn called the Crossroads. Not horribly far from Thornford. It would be in the best interest of everyone to stop there. A dragon's silence can be bought." Diaval's tone leaves no room for argument.

Apparently how he said it woke Feray up, and she nuzzles my neck. "Where are we?" She slowly sits up and looks around after rubbing her eyes.

"We've got about another thirty minutes until we are out of the Briarvale forest." Easton offers gently. Feray nods and accepts the water that Diaval passes back to her.

"Ah ha!" Khal says then looks up at us. "My informants just got back to me about Blackmoor. It's predominantly wolves with very few other species in the town." He scrolls further and stops, then looks up. "So apparently Roman is the Blackmoor Alpha and Marcus from the council is from Dunnam, interestingly enough." Khal says and Fer turns to face him.

"That is interesting. Do you think they know more than they are letting on?" Feray asks.

"It definitely would make more sense as to why they were pointing you in a certain direction." Torben states.

"What we really have to question is how many people on the council actually know who you are, and where you come from. Versus those that are willing to give us the information that we need." Khal says.

There's a silence that hangs over the car for several beats too long that makes the hackles on the back of my neck stand on edge. I look back up front and I see that both ancients seem to be in conversation with each other. It's kind of freaky how they can do that without talking or without being in a pack or a bond together. Their eyes flicker randomly to the color of their beast before Diaval turns to look at us. He takes several moments to gather his thoughts. "It wouldn't be the first time that the council or the local packs manipulated things."

Khal's phone beeps several more times as messages come in from who knows where. His eyes fly over the text on the screen, and he fires back a message almost immediately. "Blackmoor, according to my sources, is surrounded eighty percent by mountains. There are several tunnels through caves that would lead out into the wilderness through the different parts of the mountains." He scrolls through the message a little further.

"There's been several uprisings in Blackmoor which has prompted the alpha to return ahead of schedule. According to my source, he's had several younger males attempting to take the mantle of alpha from him." Khal scrolls further, then stops. "Rumor has it, it's happening across all the wolf packs. The younger generation is not thrilled with the archaic ideals." He looks up and around at all of us.

Easton clears his throat. "There has been an issue for the past hundred years that fewer females are being born. At one point, they highly encouraged it for males to be born because of the wars going on between the different species. Now, because of that selective breeding, there are fewer females to help continue on with the population."

His eyes look up into the rear-view mirror and I see Feray look back at him and nod slowly. "Well, that explains why some of us have more than one mate." She looks down and starts fiddling with the hem of her shirt again.

I rest my hand between her shoulder blades and give them a gentle rub. "My people have always birthed more males than females. It has been a common practice amongst the bears for a female to have multiple mates. Not only distributes the workload within the family. It provides greater financial stability and more to provide for the children in the family. All the work with raising the children doesn't fall on just the female when there are multiple males in the house." I offer a bit of my experience of living in my sleuth.

Khal nods along and then laughs. "With my people, it's customary for the female to choose anywhere from three to five males to be in her nest. She may not reproduce with all of them, but she has the choice of the best genetics to provide her with offspring." He shrugs and has the decency to look embarrassed.

Diaval listens and nods along. "Only the strongest females of the flights are ever chosen to produce children. I mean granted, if a mated pair wants one child, it's not forbidden. But there's always two or three females that are the strongest that give birth to multiple offspring each time they're pregnant. They have the choice of the strongest males amongst us." He smirks a little and shakes his head. "With me having my shining personality, I was never a consideration." The bastard smirks at us and then laughs a little.

"You're not that horrible. You can be a real grump sometimes and detached. But I can't see you being that dreadful." Feray says as she looks up at him.

"That could just be the mate bond talking little one." He smiles ever so briefly and then looks back at her. "I will take the compliment and I appreciate it." He reaches up and adjusts his tie like he usually does when he's uncomfortable before looking back at the rest of us. "Torben, you have the contact for the alpha of Blackmoor, correct?"

"Yes, I do." I pull my phone back out and scroll to his contact information and bring it up.

"Send him a message that we're gonna need accommodations for five when we arrive, and that we would like to discuss pertinent matters in relation to our mate." Diaval turns even more to watch as I type out the message.

I turn my phone back to Diaval and show him the message. The message was written down verbatim. "Perfect, send it." I press the button on my phone and off goes the message to Roman.

The car falls into silence as we listen to the crunch of the gravel underneath the tires. As we had decided earlier, we only pass through Norburg. The quaint little town is dark and dreary, lacking any signs of bright colors or frivolity. I watch Khal as he's on high alert, looking around all sides of the car as we pass through the village. No sooner do we get out the other side does he finally sighs a breath of relief and slumps back into his chair, relaxing.

"I hate going through there." He mutters to himself and goes back to typing on his phone. "Diaval, you were correct. Bypassing the Claw and Fang inn is a very good idea. According to my source, there's several meetings tonight that we should not be a part of."

Looking up, Diaval nods along and then taps his temple. "Sometimes the ancients know what's best, isn't that true?" Feray glances between Diaval and Khal and then back over at me before turning and looking out the window.

"So, ultimately, we're ending up in Blackmoor." Feray says as she climbs onto my lap again to watch out the window.

"To start with, yes." I press a kiss to her temple as she uses me as her personal chair.

"There are at least two other places to look after Blackmoor. Dunnum and Crescent Valley are old wolven strongholds. Crescent Valley is going to be difficult to get into. Very few know where the entrance is." Easton offers and his statement makes Feray sit up and lean over the driver's seat.

"Can't you and Diaval fly us there?" Feray's innocent question almost chokes Diaval, and Easton's eyebrows shoot up so high I thought they would get permanently stuck in his hairline.

"Well, umm…" Easton fumbles his words and Diaval coughs to clear his throat.

"There are things about flying with our shifts you must know." Diaval takes a deep breath and I already know where he's going to go with it. "For my kind it's called a mating flight." He fidgets with his tie again and looks around. "With you not being a dragon, it changes things. It makes the flight hold more meaning."

A hushed *oh* escapes Feray's lips, and she scoots back, climbing into my lap once more.

Easton seems uneasy as he drives, and Diaval keeps staring at him. "Let's table that discussion for later, shall we? For now, lets locate the information we need and take it from there." Diaval quickly changes the focus from flying and goes back to the task at hand.

My phone dings again, and I struggle to get it out of my pocket. "Roman says he will take us to dinner at the steak and ale house in Blackmoor if we have time." I read further down the message. It contains the address of the restaurant and the address of the Inn we will stay at when we get there. I message him back about the several detours we have planned along the way and that I would contact him when we are getting close.

Feray is lying on her side holding a map in her hand looking at where we are in relation to where we need to be. Her fingertips trace the path that we should follow. Her fingers freeze over the Ferryman's bridge, and she just stares at it. It's the same bridge her parents died on.

Easton stops the car and he and Diaval switch seats, allowing Diaval to take over driving for a while. With all the danger that is possible around us, it's better to have a fresh set of eyes behind the wheel. Easton turns to sit sideways in the seat, to look back and watch Feray as she looks over the map. She's so focused on the destination she doesn't realize that Easton is watching her like a bear with honey.

CHAPTER 3
DIAVAL

Sitting in the passenger seat, I could observe my old friend battling his bird over his feelings for the wolf. He's hanging on her every word, listening intently. This is exactly why I didn't want a mate. You forget yourself and slowly your world becomes about them.

The last few months have brought about some terrifying changes in my behavior. Where I once would rarely go out and enjoy a drink at the bar after a while, I found myself there frequently. Especially the nights that little siren was working.

Easton is battling himself and the feelings that his phoenix wishes to pursue. It's hard as a mythic to allow oneself to bond to somebody with so few years. I believe is the most troublesome part of all of this for him, even though we would share our life-span with her. If I'm being honest with myself, the hardest part for me is accepting the others within her bond.

Easton's twitchiness is increasing almost exponentially, and this will not bode well for the safety of our passengers. I offer for us to pull over and switch out so that way we would definitely arrive at our destination safely. Quickly he switches places with me and we're back on the road again. Out of the corner of my eye I see that Eastons turned and is watching her.

I can't lie to myself any further as much as I try to deny it. I have feelings for the little she wolf in the back seat. My eyes glance up to the rearview mirror again just to make sure that she's okay. She's curled up tightly, resting on top of her bear mate with her hands pulled against her chest, facing the front of the car.

I find myself starting to develop a little bit of jealousy. It's a feeling I have never experienced in my entire existence. The pull and need within and yet the anger that someone else is holding her. The man that I am has not come to terms with the idea that we must share our mate. Even worse, that she isn't a dragon like us.

She can't fly ... My dragon supplies.

Rolling my eyes, I attempt to focus on the road ahead until I notice movement to my right. And then it's apparent to me as I look over at Easton that he is also jealous that the bear gets to hold her. As much as my dragon is urging me to go to her, it may not be safe for her. To live as long as I have, I have enemies lurking in the shadows that may try to use her against me. Without a shadow of a doubt, they would use my soft skinned mate against me, knowing full well I would give them anything to keep her safe. Huffing out a sigh, I try to remember the safe route to the ocean.

She's never been anywhere. My dragon reminds me as I search my memory for sights to take her to see.

Norburg was as dark as I remembered it being. The dangerous sides of our communities tends to congregate here. The shops are fronts for money laundering and drug dealing for this part of the continent. Khal's people run most of the legal and illegal drug trade for the area. He pulled his hood up over his head and covered his face until we were out of the main part of town. He had explained to me earlier that it was safer if the citizens of Norburg didn't know he was leaving the area. His brief explanation said he and his brother kept the rest of the group in line. If rumors were to get out that they were gone. All hell might break loose.

We pass through some of the sketchy parts of the woods after leaving Norburg. Dark shadows of all different sizes moved deep within the tree line, and I took his warning seriously. The Fang and Claw Inn is also passed, and you can see the shady underbelly of our society lurking around the outside of the building. Motorcycles and beat up trucks are lined up out front with their colors emblazoned upon them. A body comes flying out the front window and crashes onto the hood of the truck that was there.

I make haste and get us away from the area, heading down towards the Crossroads Inn. The scenery heading south changes from having pines mixed into the woods to mostly hardwoods. The Crossroads Inn is an inn that is run by one of my flight members, Tregar. He will provide us with safe refuge for the night once we arrive and a meal fit for a king. He has a series of suites meant for groups like ours so that we may have privacy. Being that I am substantially older than he is, buying his silence will be inexpensive compared to if any of my companions would try it.

Feray starts to stretch and move around in the back seat, and I see Easton whip his head to the back, watching again. "How about we take a break before we get to the Inn? Maybe stretch our legs for a while?" I suggest the break more for Easton than the others. We really don't need him spontaneously combusting in the car. Everyone agrees with my suggestion, and I look for a suitable place to park the car.

Up ahead, there's a meadow and a stream with a patch of woods nearby that looks like it would be a good place to stop. I pull over onto the shoulder and everyone takes their time getting out. My eyes immediately lock on Feray and the way she turns her nose to the wind.

Smart little wolf. My dragon is pleased with her checking the wind.

Looking around, I study the surrounding area, looking out for danger. With everything that is going on and the attacks that seem to be aimed at Feray and Fiadh, being cautious is at the forefront of my mind. We do not know which of the sisters is the true target. My gut is telling me that my inamorata is the one that is being hunted. Perhaps that is why she has the more powerful of the mates? This is something I will ponder once we reach the inn.

The meadow stretches out before us in a picturesque display of natural beauty. It is a scene of tranquility and harmony, a symphony of colors and textures that soothes the soul. The meadow is carpeted with lush, emerald-green grass that sways gently in the breeze, its blades whispering secrets to the wind. Wildflowers of every hue adorn the landscape, their petals painted in a vibrant palette of reds, yellows, purples, and blues. The air is filled with the delicate fragrances of lavender, honeysuckle, and the sweet scent of fresh earth.

A gentle, babbling stream meanders through the heart of the meadow, cutting a sinuous path across the landscape. The water is crystal clear, reflecting the azure sky above like a mirror. Small pebbles line the stream bed. The stream's melodious murmur is a constant companion, a soothing lullaby that resonates through the meadow. Tall, graceful trees stand sentinel on the meadow's edge, their leaves rustling in the wind. Their branches offer patches of dappled shade. Birds of all kinds flit and sing among the branches, adding their cheerful voices to the chorus of the meadow.

In the distance, I can see the majestic outline of rolling hills, their slopes covered in a patchwork of forests and fields. The entire scene seems like a painting come to life, a testament to the enduring beauty of nature.

"There are several deep pools in the stream. I'm going to fish for lunch for us," Torben offers as he strips out of his clothes. His bear rips free from its human prison and lands hard on the earth before raising its head to roar. Feray giggles as she watches her mate take on his shifted form. She mentions something about him being an enormous teddy bear, and I turn quickly to gape at her. She called one of the ultimate terrestrial killing machines a teddy bear. Love does funny things to one's perception of danger. Either that or she has no sense of self preservation. For my sanity's sake, I can only hope that it is love that blinds her to the danger her mate's shift poses.

"I'm going to go find somewhere to go pee," Feray tells us before walking off into the forest. I watch Feray for as long as I can follow her path down the deer trail before scanning the area again.

Turning around, I choose to watch Torben hunt, curious about how a mammal so large is going to accomplish it. The bear's massive frame, covered in thick, dark brown fur, exudes an aura of raw strength and dominance in its natural habitat. I note its sharp claws, designed for digging and catching fish, glisten in the soft, golden sunlight that filters through the dense canopy.

The stream is surrounded by lush greenery and framed by towering pine trees. The water flows gently, gurgling over smooth river rocks. With remarkable patience and precision, the Kodiak bear lowers its massive head towards the water, its keen eyes fixed on the underwater world. The bear's senses are finely tuned, honed by generations of instinctual hunting. It has always amazed me how different species hunt. Take Feray for instance. What her wolf lacks in size, she makes up for with speed and agility. The basilisk, as huge as it is, can cover a large area quickly. Out of the corner of my eye, I catch a change in Torben's position.

As Torben watches something in the water, his body tenses, ready to strike at the perfect moment. Suddenly, he lunges forward, his powerful forepaws plunging into the water. The surface explodes in a frenzy of splashes as his massive claws snag a silvery, glistening trout. With brute force, he hoists the fish out of the water. His powerful jaws clamping down on the slippery prize. Water droplets spray in every direction as Torben triumphantly captures the trout.

Soon as his teeth sink into the head of the fish, he lays it on the bank. When he's sure it won't move he returns to the stream, walking up and down its bank searching for the next one. Khal's phone rings again and he steps away from the group to answer the call. He keeps looking up the road from where we just came from, then back down to where we are.

Easton keeps pacing up and down the roadside, looking into the woods, watching for Feray. He's anxious and I understand why. Between the symbols left at the crash site and the same one being carved into the satyr, it's definitely unnerving. Pulling the notepad, I've been keeping on the facts we have gathered is not looking good. Too many things line up that our little wolf is more than she appears to be.

The feeling of her luna gifts brushing over my skin when she calmed the masses was amazing. Like the elder had said, there are only three bloodlines that produce Lunas of that caliber. By the looks of it, having seen her fur color, I suspect we will find the answer we are looking for in the tundra. Khal returns and looks at

Easton watching the woods intently. "The path to the ocean is clear as far as I could find out. My uncle's people have taken Moors Farm to the north, so we should steer clear of that on the way back." Khal keeps typing on his phone before looking up at me again.

"Thank your informant for me. The information they are providing is quite useful." Glancing down at my notepad, then over to my phone I send a text to Tregar warning him that my party and I should be there by nightfall. He informs me he has a large suite with multiple beds and rooms we can have, and I book it with him.

Torben keeps fishing, throwing fish after fish up onto the bank. Khal eventually finishes his information hunting and goes to start a small fire to cook with. I haven't roughed it in centuries, this should be a rather interesting experience.

Easton keeps his gaze locked on the woods as he paces back and forth. *His bird is concerned. His senses aren't like ours or the bears …* My dragon supplies a fact I had forgotten. His sense of smell isn't as acute as the bears and nowhere near the wolf's. He can't use his tongue like Khal and me to taste the air for changes. What he does have is incredible eyesight that puts all of us to shame, and he can heal with a single tear.

The birds explode from the treetops to the west of where we are. Everyone stops what they are doing to focus on the spot where the birds came from. "See anything?"

"No," Easton says and somehow, I'm not convinced that everything is alright. "Something feels off. I can't put my finger on it." He turns to look at me and his eyes are balls of fire. His bird is close to the surface, and that may not be the best thing to happen right now.

"What feels off?" Khal questions as he flicks his tongue in the air several times.

"I'm not sure ... It just is..." Damn phoenixes and their non-answer answers.

"If she's not out in ten minutes, we're going in after her." I state as I move towards the head of the deer trail, watching for Feray. Easton's anxiety is getting to me. What if he's right?

CHAPTER 4

FERAY

I take several silent steps into the woods after I watch Torben shift and start fishing for our lunch. For its size, his bear is as graceful as it is powerful. The others may not see or appreciate the way his bear lumbers around, but I do. His main goal is providing and caring for the family, and it shows. He's fishing for lunch for us, so we don't have to stop anywhere for food. My big guy knows how much I love the fresh fish he catches for us. It's something about the primal hunt and being provided for that endears him to me more. One day he will make a fantastic father.

My eyes drift to the mixed signal sending doctor. Easton has his eyes locked on the woods where I entered it. The doctor is a puzzle to me; I know he feels the bond. The feather he gave me is a testament to his affection. Unfortunately, the way he was raised is the only thing I believe is holding him back from getting to know me. The fire in his eyes burns brightly and I can see his bird's gaze focused in my direction. My wolf feels the pull towards his bird, but the man is fighting it. Torben said it would take him time, so time is what I will give him.

Diaval is watching Torben as he fishes, interested in how his bear does it. The wyrm dragon is also a puzzle in the group. But now that I think about it, it was obvious he was interested in me. He was always in the bar on the nights I worked and only the nights I was there. I would hear him give Mo a hard time with the simplest order, but for me, he would smile slightly. I know the mug I gave him meant something because I saw he had packed it to bring with him. Just like the gold doubloon with his claw mark on it, it means the world to me. Not only does it offer protection, my unicorn friend told me he had never heard of it being given lightly. As much as he cares, it seems he can't bring himself to move forward. He probably has some of the same hangups that Easton does. There's also the fact that the two of them have been alone for longer than I've been alive. Change can be hard for some people to accept. I know I'm not a big fan of change myself.

Khal is pacing up and down the side of the road on the phone. He's dressed like he should be in a biker gang than in his family's business. I watch him for several beats, looking at how his expression changes as he talks. He's the nicer of the twins and I guess you can say he and his brother are like Fi and me. She's quick to lose her temper, just like Khol, Khal and I usually have to talk our siblings off the ledge. There's a tenseness to the way he's walking, and I know the guys are withholding information from me. It's probably for the best since I don't handle bad news well. Hopefully, whatever the call is about, it's good news he's getting.

I don't think I can take anymore danger for a while. My poor nerves are shot looking around every corner when we were back in Briarvale. I'm a wolf that is being hunted by who knows what, for whatever reason, I have no clue about. *What the hell makes me so damn special?* Then again, they could be hunting Fi, and maybe my journey to Blackmoor will be uneventful. *I'm not going to hold my breath hoping for that one.* Well, a girl can hope that one of her ancient mates will get their collective heads out of their asses and claim me. Laughing to myself, I shake my head and look around slowly.

My gaze returns to the deer trail before me. Old hoof prints line the trail and new ones. By the smell of it not too long ago, by the looks of it a yearling. My poor bladder feels like it's about to explode if I don't find a place to pee. The pressure alone urges me to start my trek into the woods.

The wind shifts and all the scents of the forest assault my senses. The air is alive with the sweet fragrance of damp earth, moss, and the faint hint of pine. Among the towering giants, the narrow deer trail meanders gracefully through the heart of the woods. The path is worn smooth, a testament to the countless hooves that tread upon it over the years. Each step I take is accompanied by a gentle rustle of fallen leaves and twigs. The ground has patches where a quilt of moss and pine needles silences my steps.

The trail curves gracefully, following the natural contours of the land. It leads through a cathedral of ancient trees, their massive trunks adorned with moss and lichen, and their branches creating a verdant canopy overhead. Shafts of sunlight pierce through the foliage, casting intricate patterns of light and shadow upon the forest floor. Occasional patches of vibrant wildflowers add splashes of color to the otherwise earthy palette. Butterflies dance from petal to petal while birds perch on low-hanging branches serenading me with melodious songs. My wolf and I feel at home this far away from the small town of Briarvale. Well, at least the section that Fi and I lived in between the bears sleuth and the Night District. The air is almost electric with the anticipation of what lies ahead. My curiosity sometimes gets the better of me and I continue exploring.

The trail beckons, promising a journey through a realm of untamed beauty, where the heartbeat of nature pulses in harmony with every step. Here, amidst the tranquil serenity of the woods, I feel as if I was born to be here. My wolf is at peace in the deep woods, enjoying the scents and sounds around me. I must remind myself I do not have time to hunt while I'm here.

As I walk further down the trail through the towering trees, I spot a circle of bushes that looks promising. These bushes, thick and verdant, stand as a natural barrier and a perfect spot for me to hide to pee. I wiggle my way between the bushes and find the perfect area to relieve myself. Amid this tranquil scene, a gentle breeze whispers secrets to the leaves, setting them to a soft, rustling dance. Birds serenade the world around me with their melodic songs, creating an enchanting melody. I finally feel like I can relax and enjoy this trip instead of being constantly paranoid.

A sharp, snapping sound pierces the tranquility like a thunder-clap. I freeze in my movements immediately and listen intently. Hopefully, it was just a deer being clumsy on the trail to the north. The rustling leaves still, and the woodland creatures freeze in their tracks, their senses attuned to the source of the disturbance. Staying still, I listen intently to everything around me. Even the birds fall silent.

Fear spreads like wildfire through me, and I hold my breath, waiting with bated anticipation. The forest abruptly transforms from a haven of serenity into a realm of unease. A second branch snaps, louder this time. Panic ripples through the bushes as the creatures of the forest scramble for cover. The potent scent of rotting flesh and musk drifts to me and my nose works overtime trying to figure it out. *Is there something dead over the hill?* I pull my pants up and stare in the direction of the scent. The chill that moves up my spine makes my chest tighten as fear grips me.

Just for the sake of my sanity, I get myself out of the bushes and start looking toward the scent again. More branches crack and a bone chilling roar breaks the silence and then I see it come crashing through the bushes. The creature before me is an embodiment of primal terror. It emerges from the depths of the forest like a living nightmare. Towering at an unnatural height, it appears skeletal and emaciated. Its grotesque form wrapped in tattered, rotting flesh. Its limbs stretch impossibly long, each jagged joint resembling a gnarled, skeletal tree branch. Its eyes, hollow sockets filled with malevolence, glow with a sickly, otherworldly light that pierces the shadows like eerie lanterns.

Sharp, yellowed fangs protrude from its gaping maw, perpetually stained with the blood of its countless victims. A rancid stench, a mix of decay and death, hangs in the air as it approaches, sending a wave of nausea through me. The creature's hands end in gnarled claws, each one capable of inflicting unimaginable agony. Its skin, if it can even be called that, is pallid and stretched taut over its skeletal frame, with patches of frostbitten blue and ashen gray.

It moves with an unsettling grace, gliding through the forest with a bone-chilling silence that defies its monstrous size. The sight of the creature is enough to freeze the blood of even the bravest souls, a grotesque fusion of human desperation and unquenchable hunger. Its existence is a testament to the darkest corners of my wild imagination. It takes several moments before my brain engages and my wolf rips free, taking over and we run for our lives. My fight or flight instinct kicks in and I howl for help, hearing the thundering crashes of its feet behind me.

My wolf breaks right, heading towards the open meadow. She knows full well that if my guys were coming to my rescue, the open field is the best option. I run for what feels like forever as we break into the open expanse of the meadow. I howl again as panic sets in, thinking I won't live long enough to see my guys again.

The whooshing sound of the beating of wings closes in on my location, but I dare not turn. The fear of the rotting beast that's chasing me far outweighs my curiosity of who is behind me. Suddenly, the surrounding ground illuminates and I feel heat embracing me. It can only be one person, Easton. A thunderous crackle fills the air as the heat intensifies.

A ring of fire is sprayed around me, capturing my wolf within the roaring inferno. I skid to a stop so as not to set myself on fire. The howls and screams of the creature that was following me fills the air. The scent of scorched flesh and earth fills my nostrils, and my wolf suddenly gives me back my human form. I stare at the horned skeletal beast through the flames as a cone of fire is breathed down upon it until it succumbs to the damage the fire did. I watch its burning body hit the ground and finally stills after several moments of it jerking randomly in the fire.

I huddle near the only bush naked, with my arms wrapped around me. Fear has embraced me, and I can't stop trembling as I watch the ten-foot-tall flames dance around me. Fire and flesh or fur simply doesn't mix well. Eventually, I can make out a form through the flames and it seems to pass through it. Easton walks through the fire, impervious to its damage. He stands just inside the ring of fire, not a single scorch mark on him and, by some miracle, his clothing intact. He searches the interior until his eyes lock on me. I get up without a second thought and run to him.

Our bodies crash together, and I press my forehead against his neck, wrapping my arms tightly around him. I feel him shrug off his jacket and he wraps me up in it. Tears I've held in run like rivers down my cheeks when he scoops me up, carrying me bridal style. I raise my head for a moment and watch him raise a hand and the flames lower. The charred remains of the creature smolders outside of where the ring of fire once stood. In the distance, I can see the rest of my mates running towards us.

My biggest fear has been realized. *I am no longer the hunter, but now the prey.*

67

CHAPTER 5

EASTON

I watch as my flame walks into the dark woods to relieve herself and my bird squawks, not liking her out of our sight. Pacing back and forth, I am trying not to follow my bird's instinct to chase after her and keep my eyes on her.

Standing at the forest's edge, a shiver races down my spine, while the dense canopy of ancient trees ominously looms above. Their gnarled branches form a tangled web, silhouetted against the fading light of day. Shadows dance and whisper secrets amongst the rustling leaves, and the air hangs heavy with an eerie stillness. It appears that a storm is rolling in on the horizon.

The forest beckons, a mysterious realm untouched by time. Moss-covered rocks, adorned with dewdrops, glisten like scattered jewels, guiding me further into the heart of the wilderness. Twinkling fireflies emerge from their hiding places, casting an enchanting aura with their soft glow. As I cautiously step forward, the earthy scent of damp soil fills my senses, mingling with the musty aroma of ancient trees.

Even with my phenomenal eyesight, I lose sight of Feray as she walks deeper into the woods. Reluctantly, I turn and walk back towards the road and try to watch the woods and the field. Torben's beast is charging up and down the stream, catching trout for lunch. The basilisk is typing furiously on his phone, then walking over to Diaval to show him what's happening.

If I'm being honest with myself, this isn't such a horrible group to be stuck with. The bear will kill anyone that upsets Feray without question. She seems to feel safest with him. The basilisk seems to be her emotional support nope rope. Even with as grumpy of a bastard as Diaval is, she pushes his limits and gets in his face.

Perhaps her ability to recognize danger is stunted because of how aggressive her sister is. She possibly has gotten so used to her sister's explosive temperament that the perception of real danger has been muted. I ponder this further as I watch over the field and the woods. Diaval is the only one that has eyesight close to mine and I catch him periodically scanning the horizon.

Torben's bear's head whips towards the woods and he bellows before releasing his human form. "Feray is scared."

Khal echoes Torben's words, and before I can ask the next question, we can hear her panicked howl. Her wolf's cry pierces the cold air, causing a shudder to move through my body. The way her voice resonates almost makes me feel her fear as if it's my own. Torben's bear rips free of his body and almost immediately, Khal's basilisk does the same and they take off into the woods.

Glancing over at Diaval, we know that to unleash his dragon would cause utter destruction and will alert other flights to our presence. Throwing caution into the wind, I take a running start towards the meadow and leap, letting my phoenix fire consume me.

It feels like forever since the last time I had last spread my wings. Each flame engulfed flap carries me closer to the sounds of Feray's howls. I can hear the bear and basilisk falling behind. *There's no way they will get there in time.* My flame breaks free of the woods like a little white streak cutting across the sea of green.

The Wendigo relentlessly pursues Feray's white wolf across the vast grassy field. Its grotesque form, contrasting starkly against the serene landscape, bounds forward with an uncanny grace. Long emaciated limbs move with an eerie swiftness, and its elongated fingers reach out hungrily towards my mate. Its skin, stretched thin over its skeletal frame, glints pallidly in the daylight.

Feray's wolf sprints gracefully through the tall grass. Her fur glistens like freshly fallen snow, a stark contrast to the darkness of the pursuing nightmare. Her powerful legs propel her forward with a fluidity that is almost hypnotic, evading the Wendigo's grasp at every turn.

When they get far enough away from the woods, I strike. First hitting the Wendigo with fire to stop it in its tracks.Then I surround my mate with ten-foot-tall flames to protect her. The Wendigo with its tall elk-like antlers prowls the outside of the ring of fire. Banking hard, I turn and bathe the demon in the hottest flames I can muster. Doing this, I know I will be unable to shift for a day or two depending on how much rest I can get, and how well I can eat. As long as my flame is safe, it is worth it in the end.

Once the Wendigo is reduced to a twitching, charred mass on the ground, I land and shift back. Thankfully, being a mythic has its benefits. My clothes remain intact when I move between forms. Without a second thought, I walk through the flames and search the interior for her. I find Feray huddled naked next to a bush, holding her knees to her chest.

Unexpectedly, she leaps to her feet and runs straight for me. Our bodies collide and she knocks the air out of my lungs. Her arms wrap around me like I've seen her do to Torben on many occasions. As tight as she is holding me makes my heart skip a beat and my bird for once, goes silent. I remove my suit jacket and wrap her up in it before returning her embrace. I'm having mixed emotions at the moment. Half of me is ecstatic. The other isn't ready to have to share our mate with the others.

Her body trembles in my arms as she presses her forehead against my chest. Soft whimpers escape her lips and I scoop her up without hesitation. My bird cannot stand to hear the scared tones of her whimper. She rests her head on my shoulder only a moment before I jostle her briefly to lower the flames I had erected.

With her in my arms, feeling her cling to me like I am the only man in the world, I'm doomed. This little she-wolf in my embrace has stolen my heart. Glancing down, I see the pendant I had given her hanging just above her breasts, pulsing in time with her heartbeat. Gently, I press a kiss to the crown of her head and linger there a moment.

Softly, I whisper to her. "My flame, my beautiful precious flame." She slowly raises her head, and I am lost in her gray-blue eyes. "When we get somewhere safe." I ghost my lips over hers. Pulling back slightly, I see the gold of her wolf's eyes flare to life. Woman and beast are paying attention. "I will make you mine, if you let me." The most radiant smile I have seen in my long years graces her lips and she nods as a blush creeps across her cheeks.

"I would like that very much." She leans forward and presses her pillowy soft lips against mine, and I swear I am about to combust.

Before I can deepen the kiss, her other bonded mates catch up and shift back. "Feray, are you okay?" Torben reaches for her first and she hesitates for a moment before I lower her to the ground, allowing her to go to him. Her hesitation spoke louder than all the sweet nothings her bear is uttering. *She didn't want to leave me.*

Diaval eventually meets us in the middle of the field as we walk back. "Was that what I thought it was?" He waves his hand in the direction of the remains.

I wait for the others to walk far enough away before I pull him aside. "It was a Wendigo. Not just any kind. It apparently had a mage in its chest, making it more powerful than your average demon." Depending on what being is possessed in its chest determines the wendigos strength. For the briefest of moments, I watch as the slits of his dragon's eyes become visible.

"This doesn't bode well. Our little mate is being hunted by someone powerful enough or rich enough to unleash Wendigos." Diaval strokes his chin, watching Feray walking back to the car wrapped up in the arms of both of her bonded mates.

"They are not strong enough combined to defeat the demons." I state and look down at my nails briefly.

"True, the basilisk has a chance if his stone gaze works on them. Our fire will destroy them, but until we claim her, our fire will burn her." Damn Diaval bringing up the elephant in the room.

"You know it's more than that. She has to accept my feather and your scale for it to work. Until then, we will only have her two hundred years' best-case scenario." My tone hits that haughty pitch that I know grates on Diaval's last nerve. *I did it on purpose.* He wants to force my hand so he can take his time dragging out the inevitable. Little does he know I already promised my flame that once we were safe, I would claim her.

We arrive back at the car faster than I had intended, only to find Feray dressed in a tee-shirt and leggings, leaning against the back door of the car. "We should get back on the road. It's not safe to remain here longer than we have to."

"That's probably one of the first things I agree with you on. Load up everyone." Diaval barks out his order, then heads to the driver's side and gets in.

"Who do you want to snuggle with, Precious?" Khal leans in and kisses her temple before backing off.

Wincing, she looks at me and her wolf surfaces. "Easton and Torben." Her voice wavers and I want to rip her away from the basilisk and hold her tightly to my chest. A slow smile creeps across Torben's lips as he nods knowingly. He walks over to the driver's side and slides into the back seat. Feray looks at me and I nod at her. Her nostrils flare for a moment, then she climbs into the back seat in the middle. Drawing in a deep breath, I look to the heavens and throw a prayer up to the elder gods. *Don't let me destroy this.* I say more to myself than anything else.

I slide in and close the door. "We should find food. Shifting takes a lot out of me." As I mention food, Feray looks down onto the floorboard and pulls up a sack. She smiles as she looks down into it and pulls out a pastry and offers it to me.

"It's probably not something you are used to eating. But I packed some of the honey butter crescent rolls I made for the trip in case I got hungry." Reaching out, I take the pastry from her. I watch Torben nuzzle her shoulder until she passes out one to everyone. "I hope everyone enjoys their snack." She says before fidgeting with the hem of the tee-shirt.

Usually, I don't indulge in sweet snacks. But there's something in the way that Feray is watching me that tells me this is important.

I take a bite and the decadent flavor of the butter mixed with the honey explodes on my tongue. This isn't any average honey. "This is from the giant bee's hive, isn't it?" I take another bite and there's no mistaking the flavor of nutmeg and the tang of the honey.

"It is. I harvested it the first time as my acceptance gift to Torben after all of his baskets." She blushes a brilliant shade of pink, speaking about the bear's tradition.

"Harvesting that honey is no simple feat." I finish the pastry and I have to admit it's one of the best I've had in a long time.

Feray giggles as she scoots closer to me, and I angle my body so she can lean against my chest. She snuggles herself in and sighs softly. Glancing up, I look at Torben, and he motions for me to wrap my arms around her. Phoenix females don't require being held. The minute I do as he suggested, she wiggles slightly and relaxes further. "It's easy to harvest the honey before the sun hits the hive. The cliff the nest was on wasn't easy to get to. Thankfully, my wolf and I are small enough to make it."

A hearty chuckle escapes Torben's lips. "You make it sound so easy, little wolf. She's being modest." He looks at me and I can tell he's about to spill the details. "The rock face she's talking about is the one between her cottage and my sleuth. We have been trying for years to get that honey. I'm too heavy and way too broad to fit where she did to get to the hive." He pokes a little fun at himself, and I feel Feray shake her head a little.

"It wasn't that bad." She lifts her head and I feel the loss of her weight and heat immediately. *I miss it...*

"I have known those bees to kill smaller shifters." Diaval adds.

Feray rolls her eyes and shakes her head. "Okay dad..."

A ring of smoke escapes Diaval's nostrils and I have to muffle a laugh. "Next time, please ask for me to accompany you on your endeavor. I would hate to see you suffer from the sting." Gently, I stroke her cheek and she leans into my touch, closing her eyes. She's very responsive.

"Okay, lovebirds, we're close to the Crossroads Inn. We have less than an hour to reach our destination." Diaval announces as he pulls back onto the road.

Feray lays back down using me as her pillow. Something about her body against mine settles something within me. *It's her, it's always been her* ... My bird says to me as he fights to look at her through my eyes. I relent and allow him to gaze upon her. He croons to her softly and I feel the vibration in my chest. Slowly, my eyelids become heavy, and I tighten my grip around her as her body becomes pliant.

Sleep takes us together as the world fades to black.

CHAPTER 6
FERAY

"Time to wake up..." I hear Torben's voice in my ear.

"Five more minutes." Easton says and turns us away from Torben's voice.

I feel my legs slide over his thighs and his arms band tighter around me. The warmth radiating from Easton's body keeps trying to pull me under. I bury my nose under his jaw and breathe deeply, taking in his scent. The rich scent of bergamot fills my nostrils. Its citrus-like scent is as complex as he is. It kind of reminds me of something similar to lime, but with floral, herbal, and resinous undertones.

Warm hands grip me and slowly pull me away from Easton. A whine escapes my lips as panic seizes me. My eyes fly open and I'm ready to shift to escape until I realize it's Torben that has a hold of me. Looking around, my eyes land on the Inn that we are apparently staying at tonight. Diaval takes me from Torben and tucks me under his arm and tight to his side.

"Stay close and silent. No one needs to know you're a wolf if they are looking for you. Tregar will take our secret to the grave, and I wish not to lose one of my oldest friends over a visit." Diaval's dragon croons softly and his scent becomes stronger.

Khal leans in briefly and smiles. "He's masking your scent, making his stronger. Being as ancient as he is, the others won't question his claims." Khal gives me a nod. Then he channels his best impersonation of his brother. In the blink of an eye, Khal went from sweet and happy to stone cold and angry looking with black sunglasses and all.

Diaval must have felt me flinch at Khal's change. "He's doing it for your safety. Come along, no more time for delay." Diaval heads towards the inn from where we parked, and I finally get a good look at the building.

There stands the Crossroads Inn, a wondrous establishment perched at the confluence of four winding roads. The inn was a masterpiece of grandeur, constructed from massive, gnarled oak trees that bore the marks of centuries gone by. Its exterior is adorned with intricately carved dragon motifs, each scale, and claw brought to life in remarkable detail.

Two towering dragon statues, their fiery eyes guard the inn's entrance, gleaming as though ready to unleash their breath upon any unwelcome intruders. Inside, a cavernous common room greets us with a warm hearth, where a colossal dragon's head hangs above the roaring fire, flames dancing in its mouth.

The atmosphere within is both cozy and mystical. The walls are adorned with rare dragon scales, delicate yet resilient, casting shimmering patterns of light across the room. At the heart of the inn, a massive, ornate bar was tended by a lively innkeeper who apparently knows Diaval.

"Diaval!" He jumps the bar and approaches swiftly.

An unrestrained rumble escapes Diaval's lips as his body instantly goes rigid, causing the man to stop short. "I mean your Inamorata no harm, old friend." He raises his hands in a placating manner, and I can feel the tenseness drain from Diaval.

"It's very new, forgive me." Diaval states plainly, then passes me off to Khal. "Protect her at all costs." At Diaval's command, Khal lowers his sunglasses, glaring at the room.

"You didn't need to bring a basilisk here. My people can keep you and your Inamorata safe." He says to Diaval, then turns to the rest of us. "Names Tregar and this is my inn. I have reserved the third floor for the five of you, as Diaval requested." He looks back at Diaval briefly, then back at us. "We will send dinner to your suite since my old friend seems to be very on edge. A mating drake is nothing to mess with." He again turns his gaze to Diaval, watching him.

"What do you mean by a mating drake is nothing to mess with?" I direct my question at Tregar, since Diaval seems to be super secretive.

Before Tregar can answer, Diaval is in my face, gripping my jaw, making me look up into his eyes as they shift to the silver serpentine slits of his dragon. "There are three times a drake is extremely formidable. When he has taken a mate, when his mate is in season or with child, and when he knows he's about to die." He cocks his head up at an angle and looks down at me. "Do you understand?" His tone is doing funny things to my insides. Perhaps it's the dominance pouring off of him. More than likely, it's because he's finally acknowledging I am his.

"I do." Lowering my head, I bear my neck to him, and he presses his nose over my pulse point. "I need to tend to my Inamorata.

Send the food post haste." Diaval pulls me toward the stairs and motions for Khal to go first.

We ascend the stairs, and I watch Khal taking them two at a time. He gets to the only door on the floor and points to his eyes, then mimes putting his hand over his. I do one better. I turn around and press my forehead against Diaval's chest, using his frame to block my eyes. Diaval turns us and he presses his lips to the crown of my head before spinning me. Incredible heat appears in front of me, and powerful arms pull me forward.

"I've got her." Easton's honeyed voice soothes me as he envelopes me in his warmth. He pulls me back with him and I feel his body hit the wall as he keeps my head turned away from the room. "Stay with me, my flame. Let the others do what they must."

Between his rich citrus scent and the bone melting warmth his body is giving off, I am lulled into a state of relaxation. "Are we safe, Easton?" Slowly I raise my head to look up at him. He presses my head back to his chest but allows me to look up at him. "Safe is a relative term. Can we protect you? Absolutely. Will your attackers die? Definitely." His fingers thread through my hair, working through some knots.

"Will you be safe?" Hesitantly, I reach up and cup his cheek, and he presses his face into my palm.

"Even if I were to die, I would resurrect. It's the blessing and the curse of the phoenix. Never ending life." He uses his knuckle to tilt my head back, and he presses his lips to mine, and I swear my soul ignited. I paw at him, wanting to climb him like a tree.

"It's about time!" Khal's voice breaks me out of my happy little bubble.

A deep growl breaks free from my lips, and I feel Easton's legs almost buckle under him. As I turn to face Khal, the look of shock on his face breaks me out of my anger. "I'm sorry … I don't know what got into me." Trembling, I press back against Easton's chest and try to hide.

"That's easy, my flame. You channeled the rage of Torben's shift. An alpha female becomes stronger with each mate she takes. That's why old laws dictated only for Lunas to only take one mate. The elders slaughtered everyone other than the first mate before the bonds were formed." His smooth, regal features seem relaxed as he relayed parts of the darker history of the wolves.

"That's so barbaric. Why would the elders do that?" I cling to Easton as he walks us down the hall and into our suite.

"Until about three hundred years ago, they slaughtered alpha females. Their Luna powers were proven to be incredibly stronger than their male counterparts." Diaval says as he extends a hand out to me. Easton nods and I walk over and take a hold of Diaval's hand. "It's why I suspect they hid you with the witches. There hasn't been a recorded true Luna birth in over fifty or so years." He forces a smile and motions to the room behind us. "I drew you a bath. Go relax and drink the water I left for you. We will feed you when you emerge." He walks towards the table in the room and starts pulling things out of the bag.

Nodding, I move towards the door and stop looking back at the guys. Khal is sitting in the window seat watching the road. Torben is in the kitchenette preparing a snack for everyone while we wait for dinner. Diaval is at the table spreading out our records, looking at them and the map. Easton is watching me with hunger in his eyes. "Wish to join me?" *Bold move? Yes.* Who knows how much time we have before we need to move again and get back on the road.

My question made all the men in the room stop and look at Easton. With as prim and proper as he is and his upbringing, they are curious about his response. "Yes." His terse answer catches me off guard. He removes his suit jacket and lays it over the back of the chair, then motions to the bathroom. "After you, my flame." He smiles and lowers his head slightly.

Stepping inside the bathroom, it's much larger than it appeared from the outside. The large tub in the center of the room can easily hold two to three people in it. Steam rising from the water almost puts me in a trance. The rustling of fabric catches my attention and I turn around. Easton is sliding his dress shirt off his arms, and I watch as every inch of his toned chest is exposed. He's light built. I guess that's normal for a flight shifter. My eyes lock on his hands as they go to his belt buckle. A soft laugh escapes his lips and I blush at being caught.

"If I didn't know better, my flame likes what she sees." Easton's teasing tone catches me off guard. I didn't think he could be playful.

"I do." Reaching down, I slip my hands under my tee shirt and grip my leggings and pull them down. I hazard a glance in his direction and the fire of his phoenix burns in his eyes. Slowly, I stand up and reach for the hem of my shirt. Before I can lift it, Easton's lips crash against mine and I feel his hands slide under my tee-shirt. His hands span the width of my thighs as they slide up my hips to rest on my ribs. Lifting my arms up, he breaks the kiss for a moment to pull the shirt free from my body.

My core is burning with the need for him, and he knows it. His fingers dig into my flesh as he lifts me with ease. I wrap my thighs around his narrow waist as he walks us to the tub. Breaking the kiss for a moment, he whispers. "The water is a necessary evil." His lips crash against mine again as we sink down into the hot water of the tub. He lays back, resting his shoulders against the curved side of the basin. "Phoenixes ignite when they take their mate. Until I plant my feather in your skin, you will burn." His eyes search mine, hoping for understanding.

"Wolves bite..." I run my hand over the muscle between his neck and shoulder and give it a squeeze. Smiling, I bare my canines at him, and my vision shifts as I stare down at him. My wolf is prowling so close to the surface. It's difficult to contain her.

Easton nods at me and points at the charm he gave me that rests just above my breasts. "Allow me to implant my feather so I don't hurt you, my flame." He slides himself so his chest is out of the water. Reaching over the edge, he grabs the towel and dries his hand before turning his hand palm up at me. I remove the necklace and pendant he gave me and drop it into his palm. His eyes ignite and there's no going back now.

CHAPTER 7
FERAY

THE GLASS THAT CONTAINS EASTON'S FEATHER MELTS AWAY IN HIS PALM, leaving an ornate golden feather in his hand. It reminds me of the shape of a peacock feather as I stare at it. He smiles looking at it, and then up at me. "I need to plant it where it is visible. Where would you like it? I suggest your hairline so that it's visible in wolf form." A soft smile plays at the corners of his lips, turning them up slightly as he gazes up at me.

Reaching over, I take the towel and dry my hands and reach up into my hair. The most logical place to me is my widow's peak, so I point there. "Will here do? It's very visible in both forms."

He smiles broadly and touches it. "In your wolf's form, you have chosen the ajna chakra position. It will increase your wolf's intuition and make visible things not able to be perceived with normal vision. Its placement will also open up your mind to information beyond the material world and the five senses." He reaches up and starts speaking in a language I cannot understand. For a brief moment, there is pressure, then a burning sensation where I feel the feather being pushed into my skin.

Gently, his hand moves over to where the feather was placed, and he soothes the pain away and smiles. "You look exquisite with your feather, my flame."

Smiling softly, I lean forward and brush my lips over his. "Why do you call me your flame?" Gripping the tub on either side of him, I rise up onto my knees and slide from his lap to over his groin. His thickened member rests against my folds as I rock slightly, waiting for my answer.

"A phoenix is nothing without its fire. A fire is nothing without its flame. Therefore, I am nothing without you." His eyes blaze to life and in my mind, I can hear his phoenix whispering its adoration for me.

"Do you hear that?" I tilt my head to the side and close my eyes as I angle my hips to line the tip of his cock with my core.

"Hear what, my flame?" His hands move from the tub to my hips, guiding me down to impale myself on him.

"Your shift. He's talking to me. Telling me how long he's waited for me." Tears well up in my eyes, listening to his bird's words of love and eternity. I feel the heat and stretch from Easton's cock but remain still, listening intently to his shift's words. I can feel his love wash over me as if his bird is worshiping me, wrapping me up in its wings of fire.

"He speaks the truth and always will. A phoenix cannot lie, we cannot bend or twist the truth." Slowly, Easton thrusts up into me and I feel as if every nerve ending in my body has ignited. This is so very different from my other mates. This feels different.

I open my eyes and stare down at the beautiful man below me and my hind brain finally engages. Flames begin to gently flicker over his flesh like he said it would. Easton has made me his on a spiritual level. Now it's time to make him mine on a physical level. My wolf wants to be in the driver's seat and I cannot allow it. Her intentions are good, but she's strong and her claws are sharp. I don't wish to harm my mate unintentionally.

As much as I want to touch him, I feel my claws break through my fingertips. I grip the tub as I press myself down onto him harder, meeting him thrust for thrust. Water sloshes everywhere and I don't care. His hands roam all over my body as he props himself up and draws my nipple into his hot mouth. A single flick of his tongue and my orgasm rips through me. Without hesitation, I release the tub and wrap him up in my arms. Lowering my head, I kiss where I intend to bite him. Easton knows what's coming and tilts his head to the side, allowing me access.

Swiftly, I strike and sink my teeth deep into his flesh and muscle. A surge of power rips through the two of us, and I hear what sounds like crackling as Easton follows me over the edge into oblivion. The copper tang of his blood is tinged with something else I cannot describe. The flavor is sweet, yet has a sour note to it on the back end. I feel as my core finally stops pulsing around him and we slowly come down from our high.

Withdrawing my canines, I lave my tongue over the wounds like I have with my other mates. His bird is still whispering its love for me, and that we have forever now. He thanks me repeatedly for not giving up on his human side, and it makes me chuckle.

"What's so funny, my flame?" Easton caresses my cheek as he looks up into my eyes.

"You didn't hear your bird?"

"No, what did he say that was so funny?" Easton leans forward and kisses my lips, sipping from them softly.

Both of my eyebrows shoot up, amazed he didn't hear his shift talking to me. "He thanked me for not giving up on your stubborn ass." Smiling broadly, I giggle again. "He's quite the romantic."

"Ah, I see…" He smiles, then looks around.

"It appears we made a mess." Easton helps me to stand up, making sure I'm steady before he exits the tub first. Offering me a hand, he assists me getting out of the tub and then gets himself out and wraps me up in a towel. I get ready to head towards the door and he stops me and holds out the bottle of water. "I do agree with Diaval. You need to drink your water, then eat. I will dry up all the water, then join you." Easton kisses me once more and waits for me to drink some of the water.

I walk out of the bathroom in my towel and thankfully half of the bottle of water is gone. Diaval's eyes go to the bottle of water, then looks me over and nods. "Nice feather."

I reach up and touch where it is. It's no longer as short as it was in the vial, instead it matches the length of my hair. Gently pulling it forward, I smile looking at it. Its color matches my red hair perfectly. Tiny wisps of fire dance over the edges of the feather's vanes and barbs making me squeal in excitement. Torben moves closer and examines the feather mixed in my hair. "You look very regal with your adornment, little wolf." He kisses my forehead and hands me a plate of cured meats and cheeses to snack on.

Blushing, I look over at Khal, and he motions for me to approach him. I take the snack plate from Torben, along with my water, over to the window seat. Khal moves, giving me room to sit down with my drink and snack. "It's a very becoming look on you, precious."

"Thank you." I glance out the window, then back up at Khal. "Guard duty?"

"Yeah, after our most recent adventure, I'll probably be going back to being nocturnal." He looks down, saddened by that fact.

"If we have to camp somewhere, can I sleep in your coils?" I search his stoney features and the carefree, soft lovable Khal surfaces.

"Anytime you don't feel safe, anywhere we are. I will shift so you feel safe enough to sleep." He leans forward and draws me back to sit between his legs while I eat.

My eyes drift over to Diaval, and he looks over at me and nods. I want to believe he feels the same way. The click of the bathroom door draws my attention over to Easton as he emerges fully dressed. I watch him as he heads over to our bags and digs through mine. He pulls out a colorful sundress and a matching bra and panty set, then brings it over to me. "Let's get you dressed. As much as I enjoy you in a towel and nothing else, it's not proper in case we have company." He holds his hand out to me, and I accept it.

Easton walks me over to the closest room and closes us in it. He smiles as he holds the clothing out to me. Looking it over, I take it from him and lay it out on the bed. "Are you sharing a bed with me tonight, or should I climb in with Torben?" I turn to watch Easton as I get dressed in the outfit he picked out for me.

"I will share a bed with you." He reaches up and rubs over where I bit him.

"Does it hurt?" I'm anxious that I harmed him with my bite.

"No, it seems to pulse in your presence though, it's quite interesting." He furrows his brows. "I have nothing in my memories about a wolf's mating mark reacting to its owner's presence." He shrugs his shoulders, having said it very matter-of-factly.

"Hmm, that is interesting. Let's go ask the others if theirs do the same thing." I shrug my shoulders slightly, barely raising them. None of my other mates mentioned the bites pulsing. Maybe it's because he's a mythic, and it's different for them.

We leave the bedroom that Easton has claimed as his and return to the main sitting room. Torben and Diaval are looking at the maps and Khal is still sitting in the window box. I move to stand beside him again and wait until he turns to look at me. "Does my mate mark pulse in my presence?" Reaching out, I rest my fingertips on where I bit him.

Khal tilts his head to the side, looking at me curiously. "No, should it?" Furrowing his brows, he glances from me, then over at Torben, who shakes his head no.

"Why would you ask if it pulses?" Diaval tilts his head slightly, and I can see the bone plates moving under his skin.

"Because mine pulses in her presence. I have nothing in my memories about a mate mark pulsing. Do you?" Easton answers before I have the chance to.

Diaval strokes his chin as he paces the room, deep in thought. He suddenly stops and stares at Easton and I puzzled. "Nothing in my memory to suggest that its happened before. Perhaps Dezi or Revelin would have an answer. Summon your pixie and have her inquire of the others, Feray."

Nodding, I move away from the group and draw in a deep breath. "Ro, I need you." My eyes scan the room until the pixie in question manifests before me. She looks like she recently came off a tour with a punk rock band from the eighties.

"Yes, oh fluffy one?" She flitters around and then her hands fly up to her face. Her hand slowly raises and points to the feather blended into the hair on my widow's peak. "Do you know there's a feather stuck in your hair?" She whispers like it's the biggest secret in the world.

"Actually, that's why I called for you. Can you ask Prince Revelin and Dezi if they know why my phoenix mate's mark pulses when I am near him?" I extend my hand out and offer her a place to land.

Ro lands then proceeds to sit on my palm, kicking her feet, watching me. "So, Mr. Drama Llama Picky Pants finally admitted his feelings, huh?" She leans forward, putting her elbows on her knees and her hands under her chin, smiling, looking up at me.

Khal mutters in the corner that it took me almost getting eaten by a Wendigo to do it. He slaps his hands over his mouth and whips his head in our direction. Ro's jaw drops, then she vanishes from sight. "Wonderful! Fi is going to have the mother of all fits."

My emotions spiral out of control until Torben grabs a hold of me and crushes me to his chest. "Breathe little wolf. You are safe. Nothing is going to happen." I feel the moment Easton and Khal lay a hand on me, my nerves almost instantly settle, and I can breathe again. Torben has me turned in such a way that I can see Diaval watching us intently. Slowly my nerves settle and the guys release me.

"We should probably get some sleep. I want to get up early and leave before most of the guests here awaken." Diaval says before turning and heading to the room he claimed as his.

Khal steps forward and presses his lips to my forehead and breathes in deeply. "Sleep precious, I'll keep watch over everyone." Reluctantly, he releases me and Torben takes over.

"I'm right over there, if you need me." He points to his door that is on the other side of the bathroom on the same side as Easton's room. His large hand caresses my jaw, and he tilts my head back and kisses me softly before heading to bed.

I watch him leave, then look at Easton, who suddenly seems uncomfortable. Reaching out, I take his hand and lead him back to his room. Without asking, I dig through his clothing bag and pull out an undershirt and lay it out for me to sleep in. I strip out of the sundress and lay it over the chair before slipping into his shirt. "Are you going to sleep or stand there watching me sleep?" Tilting my head, I watch him remain frozen for a few moments.

Easton bites his bottom lip and looks sheepish. "I don't normally sleep in my human form. This will be a first for me." He admits as he strips out of his dress clothing.

"Oh? Should we purchase a perch for you? I mean, I don't want you uncomfortable." I look around the room and there's nothing here that would withstand his fire.

"If you're wondering, I'm not always on fire. So that helps with finding a place for me to sleep. If I can't sleep in my skin, I'll wait until you're sleeping before shifting and leaving the bed." He forces a smile and leaves only his boxers on when he climbs into bed with me.

Easton curls his body around me, and I almost instantly fall asleep, wrapped up in his warm embrace.

CHAPTER 8
KHAL

The sun rises over the horizon, casting a warm, golden glow that spills through the window of our cozy inn's suite. I'm perched on the window seat, the world outside painted in hues of orange and pink, a breathtaking canvas to start the day. It's a serene moment, one of those rare pockets of tranquility in the chaos of life.

Amidst this peaceful awakening, the gentle snores of my room-mates provide a steady, comforting rhythm, a reminder that I'm not alone in this bustling world. The sound is like a lullaby, and I can't help but smile at the thought that even in sleep, we share this small, shared space and the memories that come with it.

A familiar clinking sound comes from the kitchen, announcing the presence of Diaval, he's making coffee. His early morning mutter-ings are quite comical to listen to as he gracefully moves around the compact kitchen. The aroma of freshly brewed coffee wafts through the air, mingling with the scent of the new day, and it's a beautiful symphony that awakens my senses.

I stretch my arms and legs, feeling the warmth of the sun on my skin as I breathe in the morning's freshness from the slightly open window. A yawn escapes my lips, a natural response to the early hour, but there's a sense of contentment that washes over me. Soon as we get into the SUV, I'll sleep and be ready to watch over everyone again.

Diaval, ever perceptive, glances in my direction, his hazel-green eyes meeting mine for a brief moment. There's a silent understanding between us, as if he knows I need a jolt of caffeine to stay awake long enough to get everyone on the road. With a nod of gratitude, I accept the steaming cup of coffee he offers. The warmth of the mug in my hands is a soothing contrast to the cool morning air.

I know I shouldn't be drinking the coffee this morning, but it smelled too good to pass up. Feray is the next one to emerge. She's rubbing her eyes with the backs of her hands, yawning. "Do we have bacon?" Without hesitation, she climbs into the window seat with me and rests her head on my chest, curling up again.

"We unintentionally overslept this morning. Tregar will deliver us breakfast post haste, then we leave." Diaval's dragon has him on edge, and I'm not sure what's bothering him.

He woke up several times over the course of the night, making sure that I was still awake. Then double checking the locks before going back to bed. If Feray hadn't decided I was her personal pillow, I would approach the grumpy dragon to see what's eating him.

Just as someone knocks on the suite's door, Torben exits his room, staring towards the sound. Diaval answers the door and accepts the tray from whomever is on the other side. The tray has every possible breakfast food imaginable on it. Diaval moves to the counter and prepares a plate and a glass of orange juice before bringing it over to Feray. "You need to eat a good breakfast and drink all of your juice." His tone doesn't leave any room for argument.

Feray slowly opens her eyes and smirks at Diaval as she accepts the tray from. "Yes, sir!" She does a mock salute, and he nods, turning away. I don't think he realizes she was being sarcastic.

"You're being naughty, Precious." I whisper in her ear and nibble on the lobe for good measure.

"I know … I also know that if I'm really bad, Torben likes to discipline me." She does the air quotes around the word discipline and then smiles.

Now I'm curious. Nuzzling her neck, I nibble the side of her jaw. "What does he do, precious? What do you like?"

Feray turns slowly, then cups her hands around my ear. "He spanks my bottom, then nips the back of my neck as he rubs where he spanked." She wiggles in her seat and the faint scent of arousal is in the air when I flick my tongue out.

I allow my snake's tongue to fully extend and watch Feray's eyes get as big as saucers as she watches me flick it. Her reaction gets the gears turning in my head about what to do the next time I get to be alone with her. The sound of shattering glass snaps my attention over towards Torben, whose eyes are that of his shift.

"Can you manage to not get her worked up before we are trapped in the car for hours?" His nostrils flair several times before he shakes his head.

The simplest thing just dawned on me. Three out of her four mates do not have heightened senses of smell. Torben is the only poor bastard that gets to smell everything all the time. Diaval and I, being dragon-kin, use our tongues to taste the air. Easton, being a predatory bird, has keen eyesight and a weak sense of smell. Oh, this is going to be fun driving the bear insane. As much as I disagree with my brother's love of chaos and doing things to disrupt the flow of things, in this case. Watching the big guy lose his ever loving mind could be the distraction I need.

A thumping on my chest draws me out of my inner musings. Feray is staring at me. Her eyes are flickering back and forth between human and wolf. "You've got that look in your eyes like you're up to something." She narrows her eyes, looking at me, then looks back at the others. "Don't mess with Torben's senses." She stares at the bear for far too long, then back at me. "It's not nice."

Before I can say anything, she gets up and goes and crawls into Torben's lap and resumes eating her food. Easton breaks away from Diaval and moves to lean against the wall near me, watching Feray with Torben. "I'll be honest. I'm a little jealous of their bond." His tone is almost clinical with the way he's processing his feelings.

Slowly, I tear my gaze away from Torben and Feray to look over at Easton. "You have to understand he helped her learn how to shift and hunt." I take a bite of the sausages that Diaval had given me. "They are both fur-bearing mammals. Diaval and I are both Dragon-kin and you're a mythical bird. Torben is the most similar to her shift." To be honest, until now, I was also having a hard time dealing with how close Feray is to Torben.

"I completely forgot her wolf was bound. She shifts so effortlessly now." He strokes his chin, watching her before picking up his bagel and takes a bite.

"She's amazing how she's progressed adapting to everything that is thrown at her in such a short time," I say, proud of how smart my mate is.

"We need to get going." Diaval hollers as he drags his bags and what looks like Feray's to the door.

"I guess it's time to get going." Yawning, I stretch, getting out of the window seat to go grab my belongings from the room I had claimed. Heading down the stairs, I feel my ass dragging as I fight the sleep I so desperately need.

"Come on Khal, you look like you're dead on your feet. Torben get in the back. I need a pillow!" Feray yells and the big guy gets in the back seat without hesitating.

Soon as Torben is settled, Feray climbs in dragging me with her. "Lay down." She lays back against Torben and then pulls me down on top of her.

Feray pulls me so I am half twisted in the chair, with my head on her chest and my arms on either side of her and Torbens hips. Her fingers thread through my hair and I hear a deep soft rumble of her wolf. It's a calming tone that immediately drags me under, making me fall asleep almost instantly.

The next thing I know, I am being gently shaken awake by Feray and she's giggling. "Wake up, sleepyhead. We've arrived."

I drag myself to sit up and I feel like someone drugged me. Looking over at Torben, he isn't in much better shape than I am. "I feel like I was hit with a sedative." Shaking my head, I try to clear it.

"It appears my flame has learned the luna gift of slumber." Easton says as he smiles fondly at Feray. "It's most effective with direct contact. Thankfully, it doesn't work with mythics unless we allow it." That holier than thou tone of his grates on my nerves, and I can tell I'm not the only one. Torben rolls his eyes, looking from Easton, then back to me as he stretches and yawns.

"We'll be here for a day, maybe two tops." Diaval says as he looks from his pocket watch, then over at the setting sun. "I need to get permission from the flight in Vasserdell for me to enter."

"Where are we at now?" Feray asks as she moves closer to Diaval, watching the plates in his face move slightly.

"We are currently in Thornford. It's a pleasantly mixed community on the way to Vasserdell, where I plan to take you to see the ocean." He reaches out and cups her cheek, looking deep into her eyes. Feray's body seems to become pliant in his gaze and she visibly sighs.

"You were serious about taking me to the ocean..." She sounds surprised that he actually meant what he had said.

"I was. You should experience everything the world offers. No more missing out on the outside world." Without thinking, he bends down and presses his lips to her forehead and closes his eyes.

Torben scoots up alongside us and nudges me with his shoulder. "Reminds me of that movie that Feray made us watch last week." Torben raises his eyebrows, hinting at the movie.

"Holy shit, you're right." My hands shoot up to cover my mouth. Wide eyed, I look between Torben and Easton. I feel like a teenage girl gossiping about the prom king and queen.

"Let nature take its course. She's patient, and he's set in his ways like some other mythic we know." Torben smiles and walks back to the trunk to grab our bags.

"I think it's time for us to go check in." Easton moves ahead and gets Diaval's attention. The two ancients walk off, leaving Feray standing there in a daze.

Seizing the opportunity, I scoot up beside her and loop my arm with hers. "Care to explore a little?" I fire a text off in our group chat before strolling down the main street in town.

Feray smiles and wraps her arm tightly around mine as we walk. She occasionally pulls me towards a storefront to look in the window. "Can we get a snack?" No sooner are the words out of her mouth does her stomach growl.

"Of course." I point a little further down the road. There's a street vendor with steak sticks and chicken kabobs. "Will that work for you?"

Feray squeals and starts dragging me down the road, making me almost trip over my own feet. As soon as we are in front of the vendor, she gives the poor woman her massive order. "I'm getting everyone a snack. Dinner isn't for a few hours yet." Her face suddenly drops, and she looks back at me, frightened. "Is that okay?" Her bottom lip quivers slightly as she waits for my reaction.

Closing the distance, I press my lips to hers and behind her back hand the vendor my credit card. "Never be afraid of trying to provide for all of your mates." Feray reaches up and wraps her arms around my neck, hugging me tightly. She whispers her thanks before slowly releasing me. The vendor hands us two boxes of sticks and kabobs to take with us.

We arrive back at the inn, and Torben is waiting in the lobby for us. "Smells divine. Good thinking guys." He smiles and takes the box from Feray and leads us up to the room.

Rolling my eyes, I follow behind them, heading up three flights of stairs. We make it to the suite and Diaval and Easton are both hovering over the maps and other books we have with us. "Snack time!" Feray shouts as she digs into the box Torben has in his hands.

She rushes over to Diaval and Easton and hands them two skewers, one chicken and one steak apiece before rushing back to the fridge. Feray grabs out a pitcher of water and passes out glasses of water to everyone. "Where's yours, Pet?" Diaval notes she doesn't have a glass of her own.

"Umm…" She bounces from one foot to the other before reluctantly pouring herself a glass.

"Good girl…" He smirks, looking at her and she arches a brow, not sure how to react. Deep down, I know her tail would be wagging at the praise. But, with as feminist as her sister is, I'm sure it's messing with her in some sense.

Feray goes and sits on the couch with her four skewers when that little pixie from hell pops into existence. "Ooooh Fluffy, Sparkles is pissed!" The little punk rock pixie stomps back and forth in her micro docs.

"Why is Fiadh pissed?" So many other things have happened that I honestly don't remember what could have set her sister off.

She stomps down the table, leaving a trail of pixie dust behind her. "One word Nope-rope: WENDIGO … Sound familiar?" She smiles, and it's creepy as all hell.

Feray gasps and then looks at the guys, then back again. "It really wasn't that bad. I promise. Easton turned it into roasted Wendigo. It didn't stand a chance against him." Feray waves a chicken kabob at Ro. "You know you want it…" Feray's voice takes on a weird tone and it's now that Diaval snaps his fingers and sticks his fingers in his ears.

My eyes dart to the other mates, and they are shoving their fingers in their ears, too. I follow along and watch as Feray's eyes slowly glow as she stares at the pixie. Her lips are moving and I know what she's saying. Soon the pixie is sitting down eating her kabob calmly. "What the hell was that?" I look over at Diaval as he smirks.

"Lunas with a powerful pack can sway others to their way of thinking. I believe Feray did it more defensively than intentionally." Diaval grabs a tome off the table and opens it before handing it to me. I read the page and sure enough, it's right there in black and white.

"We're looking for her pack, though." I'm puzzled as I stare at the page.

"We are her pack. Think about it. What is a pack, a family or a close-knit pack of animals?" Torben laughs and looks back at Easton and Diaval. "By extension, Fiadh is her soul sister, so her mates are also part of Feray's pack." Torben shakes his head trying to stop laughing. "She has three ancients, a fae, and four shifters in her pack besides her and Fi. Whoever pisses her off is screwed when she figures out what she can do." Torben almost laughs himself off the stool he's on.

Feray looks back at him and arches a brow. "Maybe that's why my wolf isn't so anxious anymore. I'm surrounded by bigger animals she knows will protect her." Feray smiles and goes back to eating her kabob, making happy little wolf grumbles.

"Oh Fluffy, I almost forgot. Count Suckula, Prince Picky Pants, and the other two shifters have no clue about the pulsing mate bite. Prince Picky Pants said he would look into it and get back to you. Count Suckula thinks it's because he's a mythic." Ro shrugs her shoulders, then poofs disappearing again.

"Well, that was not helpful at all." I say, looking down at Feray as she eats.

"Oh no, it helped tons. I have new nicknames for everyone." The evil giggle that came out of my mate's mouth makes my hair stand on end.

"That can't be good." Easton states.

"Clean up then bedtime..." Diaval barks out and for whatever reason, we listen. When Feray heads off to the shower, Diaval tells us to go to our rooms and let Feray pick where she's sleeping without pressure. I know who she's not sleeping with tonight.

This guy is on guard duty.

CHAPTER 9
FERAY

We are no closer to finding out why Easton's mark pulses in my presence. It seems even Revelin and Dezi do not know why. Looking out the window, I watch the town prepare for night fall. The sun dips below the horizon, casting a warm, orange glow across the sky. I've been on the road all day, miles upon miles of endless asphalt stretching out before us. My weary muscles ache from the hours spent cooped up in the car being Khal's pillow. The anticipation of a hot shower at journey's end has kept me going, and now, I finally step into the bathroom, ready to bask in its warm embrace.

As I turn the knob, the rush of hot water splashes onto my skin, sending shivers of relaxation up my spine. The steam rises, engulfing me in a comforting cocoon. The beads of water cascade down my body, washing away the fatigue and tension that have accumulated throughout the day.

As I turn, the jet stream of water massages my back, releasing knots and tension, and I let out a contented sigh. My shoulders drop as the soothing heat seeps into my pores, and I close my eyes, allowing the sensation to take over. The scent of my favorite shower gel fills the air, mingling with the steam, helping me to relax further.

The day's events fade into the background as I stand beneath the cascading water, lost in the sensation of sheer bliss. Each droplet that touches my skin carries away the dust of the journey, leaving me feeling cleaner and far more relaxed.

Time seems to stand still in the shower, and I relish in this moment of tranquility, knowing that the road's weariness has finally met its match. With a final rinse, I step out, my body refreshed, and wrap myself in a soft, fluffy towel. As I emerge from the bathroom, I can't help but smile, grateful for the simple, yet profound, pleasure of a hot shower after a long day on the road. Exiting the bathroom with just a towel around me, I stop to appreciate Khal's silhouette against the backdrop of the setting sun.

"Ready for bed, Precious?" Khal asks from his chair by the window. Where he's sitting, he's blocking the door and able to see out the window to the main road below.

"Yeah, I feel bad that you have to stay up all night." Pouting, I dig through my bag, finding my favorite night gown to slip into.

"I feel better knowing one of us is up watching. No one else in the group is naturally nocturnal except me." He shrugs his shoulders and smiles.

After I'm dressed, I close the distance between us and wrap him up in my arms and kiss him softly. "Thank you for watching over us."

He kisses me back gently and smirks. "So, Precious whose bed are you climbing into tonight?" He motions to the doors on the opposite side of the room.

"I think I'm going to go scare a dragon." I giggle, thinking about how bad it's going to throw him off finding me in his bed.

"I see my penchant for chaos is rubbing off on you. Go scare the dragon, just don't get burned." Khal swats my ass, sending me on my way.

Sneaking across the dimly lit suite, I move with practiced stealth, my heart pounding like a trapped bird in my chest. The carpeted floor absorbs the sound of my careful steps, muffling any noise that could betray my presence. My destination: Diaval's bedroom door, where my secret desires reside. The air is thick with anticipation, and I can feel my pulse quicken as I reach for the doorknob.

With a gentle turn of the knob, the door swings open, revealing Diaval's inner sanctum. The room is bathed in the soft glow of moonlight filtering through heavy curtains, casting silvery shadows across the polished wood floors. As I inch closer, I can't help but marvel at the sight before me.

Even in slumber, he exudes an air of regal serenity. Lying on his back, Diaval appears almost otherworldly, a sleeping prince in his enchanted slumber. His features, usually so stern and calculating, are softened in the ethereal light, and a ghost of a smile tugs at the corners of his lips. His dark, raven-like hair is still perfectly in place.

I hold my breath as I approach the bed, hesitant to disturb his peace. His hands, large and strong, are folded neatly on his chest, as if he guards his secrets even in sleep. I dare not touch him, fearing that the magic of this moment might break if I do. Instead, I slowly slide under the cool, crisp sheets, nestling beside him but maintaining a respectful distance.

The sensation of lying beside him, so close yet impossibly far, fills me with a bittersweet ache. I can't resist stealing a moment to admire the details of his face, tracing the lines of his jaw and the curve of his lips with my eyes. How is it that such a formidable man can appear so vulnerable in his slumber?

As I lie there, I can feel the rise and fall of his chest, a rhythmic reminder of his living presence. In this stolen moment, I feel closer to him than I have ever dared to hope. Diaval, the ancient dragon shifter. The fancy drink loving grumpy puss, now lies before me, a mysterious enigma that has captured my heart. And in this silent, moonlit bedroom, I find solace in simply being near him, even if it's in the hushed stillness of the night.

At some point I fall asleep watching him, only to slowly awaken, wrapped tightly in his embrace. His nose is buried in my auburn locks and his arms feel like bands of steel surrounding me. The heat from his body is slightly warmer than Torben's, but not as hot as Easton's.

Diaval's warm breath caresses the nape of my neck, a gentle, tantalizing sensation that sends shivers down my spine. I'm enveloped in the alluring fragrance of geraniums, a scent that I've come to associate with him. It fills the air, becoming stronger as his muscular arms band tighter around me. It's as if I've been ensnared in a cocoon of desire and enchantment.

"Sneaky little wolf climbing into my bed," he murmurs, his voice like a sultry whisper in the night, laden with a mix of amusement and desire. His lips brush against my ear, igniting a fire within me. He's playful and seductive all at once, a combination that makes my heart race.

As Diaval rolls away, the loss of his warmth against my back is palpable, and I let out a soft sigh of longing. His absence leaves me feeling vulnerable and exposed, like a lone wolf without its pack. I watch in the dim, silhouetted morning light as he exits the room, his movements fluid and graceful, a testament to the dragon within him.

The room falls into a hushed stillness, but the imprint of his touch lingers on my skin, a reminder of the intimate encounter. I reach out, my fingers grazing the space where he was, as if trying to capture a fleeting moment of connection. The sheets still bear the warmth of his presence, and I can't help but wish for more.

The memories of the moments we've shared flood my mind like a vivid tapestry of passion and longing. Diaval, with his enigmatic allure, has woven his way into my heart, and every stolen moment with him is a treasure.

I listen to the distant echoes of his footsteps, each one taking him further away from the room, from me. The longing for his return is undeniable, and I yearn for the sensation of his arms wrapped around me once more.

I stare at the door for far too long before I remove myself from the bed and his room. Stepping out, I look around to find him and Khal at the table sipping their orange juice like nothing had happened. Diaval tilts his head to the side then reaches back, grabbing a third glass of orange juice and wiggles it at me. "Come, drink your juice and wait for breakfast." His tone still holds that rough early morning quality to it.

Without putting too much thought into it, I walk over to the guys and take the juice. Khal pats his thigh and I climb up and sit snuggled in his lap. Easton is the next to emerge, and he stops taking in the scene. "Where did you sleep last night?" He stops on his way past me to kiss my temple before pouring himself a glass of orange juice.

"Some sneaky little wolf found herself in the dragon's den." Diaval's grumpy tone has a hint of playfulness to it that wasn't there before.

Shaking my head, I just stare at my orange juice. I will not rise to his baiting this time. Before I get to say anything, Torben walks in with a tray filled with breakfast foods. "Where did you sleep last night, little wolf?" He drops a spinach and cheese omelet and bacon in front of me before kissing my temple.

"I invaded grumpy's room. This morning I woke up being held like a woobie." I raise my gaze, staring defiantly at Diaval, waiting for his retort.

Torben's head whips back and forth between Diaval and me in shock. "Oh ... Okay then." Shrugging his shoulders, he sits down and eats his breakfast.

Clearing his throat, Easton gets everyone's attention. "It's approximately twelve hours between here and Vasserdell." He retrieves the mini map so we can follow along. "Taking into account that Torben, Feray, and Khal need to shift and hunt at some point. I figure if we stop about here," he points to a spot approximately in the middle between the two towns. "We should be able to shift safely and allow their animals to hunt." He then turns his gaze to Diaval. "Did you hear from the elder in Vasserdell?"

Diaval pulls his phone out from his pocket and stares down at it as he taps away. "They have a waterfront home for us to use for a few days. I requested to be allowed to take everyone to the ruins while we are there." His normally grumpy demeanor shifts and I see pain in his eyes. I study his features for several more minutes and decide now is not the time to ask what's wrong.

"It sounds beautiful." My words catch him off guard as he stares openly at me. It's now that I notice he's using the mug that I gave him for his coffee. I smile and go back to eating my breakfast.

"What was that smile for? It was beautiful." Easton shocks me by asking.

It takes me several moments to parse together an answer that won't give away anything. "Just a happy thought about how things mean something to everyone. Torben, it's the honey from the giant bees. Khal is physical contact. You, it's when I don't hide how smart I am and say things that shut people up." I smile again and laugh a little. "Diaval, it's his horde, his most valued possession, never far from him." I watch as his finger taps the mug and the corner of his mouth ticks up for a brief moment.

"Precious, a dragon's horde is enormous. He can't possibly bring it with him." Khal says as he threads his fingers through my hair.

"What he considers his horde is relevant. It can be a room full of treasure or as small as a thimble. Whatever his dragon focuses on as its prized possession is the only thing in its world that matters." As I speak what I know to be the truth, Diaval looks up and his eyes shift to that of his dragons. Man and beast stare at me openly and he smiles.

"For not being a dragon, you have a better grasp of how things work than most. Good girl..." He slides more bacon over to me and returns to studying the maps.

For whatever reason, his praise makes butterflies flutter in my stomach. Torben reaches over and pulls me off of Khal's lap and onto his. Torben's bear rumbles to me, and I sigh. I feel safe and secure in his arms. Leaning back, I close my eyes and just breathe in deeply. His rich scent of sandalwood envelopes me and I melt in his embrace.

"Don't forget, little wolf." He pulls his phone out, making me open my eyes. On the calendar it's marked that I need to get my birth control tincture for next week. I'm so glad my gentle giant is keeping track of these things. "Guys, we need to stop at the herbalist before we head out." Torben says, and then everyone looks at me.

Rolling my eyes, I shake my head. "I need a refill for my birth control. Last thing we need is for me to go into full-blown heat on our adventure." Torben kisses my cheek and gives me a hug, comforting me. He knows I want a big family someday. If I wasn't afraid of almost getting murdered at every turn, I would start now.

"The herbalist is the first stop then. After that, we'll depart." Easton offers.

"Let's kill two birds with one stone. Torben take Feray to the store while the guys and I get everything settled here." Diaval offers then slides a credit card across the table to us. "Buy as much as the herbalist has in stock. We don't know what lies ahead of us. I would hate for Feray to be put in danger over her heat." Diaval pauses between sentences as he stares at my hand, moving forward for the card.

"Thank you." I say as I slip off Torben's lap to go get changed. I pause at Diaval's side and look up into his eyes. The green in his hazel eyes seems to burn. With him sitting, he's just slightly taller than I am. Leaning in, I kiss his cheek then head to the bedroom to get changed. Onto our next adventure, I suppose.

CHAPTER 10

TORBEN

Feray's bold decision to venture into the dragon's den was not lost on any of us. As she emerged from my room after changing, a radiant smile graced her face, flooding the room with her warmth. Her arrival had a magnetic effect on the rest of the group, making us pause to admire her vibrant spirit.

"Be careful," Easton advised, a fond smile gracing his lips as he pressed them to Feray's forehead. Her smile in response was all the reassurance he needed; their connection clear in the way they gaze at each other.

Diaval, ever the stoic and grumpy one, made his way to Feray next. He meticulously adjusted a few stray strands of hair and gave her some essential supplies—a water bottle and a handful of snack sticks. His fingers lingered under her chin, gently lifting it with his index finger while his thumb rested atop her lower lip. The unspoken affection in the air was undeniable, and it gave me hope for the grumpy bastard. Diaval sealed his care with a kiss on Feray's forehead, passing her to Khal.

Khal, in his playful nature, couldn't resist a bit of levity. He scooped Feray up into his arms, spinning her in a joyful circle before entrusting her to my care. "I'll probably be asleep in the front seat by the time you get to the car," he teased. "Can you grab a few spray bottles of Shed Spray? It's almost time for my shift to shed his skin."

Feray's laughter echoed through the room. Her joy and happiness made me truly appreciate the bonds that had been forged among us during these trying times. As I agreed to Khal's request and made a mental note to retrieve the shed spray. Feray's departure marked the beginning of a new adventure. I can't help but feel a sense of hope and optimism about our unconventional family.

Feray's small notebook made a reappearance, and she added the shed spray to her ever-growing list with a mischievous grin. "Yup, just added it to my list. See everyone soon!" Her cheerful farewell echoed through the room, mingling with the last words of our makeshift family as they wished her well. With swift efficiency, Feray seized my hand and whisked me out of the door, her eagerness contagious and setting the morning's tone.

The early light of dawn filtered gently between the small, weathered buildings of this peaceful little town. The world roused itself in a soft symphony of muted colors, painting the cobblestone streets with a delicate palette of pinks and oranges. Hand in hand, we strolled through this serene tableau, we're on a mission that carried an unusual blend of responsibility and affection.

As we ambled along, I couldn't resist stealing sidelong glances at Feray, captivated by the grace in her every step. She glided with a natural elegance that leaves me spellbound, her silhouette etched against the backdrop of the pastel dawn. Her fiery hair, touched by the first rays of sunlight, shimmered like embers in a fire, radiating a warmth and vibrancy all its own. Her laughter, like a melodious tune, dancing on the morning breeze, wrapping around us and adding to the enchantment of the moment. In the gentle, early light, she was nothing short of a living, breathing masterpiece. Every second spent beside her feels like a treasured moment in our ongoing love story.

I squeeze her hand gently, and she looks at me with eyes that mirror the sky above—a soft, endless blue that makes my heart skip a beat. It's moments like these, in the quiet intimacy of dawn, that I realize how profoundly I love her. Her smile, so tender and filled with a touch of vulnerability, is my favorite sight in the world.

The apothecary's shop is nestled on the corner, a quaint little establishment with its aged, creaky door. A bell tinkles as we enter, announcing our presence to the elderly apothecary behind the counter. He greets us with a warm, knowing smile, probably having seen countless couples like us before. It's a subtle reassurance that eases my racing heart.

"Good morning sir, I need a birth control tincture meant for wolf shifters." Feray asks in a low tone and the shop keeper smiles softly back at her.

"Of course, dear let me grab the two types I have and you can pick the one you need." The apothecary fetches the two small glass vials filled with a precious elixir that has become a part of our lives.

Feray looks them both over, then chooses the purple one. "Can I get as many of these as you have?" Feray's question catches him off guard and he heads back into the back room. "Oh and I forgot, we need a few bottles of Shed Spray as well." She says quickly as it dawns on her she forgot Khal's order.

"You know that's not meant for wolves, correct?" The shopkeeper asks.

Feray giggles and nods. "I know. I was asked to pick it up while I was out." The way Feray doesn't mention it's for her mate makes me look at her oddly. Her eyes lock with mine and flare for a moment. I can feel the warning in her gaze wash over me, as if she shoved me physically. There has to be a very good reason why she didn't say who it was for. The shopkeeper returns with several bottles of spray and Feray picks three different ones, not sure which would be best.

"If you told me which shifter you were shopping for, I can point you in the right direction." The shopkeeper smiles sweetly. The wrinkles in the corners of his eyes creasing as the smile met his eyes.

"She's dragon-kin, that's all she wanted me to say." The smoothness of Feray's face and the even tone she held shocked me. She's lying right to the shopkeeper, and it appears she is telling the truth.

"Ah, that makes all the difference." The shopkeeper reaches under the counter and pulls out a different kind of spray and places it on the counter. "Dragon-kin's scales are very difficult to shed. This should help her immensely." He offers Feray the bottle and she untwists the cap and sniffs it.

Smiling, she puts the top back on. "I'll take six." The shopkeeper pulls out five more and boxes them in with her tinctures. We complete the transaction, leaving the shop with the stash of tinctures and sprays held securely in my grasp.

Our footsteps carry us toward a nearby park, where we find a quiet bench under the shade of a sprawling oak tree. We sit down, our fingers still entwined, and she takes the tincture immediately.

She makes a disgusted face as she shakes her head. "Yuck, I was hoping it was grape flavored, boy was I wrong." She laughs a little and stares at the little vial in her hand. I know she hates it. Her instincts, much like my own, are to start a family. It's not safe yet, sadly. Hopefully sooner than later we'll figure out why she's being hunted. For now, my number one job is to keep my mate happy and safe.

"We should probably head back, little wolf." Leaning over, I kiss her temple and pull her into my lap for a moment. I hug her tightly, missing the feel of my mate in my arms. "Will you hunt with me later?" Gently, I nuzzle her cheek before placing a kiss there.

"Of course." She stands up suddenly and starts dragging me back toward the inn. Her sudden enthusiasm to leave earns her a hearty chuckle from me as I'm dragged up the road.

"Why didn't you tell the shopkeeper it was for your mate?" Her omission of the truth is bothering my bear and me both.

She pauses in her steps, drawing in a deep breath. "If we are being hunted and watched. If someone asks around about me or who I'm traveling with, dragon-kin is not an exact answer. There are dozens of subspecies. They wouldn't know about Diaval or Khal, since that's species specific. Saying she instead of he also throws things off." Her eyes glow with the power and light of her wolf as she looks up at me. "I may not be as strong as everyone else, but I protect what's mine, however I can."

What she said makes sense. If we are being followed or tracked saying it was for her mate or for a basilisk would be like flashing a neon sign over our heads. "Makes sense, little wolf. I just didn't understand why you did it." Smiling, I kiss her temple before continuing on our way.

As we approach, we get to watch Easton and Diaval loading the car with a sleeping Khal in the front seat. When we get close, Feray climbs into the car, sitting herself in the middle of the back seat. She leans forward and fastens Khal's seatbelt and snuggles him into place for the ride. I help finish loading the SUV then climb in the back with Easton and Feray.

Feray shocks me by placing her back against Easton, allowing him to hold her while she stretches her legs out over my lap. "Diaval, what can you tell us about Vasserdell?" Since it appears our mate has decided to sleep more, I need to learn about our next stop.

"It's an old draconic stronghold for the older species of dragons and dragon-kin. Unlike Norburg you will find many species versus only basilisks." He glances back, using the rearview mirror. "There are ruins near the town where several of my ancestors are laid to rest. I haven't visited in decades, mainly because the female I was almost forced to be mated to is the matriarch." Diaval visibly shivers, thinking about what we are walking into.

"Is it safe to bring Feray there?" I look over at my sleeping mate wrapped up in Easton's arms. His eyes burn with the fire and intensity of his shift watching over her.

"She has two mythics, a basilisk, and a Kodiak Berserker in her nest. She can't get much safer than she is right now." He glances down quickly. "I'll give her my scale before we get there. The rest will have to wait." Diaval goes silent as his stony mask falls back in place.

"She has to accept his shift and fly with him." Easton whispers so as not to wake Feray. "A Skull Dragon's natural intimidation ability is very hard for a smaller shifter to withstand." Easton glances up and watches Diaval nod stiffly. Come to think about it, I've never seen him shift either.

"Have you seen his dragon before?" Looking back at Easton, he nods and looks down.

"Yeah, it scared me to death." He looks down at Feray and a single tear rolls down his cheek. "I'll make the sacrifice to walk with her when it's time. I can resurrect." He runs his fingers through her hair, playing with her feather.

"So, it can kill her?" I try my best to quell the fear building up in my chest over it.

"It's why it's imperative I plant my scale first. The intimidation shouldn't affect her once it's in place." Diaval's tone is rough and the feeling inside the car becomes almost oppressive.

Feray half wakes up and yawns before sitting up and reaching out to touch Diaval. "Shhh ... you're okay." Her tone is almost hypnotic when she speaks and the oppressive feeling fades away. Soon as it does, she lays back down and goes back to sleep.

"She shouldn't be able to do that." Diaval whispers.

"Why?" I glance between him and Easton.

"She's not bonded to him yet." Easton glances down, then his head whips towards me so he can look me in the eye. "It's because of me, my feather." He brushes his knuckles over her hair, touching her feather.

"What does that have to do with anything?" His answer has confused me more than I was before. The sudden left turn we just took mentally threw me off.

Diaval sighs and pulls over for a moment. "What my old friend is so tactfully trying to say is that it is because of his feather. She's gotten stronger. Well, her luna gifts. From what I know of the lass, she is not a warrior, but she will go to war if someone she loves is threatened. Thankfully, unlike her witch sister, she does have the self-preservation instinct." As much as I want to let Diaval's tone piss me off, he's right.

Feray studies the situation before she reacts that coupled with how scary intelligent she is. She's more formidable than some of the alphas I've met over the years. I watch as my little wolf snuggles into Easton's chest. "So, between his feather and your scale, you believe she'll survive meeting your dragon?" My heart is beating erratically in my chest as I watch the minute changes in the creases around Diaval's eyes.

"She has to." His terse, definitive answer doesn't exactly comfort me.

"What do you mean, she has to? You aren't bonded to her fully. Her dying won't destroy you the way it will the three of us." My bear is clawing at my chest, wanting to be released. He feels he needs to protect Feray from the dragon. *What the actual fuck is he thinking?*

"What Diaval is failing to express..." Easton gets ready to explain when Diaval cuts him off.

"My dragon will go insane if he accidentally kills his mate. The rampages written in the history books will be nothing compared to what he will do." His tone sounds broken as he glances between the two of us. "The literal fate of the world rests in her little hands." His voice softens as he turns further to look into the backseat at Feray while she sleeps. He watches her for several more moments before turning back to face forward. With a sigh he gets us back on the road again. Taking my cue, I close my eyes, hoping against hope that whatever needs to happen at the next stop, my love, my heart survives.

CHAPTER 11

DIAVAL

The countryside stretches out before me, a patchwork quilt of vibrant greens and golden yellows. As the sun climbs higher in the sky, its gentle rays casting a warm, honeyed hue on the landscape. The air is crisp and clean, carrying with it the earthy scent of freshly plowed fields and the faint fragrance of wildflowers that line the roadside.

I grip the leather-wrapped steering wheel of the car, the smooth texture cool against my palms. The engine purrs a comforting background hum, and the tires whisper over the gravel stone. The road stretches ahead, winding through rolling hills and quaint, picturesque farms, each with its own barn and weathered picket fence.

My travel companions, cocooned in the tranquility of slumber, rest peacefully while I make the drive to our next stop. The soft, even breaths of the basilisk in the passenger seat are like a gentle metronome, a reminder of all the danger that surrounds our group. I will not forget his sacrifice of remaining on watch all night. One awake, four asleep. It seems to be the way we are being forced to operate these days. My mate nestled in the back seat, her head resting on Easton's chest, is a vision of serenity.

I steal occasional glances at her, my heart swelling with affection. Strands of her auburn hair cascade gracefully over her shoulders, framing a peaceful expression that dances with fleeting dreams. Her lips, parted ever so slightly, form a delicate, contented smile. The morning sun plays upon her face, casting a soft, ethereal glow that accentuates the flutter of her eyelashes.

Outside, the world continues to unfold. I pass a meadow where a family of deer grazes, their white tails flicking in the morning light. The birds above, heralding a new day, serenade us with their melodic songs. In the distance, the old oak trees stand like ancient sentinels, their gnarled branches reaching for the heavens.

As we journey through this idyllic countryside, I am filled with a deep sense of foreboding. At some point during our next stop, I need to convince Feray to allow me to implant my scale on her chest. How in the nine hells am I going to pull off that miracle? Shaking my head, I return my focus to the road ahead of us. Danger lurks around every turn. The most dangerous part heading into Vasserdell, and facing Myra, is more terrifying than meeting this unseen danger.

-Several hours later-

Feray stirs from her slumber and pulls herself free of the Doctor's embrace. "I need to pee." She yawns promptly after making the statement.

"Remember what happened the last time you went pee?" Arching a brow, I playfully remind her of her last misadventure.

Feray looks taken aback by my statement and lowers her eyes. Glancing back to the road, I find a nice area for us to pull over and let everyone stretch their legs. "Allow one of us to accompany you into the woods so we can be within reach of you." I turn in the driver's seat to reach back and take her hand in mine. "You are far too important to us to lose." Easton is the first to awaken, having heard me. He gives me a slight nod out of respect and rubs her back.

"We just wish to keep you safe." He offers gently.

"That makes sense." She pulls at some of her hair and sighs. "I'm sorry I reacted poorly. It's been a lot to adjust to." She huffs out a laugh. "The predator is now the prey." Her tone turns sour, and she lowers her head again.

Reaching back, I grip her chin and raise her eyes to face me. "You are no one's prey." I wink at her, then smile. "Unless you want to be." Her pupils dilate immediately at the dark promise. I think my little mate may have a bit of a kink.

"I can go with you if you want." Torben offers her, and she looks between me and Easton, then over to a sleeping Khal.

"No offense Tor. Easton can torch the bad guy; it may be more effective than your bear. Depending on the foe, of course." She stares down at her hands and it's now that I notice she is shifting her nails back and forth between her claws and her nails.

"You're not defenseless Feray." The words tumble from my lips without a second thought. I'm just as surprised as she is when I say it.

"I can't kill a Wendigo." She flexes her hands again, shifting her nails back and forth, watching her claws come out.

I hazard a glance at Easton and Torben and they exit the car, leaving me with Feray and a sleeping basilisk. Reaching back, I take a hold of her hand and exhale slowly. "If my guess about your bloodline is correct, you are more powerful than you think." Her eyes lower and she stares at our joined hands.

"I hope for my sake you're right." She lays her hand on mine and gives it a pat before exiting the SUV.

My hand still tingles from where we had made contact. I remain seated for several moments longer before exiting the car. Feray is walking hand in hand with Easton into the brush close to where we parked. "She's so timid. There's a demon locked in her chest and yet she acts like a frightened doe." I say as I move to stand alongside Torben.

"What do you mean by that?" He quirks his head to the side and looks at me oddly.

"You don't feel the dormant power within her?" I shake my head, puzzled by this revelation.

"No, should I?" He scans the wood line, watching for fire like I am.

"She's not on edge around you, so it probably remains suppressed. With me, I feel the surges of power within her. It's as if her wolf is railing against my dragon for dominance." A hearty chuckle escapes my lips as I watch the horizon.

"What's so funny?" Torben moves to stand in front of me. His bear is close to the surface.

"Remember what your book about her Luna line said?" I tilt my head, looking at him, waiting for reality to set in. He shrugs his shoulders, looking at me, then shakes his head no. "A luna is only as strong as her pack. A wolf's pack is its family."

His eyes flair with the power of his bear as his head whips toward the woods, then back at me. "Shit..." He paces, then looks at me again. I think he finally connected the dots.

"She has a wyrm skull dragon mate, an ancient phoenix, a basilisk, and a berserker Kodiak. We are the most powerful of each of our species. Imagine when she accepts my scale and bonds with me properly." I tilt my head, looking down at him. My dragon rises to the surface to greet him.

Torben takes a step back, then almost jumps out of his skin when Feray touches him from behind. The melodic giggle that escapes her lips makes my smug dragon tilt his head, listening to her. The brazen little wolf steps into my personal space and stares up at me, her eyes burning yellow. "Don't laugh at him." She slaps my chest, then moves past me.

"You like living dangerously, don't you, little one?" My voice drops octaves lower than I usually allow it to be. My dragon wants to be in control and he's trying to croon to his mate. The change in the pitch of my voice makes white fur race up her arms and she stops. She glances over her shoulder at me. Her eyes are her wolf's and I can see the shifting of bone plates under her skin. Without warning, she throws her sundress off and shifts suddenly.

Her wolf walks up to me without fear and stares defiantly into my eyes, challenging my dragon. *She's worthy* ... The cantankerous bastard finally speaks to me after centuries of silence.

"Enjoy your hunt, Feray. When you return, I would like to offer you something very valuable." She glances towards Torben and barks at him. The bear walks off and starts stripping. A cold wet nose touches my hand and it's Feray trying to get my attention. "I can't hunt with you yet. There are things that need to be done before I introduce you to my beast." Smiling, I take a knee before her. "He wants to meet you very badly. Both your human and wolf intrigue him." Stifling a laugh, I listen to my dragon remind me about the mug. "He says thank you for our mug. It's the most precious thing in his horde."

Feray's wolf tilts its head, studying me, then steps closer. When she's finally within reach of me, I slowly extend a hand out and run my fingers through her thick pelt. Her fur is as soft as I would imagine petting a cloud would feel like. Unlike the run-of-the-mill wolves I am used to seeing, her coat has two distinct layers. The outside layer gets thicker for winter to provide added protection as the weather turns harsh. The inside layer covers the skin closely and acts like a waterproof barrier to keep their skin dry and warmer.

Having felt her fur, I know without a doubt she comes from the Crescent Valley Pack. The Dunnum Pack migrates south when the harshest part of winter hits, or they remain in their human forms. They do not have the same pelt as she does; theirs lacks the second layer. The Crescent Valley Pack shifts to their wolf forms and remains as their wolves all winter.

"You are exquisite, Feray." My words come out softer than I had intended.

Her wolf cocks its head but doesn't pull away as she stares into my eyes. Hesitantly, her wolf takes another step forward and presses its lips to my cheek like a human would before she turns and bounds off.

"That could have gone very badly..." Easton's cocky tone makes me want to roast him on the spot.

"Thanks fire chicken..." Rolling my eyes, I shift my hand, allowing scales to erupt over my human flesh. I stare at my armored scales, noting the damage from wars gone by. "I wonder which scale she would want more..." I muse as I turn my hand over, slowly scrutinizing every scale.

"I'm sure any of them would be valuable to her if you explain to her the meaning behind it." Easton turns his gaze upon me and the fire in his eyes tells me his bird is the one offering the advice, not the man.

"How did you choose which feather to give her?" Now's the perfect time to put him on the spot as any.

Easton's steady movements falter and it's now that his normal nervous tick kicks in. His fingers move to every inch of his pressed shirt, making sure not a button is out of place before he turns to look at me. "I didn't. My bird forced the shift one night after work and we flew home. When we landed on the rail of my balcony, he plucked a feather and left it on the table."

"You know perfectly well I cannot shift in front of her until she has my scale." My voice is a rough growl, making my throat feel raw from the exertion.

Take one from our chest ... My dragon growls in my head and shifts the flesh over our sternum. *It will grow back* ... He's right, these scales grow the fastest and rejuvenate the quickest.

Glancing up, I look at Easton. "I'm going to need your help upon her return. Heal her once I implant the scale." I unbutton my vest and then remove my tie. Nimble fingers go to my dress shirt, and I undo several of the buttons exposing my battle-hardened scales. Each one with its own damage from years of war.

"You know I will," Easton responds as he looks my scales over. "It would be wise to let her choose. After all, she is the one that will wear it."

"Who will wear what?" My Inamorata's sweet voice shocks me that she is so close to me.

How much of our conversation did she hear? My hands rise of their own accord to adjust a tie that is no longer around my neck. "Well, a dragon's mate is adorned with one of his scales. It is as symbolic as your bite is for the wolves." Feray cocks her head to the left, then the right until her eyes lock on my opened shirt.

"May I?" Her eyes begin to glow with the power of her wolf as she steps cautiously into my personal space. Her hand motions in the air towards my half-opened dress shirt and her eyes lock on my scales underneath.

Don't mess this up meat bag or you will never fly again ... My dragon threatens me. Me, of all the beings in the world, he chooses me to be the focus of his aggression. *You have denied us taking a mate for hundreds of years. Don't scare our female ...* I feel him retreat to the depths of my consciousness almost to the point I barely feel him.

"Diaval? Are you okay? One minute I saw your dragon's eyes and the next he's gone." She rests her dainty hand on my chest over my heart, and I swear the damn thing is going to explode.

"Um, yes ... We are fine. He was threatening me to behave and not scare you." I stare down at her hand and out of the corner of my eye I catch Torben motioning for me to put my hand over hers. I mimic his action and Feray smiles brightly.

"Well, I don't know what you said to him, but I feel like he's not happy with you." She smiles as her free hand slowly raises and pushes open my shirt. Her eyes widen, looking at the armored scales over my chest. Hesitantly, her hand reaches out and lightly touches one.

It's then that my dragon surges forward, and she leaps back, feeling his sudden presence. *Damn it ...* Did his excitement ruin our chance at being with our mate?

CHAPTER 12
FERAY

The feel of Diaval's scales is so different from Khal's. Where Khal's is cold and hard yet smooth to the touch. Diaval's runs hot and rough like sandpaper under my fingertips. There's a surge of power from him and I leap back, half shifting. My legs are that of my wolf, as are my forearms and hands. I stare at my claws and feel my elongated canines in my mouth.

My tail swishes behind me as I study Diaval. His eyes are lined with tiny black scales and his eyes have a malevolent glow to them.

"Careful Diaval. Your dragon is close to breaking loose. Look what it did to Feray. Her fight-or-flight instinct kicked in." Easton warns, stepping between Diaval and me.

It only angers his dragon further and a deep growl escapes his lips, making my wolf whine. I force myself to draw in a slow breath. Reaching out, I take a hold of Easton's shoulder. "I'm alright. Step aside." Gently, I give his shoulder a reassuring squeeze before he steps out of the way.

"Naughty dragon…" Each step closer, I shift back to being completely human. I watch every shift of the bone plates in Diaval's face. "We understand you're excited to see us. Remember, we are probably no bigger than your largest scale when you emerge." Having no experience with an actual dragon, I can only assume he's enormous.

Diaval chuckles. "You've gone and done it now."

"What did I do?" I tilt my head to the side as I rest both palms against his chest, looking up at him.

"You have somehow made him even more protective of you. Thinking of you being no bigger than one of his scales, he wants to place you with his horde and burn the world to ash to make sure you're safe." Diaval's hand rises slowly, and he cups my cheek.

His warmth seems to envelope me and I hear what sounds like a low, humming purr. "My Inamorata, I need you to choose the scale you wish on your body." Diaval nuzzles my cheek and I feel my canines break free of my gums.

The taste of iron makes my eyes pop open, and I know I am looking at him through my wolf's eyes. Shaking my head slightly, I break free of the trance I was falling under. Cautiously, I slide my hands down his chest to his open dress shirt to look at the scales again. "May I choose a scale from somewhere else? This is far too close to your heart. I don't wish to be the reason you are left defenseless."

Diaval tilts his head, looking at me, then smiles. "He says we have chosen wisely." He smiles and steps back. "Anywhere you desire, I will shift and you may pluck the scale yourself."

My eyes roam his body, and I didn't realize just how toned his shoulders are. Sliding my hands up his chest, I make his jacket and vest slide off his shoulders and down his arms to pool at his feet. A richer version of his chamomile scent hits my senses like a freight train. The simple act of removing his vest and jacket is turning him on.

Staring at the remaining buttons on his shirt, I make quick work of them, opening his shirt wide. I can hear his breath hitch when I touch his skin and I freeze briefly. My eyes remain locked on his shirt before I slide my right hand under it and move his shirt off his left shoulder. "Shift here…" I touch the thick ball of muscle that surrounds his shoulder joint.

One by one, blackened scales emerge from his tan flesh. It amazes me, watching them as they ripple across the muscle, giving me several dozen to choose from. Leaning in closer, I sniff at the scales taking in their scent. If danger had a scent, it's his. The chamomile scent has morphed to be rougher, edged with a hint of leather and burning wood. The hairs raise on the back of my neck as I move closer and inspect the scales. "How do I do this?" I stare at the one scale that seems to be battle hardened, the one that has a scar.

"Use your claw tip at the top of the scale and pull down." Diaval's tone is smooth and even as he turns his head to look at me. A gentle smile graces his lips and he for once, doesn't look like he's scowling at the world.

Nodding my head, I draw in a fortifying breath and shift my index fingernail to a claw. Staring at the scale I want; I strike quickly and pluck the scale from his shoulder. Without thinking about it, I lean in and lick the wound, sealing it. My mouth opens of its own volition and my canines descend.

Bite him … Make him ours… Pretty pretty dragon… Strong mate… My wolf for once utters words and I can't help but do as she desires.

I strike without warning, sinking my canines into the meat of his shoulder. The burst of iron upon my tongue gives me a sense of euphoria. Panicked shouts are droned out as I focus on Diaval's heartbeat. Strong fingers thread through my thick red hair and pull me back, making me release his shoulder. His blood coats my lips and before I can say anything, he mashes his lips against mine. Diaval dominates the kiss, his tongue teasing the seam of my lips until I open for him. He controls the kiss as our tongues slide and caress each other. My greedy core tries to grip something that isn't there before he slows the pace of the kiss.

He leaves me wanting as I finally open my eyes to see his dragon is on the edge. "I need to plant my scale..." He forces the words out, and it seems like he's battling his dragon for control.

I know something else I would like him to plant ... I say to myself and my wolf fully endorses the idea. Turning my hand palm up, I expose the scale to him and he looks at it, shocked. "Are you sure you want that one? It's damaged." His brows knit together in the middle as he glances from me to his scale in my hand.

"We're all a little damaged if we're being perfectly honest." Smiling, I look fondly down at the scale in my hand. "I'm a wolf raised as a witch, bound and hidden for over twenty-some years." I slowly look up and make eye contact with Diaval, Torben, and Easton, since Khal is still sleeping. "Torben was ready to go live as his bear. Easton buried himself in his burn unit. And you..." I turn my gaze back to Diaval. "You left your flight to escape a forced mating."

Moving my hair to the side and motion to my upper chest. "Make my wolf and your dragon happy. Plant your scale." I take his hand and rest it over my heart and give him a nod.

Diaval hesitates, staring down at where his hand is resting. "I don't want to hurt you." His voice is barely above a whisper as he stares at my lightly tanned skin.

I bring my claw up and press it into my skin. A rivulet of blood rolls down my chest and his eyes flair to life. Quickly taking the scale from me, he shoves the meaty side into the hole I made. "Easton, heal her..." Diaval's head whips up and his eyes lock on the now skittish doctor. He places his hand over the scale and a warmth washes over the area. Soon the minor pain I was feeling passes, the warmth slowly recedes.

Easton dips his head in my direction before backing away. "Torben, you need to take the car and park it in the woods and not come out. Diaval's dragon is going to break loose soon now that the scale lives on his mate."

"What about Feray? You said it could kill her..." Torben's panic echoes through the bond, and I try to send soothing feelings down through our shared connection.

"It won't kill me. Besides, Easton said he will stay with me. Even if it kills him." I look over at him sadly, knowing what he's about to sacrifice.

Easton grips my hand and gives it a squeeze. "On the bright side, you get to see a baby phoenix." He forces a smile and shrugs his shoulders.

"Not exactly the way I wanted to see one." I feel a soft blush creep across my cheeks, warming them.

"I know." He smiles.

Turning back to Torben, I give him a hug and smile up at him. "I'll be okay. My wolf says we'll be fine." I try to imbue as much strength as possible into my voice as I talk to him.

"If you're sure." My big guy bends down and kisses me tenderly. I can feel the slight tremble of his hand against my cheek. He's scared for us.

"I'm sure. Go hide the SUV out of sight. Stay there until I come and get you." I kiss him again and hug him tightly before I playfully start shoving him towards the vehicle. "Go, I'll be alright." Torben nods and lowers his head before getting in the SUV and driving out of sight.

"Feray." Diaval calls my name and I turn to face him. "It may be easier for your wolf if you keep your eyes closed while I shift."

"I'll hold her with my back to you." Easton offers and I nod.

There's a curiosity and a terror that is creeping up my spine, thinking about how huge his dragon is. Black dragons are known as skull dragons and are nightmares in scales. Stepping into Easton's embrace, I press the bridge of my nose against his throat so that his neck hides my eyes.

There's a distinct popping and a shift in the pressure in the air. The beast has emerged. I can feel it in my very soul that he is looking at us. The scale on my chest feels like a gentle tugging sensation. "Keep your eyes closed. I'm going to step away, Easton."

I feel him nod his head and I do as I had said. I step away, keeping one hand on him. Lowering my head, I open my eyes and stare at the ground. Inch by inch, I slowly look in the direction of the tugging. Black talons are sunk into the earth and are easily half the size of my wolf. The front hand can easily engulf my wolf and carry her off, probably even Torben's bear. My eyes slowly inch up his battle-hardened scales following the lines of his front legs up to the massive black armored chest of his dragon.

My breath catches in my throat as I stare at how wide his dragon's chest is. It's easily as wide as the house I live in. Bloody hell, his dragon is the biggest thing I have ever seen. The moment of truth is when I look up to face the dragon in question. The raised bony prominences of his skull are white like bone, denoting his wyrm status. His maw is whitened from age and battle. Several large, jagged scars cover his maw up to his bony eye ridge. His horns are huge and curled similar to a ram's horn.

"I'm okay, Easton. I'm looking at him and I'm safe."

"I'm going to shift and fly off so you two can get to know each other." With that, he shifts immediately and takes off toward where Torben parked the SUV.

Diaval lays down in the field and rests his head on the ground. Slow, steady steps carry me across the grassy meadow. My heart beats erratically in my chest as I approach him. All of his scars seem to stand out further than they did when I first looked at him. "Who hurt you?" I say as I rest the palms of my hands on his face.

His giant yellow green eye closes slowly, and I hear him exhale the breath he was probably holding. "I'm tougher than I look, Diaval." His eye pops open and he wiggles his eye ridge.

"Don't give me that look. Yes, the thought of meeting this side of you terrified me. Mainly because everyone kept telling me I could die." Shifting my hands, I use my claws to preen his scales closest to me. In several crevices on his face, there's a buildup of old scales that didn't shed off. His dragon makes a deep rumble that sounds almost like a purr as I clean away the old scales.

"I bet this feels good, huh? The old scales have to be itchy." His eye closes again and next thing I know, I have the man standing before me. Double blinking, I retract my claws before I accidentally hurt him.

"Did I do something wrong?" Before I can pull my hands back, he grips them both closely.

"No, you did everything right." He reverently kisses my knuckles, and I laugh. "What's so funny?"

"It's not fair you get to keep your clothes when you shift like Easton does. Damn mythics." I giggle playfully, so he knows I mean no harm.

"You bear the marks of two mythics. There's no reason why I shouldn't be able to teach you to keep your clothing after we…" He leaves the word mate unspoken. He's not ready for that step for whatever reason. But that's okay. If I'm being honest with myself, neither am I.

We walk hand in hand across the field to where the others are waiting for us. They're probably waiting to see if I lived or died or not. Won't they be pleasantly surprised to see us together?

CHAPTER 13

EASTON

I left my mate to die alone ... What am I thinking? Why would she send me away? I do as Feray wishes and I fly over to where Torben and the SUV are. I shift back as I land, and Torben is on me in a millisecond. "Where's Feray?"

He grips my shoulders firmly, and shakes me almost violently. "She said she was fine. If she wasn't, we would feel it and or I would be dead." I stare him in his eyes, trying to imbue him with some sense of security.

"I hope you're right." He practically growls out and stomps back to the other side of the car and starts pacing.

My bird is tearing me apart from the inside and I swear I feel like I'm going to spontaneously combust on the spot. Khal has, by some miracle, slept through the entire ordeal. In some ways, he's the lucky one. He doesn't know what we are anxiously waiting for. Any sign of life.

"Don't look so stressed out Doc..." Feray's musical tone makes my heart stop dead in my chest.

"Little Wolf!" Torben bellows before running over to her to pick her up and crush her to him.

Feray is giggling in his arms as he spins her around. She's kissing him back, just as excited as he is. You would think they were separated for months instead of barely thirty minutes. "Put me down you big lug, I have to see the others too." Her giggles are infectious as he carefully puts her on the ground.

"Sorry, little wolf. When they said you could die..." He looks down and away until she pulls his face back towards her.

"Yeah, that didn't exactly help set my nerves at ease, either. But, it's like Diaval said. Once his scale was implanted and I bit him, we were okay." Feray says as she strokes his cheek, trying to soothe him.

"I would never hurt my Inamorata." Diaval says definitively.

"What does that word mean? I know it's not in English," Feray gently extracts herself from Torben's grip to go stand before Diaval.

"Yes, please do translate that for her." I decide to help put the old grump on the spot. After all, he stole the word from my people that we use for our mates.

He adjusts his tie and openly glares at me. "It comes from the Phoenixes. It means in flames in love." Smoke bellows from his nostrils as his eyes flicker between human and dragon. Maybe I pushed him too far this time?

Feray looks from Diaval, then over at me, then back at Diaval. "What do dragons say to their mates?" She tilts her head several times, watching Diaval fidgeting under her intense scrutiny.

"Usque ad mortem." He moves closer to her, and his eyes take on the glow of his dragon. "Until death. It means as long as my heart beats, you are it for me. You are the beginning and end of all things. The sun rises and sets according to your every desire." It's like watching one of those hallmark movies. The arrogant asshole changes his ways and finally earns the woman's love. Diaval leans down and kisses her lips and I hear Torben sniffle. The big guy is over there watching them have their moment moved by how Diaval just made his feelings known. I thought the fae were bad with how they ooze sex appeal. The old grumpy bastard just incinerated her panties.

Slowly, they pull apart, and she looks over at me. Her steps carry her across the distance, and she grabs me by my tie and pulls me down to her level. "Thank you for being so selfless to sacrifice yourself to ensure my safety." She kisses my lips so softly and it's the most erotic thing I have ever experienced in my life. I can feel the surge of her wolf under her skin, and she's become more powerful.

Feray pulls back and smiles, looking up at me. "Anything you need of me, ask, and it shall be yours." I caress her cheek and kiss her forehead. I allow my lips to linger there for several beats before pulling away. "We ought to get back on the road." I whisper against her skin before backing away and taking her hand.

"Why don't you let me drive? You and Diaval sit in the back with Feray." Torben offers, smiling and motioning to the car. The bear, her first mate, is so selfless with his time. He is willing to forsake his place at her side to allow Diaval and me to have ours.

"Are you sure?" I question as I pull the keys out of my pocket.

"I'm sure." He reaches out and takes the keys from me. "You're newly mated and Diaval is half mated to her. You both need your time to let the bond strengthen and deepen naturally."

I extend my hand out to him and shake it firmly. "I can see why she accepted you as her first mate. You lead from a place of self-lessness. Torben, you are wise beyond your years."

"What do you mean I accepted him as first mate? The order makes a difference?" Shit … Her innocent question I know will not be able to be derailed.

"Let's talk about it while Torben drives, shall we?"

"I need answers, many detailed answers." She looks up into my eyes as she grips my tie firmly in her hand.

"Answers you shall have." Diaval states as he offers her his arm.

Feray releases me like I had set her hand on fire and takes hold of Diaval. He leads her back to the car and then to the trunk. Popping it open, he pulls out a bottle of water and a bag of snacks. "You need to eat and drink once we're in the vehicle again. Then we will give you the answers you desire." He doesn't give her the option to refuse the food and drink. Instead, she smiles slightly and nods, taking what he's offering.

Without hesitation, she gets into the car and I stand here stunned, watching what's happening before me. Feray is strong and dominant when she has to be, otherwise she enjoys feeling safe and cared for. Her preference for being sheltered versus having to wage war is interesting. I get into the back of the SUV from the passenger side and close the door.

"Are we ready to get going?" Torben turns with a big smile painted on his face. The big guy seems happy with the way everything is progressing.

"Let's get going." I laugh a little, watching Feray eating her snack and Diaval watching her like a hawk. "What is it with you two and stuffing food in Feray's face?" I look between them as Torben pulls back out onto the road.

"For bears a well fed and happy mate is a sign of a powerful male. A good boar provides food and protection for its mate. If she feels safe and is never hungry, then I have done my job." Torben says it with such passion that I sit up and take notice.

"Dragons believe that if our female wants for nothing, we have done our job." I watch him brush the hair away from her face as she eats the second bag of snacks.

"What of your horde? Which means more to you? Your mate or your horde?" I pose the question, curious about what his answer is.

Diaval laughs as he hands Feray her bottle of water back. "That's easy ... A dragon's mate trumps its horde. Since my mate gave me my prized possession, it's always going to be her."

"I did?" Feray angles her body, leaning back against me to watch Diaval. She obviously didn't realize how important her gift was to me.

"You did." The smirk he was wearing earlier fades, and a genuine smile appears for a moment as he digs in the satchel that is never far from him. He pulls out the black mug Feray gave him.

He hands it to her like it's the most fragile thing in the world. She turns it over in her hands several times and then notices the inscription. The same Latin phrase, until death written in a beautiful script. "You didn't know it. But the day you gave me that mug, my dragon decided you were meant to be ours. Instinct told me you were mine, but that cranky bastard doesn't always agree with me. For once he did."

"But you set it aside..." She sets the mug on her lap before she wrings the hem of her sundress.

Torben's eyes find the rearview looking back at Feray. "Deep breath, let him explain."

Diaval nods his thanks in Torben's direction before speaking. "Your thoughtful gift stunned me. I'm usually so unapproachable that no one has ever gifted me anything." I watch him reach down and extract her hands from the hem of her dress and he rubs his thumbs gently over the back of her small hands.

Slowly, I run my hands down her arms, trying to soothe her. "You are a massive asshole most of the time, Diaval." I chime in.

"Easton!" Feray looks over her shoulder at me and lightly smacks my hand.

"What? it's true."

"He is right. Diaval can be a dick at times." Torben adds.

"Now that we've determined I can be a dickish asshole, may I continue?" Diaval stares at each of us then proceeds, taking our silence as permission. "My dragon started fighting me, wanted to be released in that little room for you to see him. Before I accidentally crushed the mug in my hand, I set it aside to keep it safe." He draws in a deep breath and looks over her shoulder at me. "As Easton can attest. It's difficult when you have spent most of your existence alone."

A smirk ticks up the corner of his mouth for a moment. "In dragon society, the female picks the males in her nest. My dragon chose you. It was a shock when he was urging me to claim a female that he only knew from the bar. One who seemed to know exactly what flavors would please us the most." He gazes affectionately down the bridge of his nose at her.

"It wasn't hard to figure out. Your choice in whiskey or bourbon told me exactly what to put together. The rest was watching and learning." Feray leans back and presses herself into me further. From what I can tell, she does this when a topic makes her uncomfortable.

I stop running my hands up and down her arms and I wrap an arm around her waistline, hugging her. "You are very observant and highly intelligent. I would expect nothing less from you." Leaning in, I kiss the shell of her ear and nuzzle her cheek after, like I had seen Torben do to soothe her. Slowly, the tenseness I was feeling in her rigid frame relaxes and she sighs softly.

Leaning her head back, she smiles at me. "I'm not the only one watching and learning what my mate needs. You did good." Her praise is followed up by a kiss as she remains leaning against me.

"I would not be a suitable mate if I didn't notice what does and doesn't make you happy." Glancing towards the front of the car, Torben makes eye contact with me using the rear-view mirror. He gives me a terse nod and I assume it's his way of showing his approval.

"So back to this mate order thing. Someone needs to start explaining because I'm confused." Feray makes the give me movement at Diaval, and he hands her back her water bottle.

"Well, way back when." I gesture in the air, rolling my hand slightly. "Most families were like how this one is shaping up to be. The female having several mates in her nest. In the grand design, it makes more sense." Shrugging my shoulders, I look between Diaval and Torben.

"What Easton is trying to say, given everyone's chosen profession. Someone will always be with you. Not that anyone would tell you to quit your job, but you could if you wanted to.

Combined, your mates make enough to support everything."
Torben offers.

"Or if there's something you always wanted to do, we could help you achieve it." Diaval interjects.

"Is there anything you always wanted to do?" Leaning forward, I hug her tighter. Hopefully, she will let us in on what her deepest desires are.

CHAPTER 14

FERAY

WHAT IS IT I WANT TO DO WITH THE REST OF MY LIFE ONCE THIS IS OVER? I've never thought about what the future holds. All I've ever known is struggling from paycheck to paycheck, hoping to keep food on the table and a roof over our heads. Now my mates are asking me what I want to do with my life and I'm not sure.

"Can I think about it? It's a big decision." Do I want to be just a housewife? Do I want a business of my own that I can run out of another building close to the house? Will Fi and her mates want an entire house of their own in the future?

"Of course, little wolf. It's something to think about," Torben says, glancing up into the rear-view mirror.

A yawn echoes from the front seat. "What did I miss?" Khal says as he rubs his eyes, turning in his seat to look back at me.

"Feray bit me and accepted my scale. We are currently looking for a safe place to camp for the night." Diaval sounds positively bored, relaying what's happened since Khal was last awake.

Reaching down, I grab one of his energy tonics out of the mini cooler and pass it forward. "Is it still okay for me to sleep in your coils tonight?" I scoot to the end of the seat, coming up between the driver's and passenger's seats to look at him better.

"If that is what will give you peace of mind tonight, then that's exactly what we will do then." His voice is still gravely from just waking up and I blush slightly.

"What's the blush for, precious?" Khal teases me as I slide back into the back seat.

"Just had a naughty thought, that's all." I scoot back and lower my eyes before carefully passing Diaval his mug back.

"Now, I am truly curious." Easton reaches out and caresses my cheek, sending molten heat straight down to my core.

"Seriously! I'm trying to drive…" Torben growls out. My eyes immediately find his in the rearview and they are glowing.

"Oh, shit…" His bear is hungry, and it's not for food. I squirm more under his intense gaze.

"For goddess's sake, why are you two acting so weird?" Diaval's serious tone gets Khal to turn and flick his serpent tongue out, tasting the air.

"Damn precious … Be thankful the rest of us have dull senses in our human forms." Khal winks at me and then stares at Diaval. "Flick your tongue out, old man, and figure it out. Don't play stupid, it's unbecoming someone of your age."

Diaval mocks Khal and finally flicks his dragon's tongue out. Holy hell, that thing is thicker than Khal's… "How many penises do dragons have?" I arch a brow, looking at him as I hear Khal choke on his drink.

Diaval chokes on thin air and coughs several times, clearing his throat. "What would possess you to ask that? One, I have one…" He still stares at me in shock, and I turn my gaze towards Khal.

"Someone, I won't mention his name…" I hike a thumb in Khal's direction. "Hid the fact he has two!"

Diaval shakes his head and huffs out a laugh. "The second one really isn't a penis, so he also has one. The other is purely for mating purposes. Its venom makes your womb ready to accept his seed."

My jaw drops hearing what the snake dick is really for. Slowly, I turn to face Khal again and stare at him. "Interesting fact to know…" Pouting, I slide back in the seat feeling stupid for not having been raised a shifter.

No one dares to say anything until Torben finds a place to park and camp for the night. "Little wolf … Let's take a walk until the others have camp set up." He still has that deep rumble of his voice, and it sends a chill down my spine.

The meadow stretches out before us, bathed in the golden hues of the setting sun, painting the sky with streaks of orange and pink. Diaval, Khal, and Easton are busy unloading the SUV, their voices mixing with the rustle of the evening breeze. Together, we're preparing our camp for the night, the air tinged with the scent of pine and wildflowers.

I come alongside Torben and slip my little hand into his. Slowly, his huge hand engulfs mine, and he smiles. His amber eyes meet mine, a silent understanding passing between us. With a gentle tug, I guide him toward the edge of the meadow, where the trees stand tall, their branches reaching for the darkening sky.

The transition from the meadow to the new growth forest is marked by a change in the soundscape. The whisper of leaves replaces the chatter of the birds in the meadow in the trees. Light filters through the canopy, casting dappled patterns on the forest floor. My steps are light, and senses are attuned to the surrounding wilderness, my ears picking up the slightest rustle or chirp.

As we delve deeper into the woods, the air grows cooler, and the scent of earth intensifies. The trees seem to cocoon us, embracing us in their natural fortress. Moss-covered rocks and fallen logs create a picturesque scene.

We move along a winding path, guided more by the subtle shifts in the landscape than any distinct trail. Torben nudges me, drawing my attention to a small brook, its waters glistening under the waning light. The babbling of the stream adds a soothing rhythm to the symphony of nature that surrounds us.

We walk on, our pace unhurried, simply relishing the tranquil ambiance and the connection between us. The forest feels alive, vibrant in its own way. The occasional rustle in the underbrush reminds us we're not alone.

Eventually, we find a small clearing, a natural alcove bathed in the remaining light of the day. Torben and I settle down, leaning against a large tree, feeling the pulse of the surrounding forest. As the stars emerge in the darkening sky, we sit close, absorbing the serenity of the moment, lost in the tranquility of the wild, together.

His lips lower and nibble at the back of my neck, and I feel my core pulse in response to his teasing. "I've missed you..." His hand rubs my sides and I arch my back in response.

Rolling my head to the side, his bites become harder and his bear growls low in his chest. His hands slide forward and he cups my breasts, hitting the gold bars in my nipples. "You know I love what these do to you." He rubs the tips of his calloused fingers over my nipples before tapping the bars.

That simple motion makes my core tingle and flutter, wanting to be filled by him. "Tor…" My voice is strained and breathy as I lean back against him, feeling his length thickening behind me.

"I know, little wolf…" His hands move from my breasts down my stomach, then to my hips. Gently, he rocks me forward and raises my dress over my hips. His hand moves from me, and I hear the buttons on his pants come undone. My core pulses with anticipation, knowing Torben is going to give me what I need most.

The thick head of his cock slides up and down over my slick lips before teasing me, dipping into me briefly before pulling back out again. "Please Tor … I need you…" I whine and lower down onto my forearms in full submission to him. The deep appreciative rumble of his bear makes my core pulse again.

"You're so wet for me, little wolf." He caresses my ass reverently.

Without warning, he sinks in deeply, burying himself to the hilt. I rock forward and moan from the sudden fullness and heat of his thick cock. My nails shift to claws as I grip the soil. "Be a good little wolf and stay quiet. Good girls get orgasms." He rocks his hips slowly, drawing out ever so slightly before pushing all the way back in.

Torben moves slowly, sliding almost all the way out. I can feel him just barely still in me and I'm missing his heat. A low whine escapes my lips, afraid he's going to pull out. Inch by inch, he slides his length back into me and I arch my back, feeling how full I am. The warm tingling feeling stirs low in my belly. I try to move against him, only to have him put his hand flat across my shoulders and press down.

He must have sensed my impending orgasm because Torben changed his angle and sends me plummeting over the edge. My orgasm washes over me like a tidal wave, stealing my breath and making every inch of me super sensitive to touch. Every thrust seems stronger than the last, drawing out the pulsing of my core.

"I'm so close, little wolf," he pants as he bends over me, caging me in his arms. His thrusts become erratic, rocking me almost to the point of collapsing from his weight.

Whining, I dig my claws into the earth deeper, trying to keep my balance. His thrusts shudder, and he throws his head back, roaring into the night air as he buries himself deep within me. I feel every single pulse of his cock as he fills me with his seed. His orgasm triggers me to tip over the edge with him. A howl escapes my lips as I tip my head back, joining my voice with his.

Carefully, Torben wraps his arms around me and rolls us to the side, and starts laughing. "What's so funny?" His laughter turns into muffled giggles.

"Would it be wrong of me to say I'm jealous sometimes of the others? I don't have the wealth of the other pack mates. I can't give you what they can." He hugs me tighter and sighs.

"Unlike everyone else, you can read me better than they can. Their noses aren't as acutely tuned to scent as ours are." When I feel his cock slip free, I roll in his arms to face him. "You taught me to shift, how to hunt and all the important things I needed to be a good wolf. Khal showed me all the plants that can hurt or kill me at the botanical gardens." Smiling, I pull Torben to me and kiss his lips gently. "You don't give yourself enough credit. Your gifts can't be measured because they are what keep me alive and safe."

"You are too good to me, little wolf." Torben kisses my lips gently and caresses my cheek before speaking again. "We should get back and have dinner, then get some sleep. I have a feeling tomorrow is going to be an adventure." There's a bit of sarcasm in his tone and I nod, not wanting to poke the literal bear.

"Okay." He hesitates, opening his arms, and allows me to roll to my feet. We walk back to camp much faster than we had taken to get to the meadow. As we emerge from the darkness to where the guys have the fire going, Khal arches a brow and gives me a knowing smile. Torben has been putting everyone else's needs before his and I finally had the time to make things right with him. I didn't want him to feel neglected.

"Come eat." Diaval waves me over and sets me down on one of the few chairs we have with us. Within seconds of sitting, he has dropped a plate of rare meat and assorted veggies. Before I can say anything to him, he raises his hand to silence me. "You need to eat well. After all, we do not know what lies ahead for us."

"I have to agree with him, Precious. Please eat." Khal backs Diaval up without question and it makes me look between the two of them, puzzled by their actions.

Shaking my head, I decide this is not the hill to die on today. "Where did we get the fresh venison from?" I look curiously at the guys, and Easton won't meet my gaze.

"Does it honestly matter?" Torben waves his fork in my direction, trying to get me to drop my line of questioning.

I study Easton's body language and I can tell my prying is making him uncomfortable. "No, I was curious who did such a good job hunting." A half of a smile creeps across Easton's lips and I know he received my praise well. I return to eating my meal and every time I look away, either Diaval or Torben has refilled my plate. This whole needing to eat a lot as a shifter isn't a joke. I'm just grateful that someone besides me can hunt for our food.

CHAPTER 15
KHAL

Sleeping when everyone else is awake absolutely sucks. I've missed out on so much since I've flipped my sleep schedule. The only positive is that I know, unlike the others, my night vision is unrivaled. Diaval comes a close second, but he's not naturally nocturnal like I am. Feray sits there and eats two whole plates of food before she tells the others to stop refilling her plate. Affectionately, she rubs her stomach, calling it her food baby.

Everyone, including myself, stops and stares at her as she smiles, looking down at the slight distention of her stomach. I can imagine her swollen with my child, looking down at it with so much love that it makes my heart want to explode with joy. Shaking my head, I clear those hopeful thoughts. One day in the future, once we are sure all the danger is far behind us. I can worry about creating life with my mate.

Diaval uncharacteristically pulls Feray to him and then points to the stars in the sky. I'm guessing he's teaching her about astronomy and how his people used to navigate the night skies.

Every once in a while, words drift to me as I look at the area in the meadow that we've chosen for the night.

"Something on your mind, Khal?" Easton makes me jump at his sudden intrusion into my thought process.

My eyes drop to the earth below my feet, then I look around. "If it's not too much trouble, can you scorch this section of earth?" I motion to the area I intend to shift in and coil up with Feray. "It would be easier to watch for danger and give me level ground to coil up for Feray to get a good night's sleep."

"Not a problem. Just have a drink and some food ready for when I shift back." Easton steps away from the group and literally bursts into flames.

Feray gasps and jumps because of his theatrical shift. The next thing I know, lithe hands are gripping my tee-shirt tightly and I feel the heat of her body pressed into my back. "I saw him in flight when he rescued me. It was as terrifying as it was intensely beautiful." She whispers as he takes to the air and starts circling before laying down a stream of fire like a flamethrower.

I pull her alongside of me and tuck her under my arm. Looking over my shoulder, I notice Torben is having a similar reaction to the fire as Feray. It must be something to do with fur-bearing mammals having a fear of fire. Diaval steps up beside Feray on her other side and takes her hand in his.

"He would never hurt you." His voice is pitched low, and she looks over at him and nods, still occasionally trembling in my arms.

"Is the fear of fire a mammal thing?" I glance over at Diaval briefly before watching Easton practically glassing the area for Feray's safety.

"Yes, their fur will burn in seconds and their soft skin will peel off their muscles, eventually exposing bones and tendons." Diaval's clinical approach to explaining their fear almost turns my stomach.

Feray's reaction takes the cake. She's standing there looking up at him like he's a hydra. "That wasn't even a thought!" She screeches at him, then moves to the opposite side and tucks herself back under my arm. Her reaction, however, got Torben to step forward and press himself against her opposite side and rub her back.

"Then what is it?" Diaval queries.

"Her friend was badly burned in a fire." Easton says after he shifts back and adjusts his tie.

I remember hearing mentions of the satyr and what had happened to him, and it didn't make sense until right now her fear of fire. Easton approaches and offers her his hand. Feray gives me a squeeze before going to him. He runs his hand over her hair and her feather ignites in her hair. "My flames can no longer harm you. You are their life and reason for living." A small font of flames manifests in his hand and he holds it out in front of her. For several moments she stares at the fire, then hesitantly reaches out. The flames wrap around her hand, not touching it at all. It's almost like there's some sort of shield around her skin.

"That's amazing..." Her breathy tone makes all of us pause as she plays with his fire.

"Keep in mind my flame. Regular fire can still burn you. Mine cannot there is a difference." He tilts her head up and then presses a kiss to her lips gently. "We should turn in for the night. Khal, what do we need to do?"

I glance from Diaval, then over at Easton. "Cover your eyes until I thump my tail on the ground. I need to get the membranes over my eyes. After that, whenever Feray is ready, she can climb up and get herself comfortable." As I walk away, I see Torben coming over with a sleeping bag that looks to be extra fluffy.

Torben walks over and takes a hold of Feray and spins her away from where I am. He pulls her close and, looking at him from the back, I can't see her at all. When the others turn away, I start my shift. My shift feels excited, happy to be able to tend to and care for our mate. I'm not sure how the other species feel when they shift, but for me. It feels like stretching taffy, the pull of my skin and stretching of my muscles and a warmth that flows over me. Out of habit, I close my eyes so as not to accidentally turn anyone to stone.

When I feel my shift is complete, I make sure all six nictating membranes cover my eyes before I open them slowly. I rise above the others and tap my tail on the ground to get their attention. Diaval looks me over, then touches my scales. "Good strong armor." He rapped his knuckles against the scales and then nods his head. "Definitely strong armor. I'm sure Feray will be safe within your coils." Having the wyrm's seal of approval makes my shift feel pride for once instead of shame for what we are.

Torben releases Feray, and she rushes over to me, and I lower my head. "There's my giant spicy danger noodle." She shifts her nails to claws and starts preening my face as I move my body to form coils.

"Can you tighten your coils a bit more? I'm going to lay her open sleeping bag in the middle." Torben says as he motions to my body. Feray releases my face and I coil up tighter, making sure to leave a protected area in the middle. "Looks perfect, man..." Torben uses my scales to climb my coils. He looks down into the dish I've created and lays out the sleeping bag for her.

Once the bedding is complete and he's satisfied with what he's made, he climbs back down. Feray goes between her three other mates and kisses them each good night before she comes to stand alongside me, looking up at my coils. I watch with bated breath as Feray, my dearest mate, begins her ascent up my basilisk's armored coils. Each scale is a dark, ink-black masterpiece of nature's design, rough and rugged from countless battles. The moment her fingers touch the first scale, I can see the determination in her eyes, and I'm filled with a profound sense of pride.

She's not afraid of us.

As she continues her perilous journey upward, I can't help but admire the intricate pattern of my scales. They overlap like shields, offering both protection and a striking visual display of power. Their texture, rough to the touch, reminds me of all the challenges I've faced and overcome. Criminal and as a creature has been put through hell to get to this point.

I feel the weight of responsibility on my serpent-like form, knowing that she trusts me in my most deadly manifestation to keep her safe. It's a bond of profound trust, a testament to the unbreakable connection that binds us together as mates. My heart swells with pride as I realize that, even in this deadly form, she sees not just a fearsome creature. She sees me as a protector who would move heaven and earth to keep her out of harm's way.

I watch every movement she makes, my senses attuned to her safety, my loyalty and love unwavering. In this moment, as she conquers the perilous journey up my scales, I am filled with a sense of awe and love for my remarkably brave and trusting mate.

Once inside my coils, she strips out of her sundress and shifts to her white wolf. She shakes out her fur before circling around the inside of my coils before laying down. Lowering my head, I grip her dress with my teeth and lay it outside of my coils over a lone bush. If anything is hunting by scent, her dress being down on ground level will distract them.

"Expecting guests?" Easton moves to stand before me and the lone bush that was untouched by his flames. Nodding my head, I look in the direction that we came from staring in that direction. "I don't trust them either." Easton says as he looks in the same direction that I do. "Turn this place into a sculpture garden if you have to. Diaval and I will clean up whatever mess you make protecting Feray." I nod my head again and lower it over Feray, protecting her the only way I know how.

-Later in the night-

My basilisk's coils, sensitive to the subtlest vibrations, twitch with an eerie awareness that something wicked slithers closer to our camp. I tense, feeling a shiver of unease ripple through my bond with my creature. Gently, I raise my head, careful not to make a sound, and my gaze darts across the shrouded wilderness that envelops us. The night is alive with shadows, a theater of obscurity where unseen danger lurks.

Through my basilisk's keen eyes, or rather, the gift of its thermal vision, I discern bluish, ghostly shapes shifting and advancing in our direction. I narrow my eyes, confirming my worst fear—vampires, the sworn enemies of our mate's kind. The icy grip of dread tightens around my heart.

Without hesitation, I raise the alarm, issuing a low warning hiss that reverberates through the quietude of the night. It's a signal to my bond mates, a clarion call to brace for the imminent onslaught. Our shared connection to Feray pulses with a primal urgency, conveying the impending peril.

Diaval, Easton, and Torben, wrapped in a fitful slumber, are awakened by my basilisk's ominous cry. Their eyes snap open, pupils dilating with instinctive readiness. In the dim moonlight, their expressions harden with determination. As they scramble to their feet, Easton's and Torben's shifts burst free of their human forms. The four of us form a vigilant circle, united by our shared bond and a deep-seated resolve to protect Feray.

In the black canvas of the night, the approaching vampires draw closer, their malevolence, and thirst for blood palpable. We stand as a formidable wall against their impending assault. The clash between our species is an ancient one, steeped in blood and shadow, and tonight, it will be written anew.

As the first wave of vampires lunge from the shadows. Easton unleashes the fiery fury of his phoenix. With a powerful beat of its wings, it rises above us, its feathers aflame, casting a brilliant inferno across the landscape. The night itself ignites, and the vampire horde is engulfed in a searing cascade of flames. Their agonized howls pierce the air, a stark testament to the destructive might of Easton's elemental form.

Torben's Kodiak, an embodiment of sheer power and ferocity, rears up on its massive hind legs. Its colossal form dominates the scene, and with a deafening roar that reverberates through the forest, it bellows its war cry. The ground trembles beneath its immense weight. He charges headlong into the throng of vampires, slashing and mauling with primal, untamed might.

Diaval, ever the strategist, quickly retrieves his concealed cane from the back of the SUV. With a flick of his wrist and a swift pull, a gleaming saber blade springs forth from its hidden sheath. He moves with the grace of a seasoned duelist, striking down vampires with a dancer's precision. The gleaming blade slices through the air, a swift, and deadly instrument of defense.

Behind me, I hear the eerie sounds of vampires closing in. In an instant, I lower myself, shielding Feray with my body, and my nictating membrane flickers down freeing my eyes. With a swift, practiced motion, I lock my gaze on the approaching foes, and the ancient power of my basilisk surges through me. Several vampires are caught in its irresistible grip, their forms gradually hardening into stone. The transformation is a gruesome spectacle, their expressions of malice forever etched into their stony visages.

Amidst the chaos and the clash of elements, our bond mates and I stand as a united front against the vampire onslaught. Our unique gifts give us an edge against our attackers. Thankfully, Feray remains curled tightly in a ball, secure in my scales. I don't sense any fear from her. The only thing I can sense is anticipation and the desire to get out of my coils. We wait almost twenty minutes since the last attack before we finally lower our guard and I let Feray's wolf out of my coils. Her wolf walks straight over to her sundress and she shifts back and gets dressed. Her eyes search the battlefield, and I can almost see the moment she withdraws. Deep down, she's blaming herself for putting everyone in danger.

How are we going to convince her otherwise?

CHAPTER 16

FERAY

WHAT HAVE I DONE?

My mere existence has put my mates in danger. These poor, wonderful men deserve better than what I can give them. My eyes scan the battlefield and whatever isn't painted vermilion or covered in ash has statues of horror movie quality vampires frozen mid attack. *They would be safer without me.* Some luna I am, I can't keep my mates safe from the monsters pursuing me.

I walk around almost in a daze, barely able to understand the words coming out of their mouths. It sounds like a speaker under water with static. *Why do they want me so badly?* Walking close to one of the vampires, I stare up into his frozen gaze.

Warm hands palm my shoulders and then pull me back against a much larger, firm body. By scent I know it's Diaval. His soothing chamomile scent envelopes me and starts draining the tension from my body. "Stop beating yourself up. We all knew what this trip would entail. As your mates, it is our honor bound duty to provide and protect you." He spins me in his arms and places my palms flat on his chest. "You are not removing yourself from this equation. Do you understand me?" His tone darkens and I am painfully aware that he knows where my darkest thoughts had gone.

"But..." I motion to the field.

"No but's ... You are my greatest treasure. Our love eternal. The one being in this entire sea of time that has called to my dragon. He's a fucking picky ass bastard." He tilts his head, looking at me. "You die. I die. Easton dies. The other two will mourn themselves to death." His statement has drawn the attention of the others, and they gather around.

"No no no no. Please, Precious, don't think like that..." Khal looks panicked, his eyes darting all around.

"Little wolf, I don't know what I can do to make you feel safe. Tell me I will do it." Torben's words hold an unfathomable strength, yet the vulnerability in his eyes shows that he's scared.

"My flame, none of this is your fault. Once Diaval and I started suspecting what your true bloodline is, we started preparing for war." Easton reaches out and places a hand on my shoulder.

"What is my bloodline? What makes me so valuable?" Diaval pulls me closer and presses my head to his chest. The deep slow lub-dub of his heart sounds like a metronome ticking in an ever-constant beat.

"We are not sure which exact bloodline you are from. But what we do know is you are a true born Luna. When you learn to focus your gifts, you can control an entire army of shifters. They will obey without question and die without a second thought to keep you safe. A true born Luna inspires absolute devotion to whatever her cause is." Diaval hugs me tighter as he explains what he and Easton have kept secret from the group.

"I barely know how to be a wolf, let alone some almighty leader." I laugh, and it sounds almost like I've become unhinged. "A bear taught a wolf to be a wolf. I'm no Luna." I shake my head and slam my eyes close trying to get a grip on the maelstrom of emotions battling within me.

Suddenly Torben rips me away from Diaval and holds me tightly by my shoulders, making me face him. "You're right. You're not a Luna because you have not tried to be. You can be anything you want to be." The way his hands come up and cup my face, making me feel tiny tears prick my eyes, making me want to cry.

"I'm so scared…" My voice sounds weak and broken as I admit to what's really wrong.

"Change can be scary. You have four supportive mates willing to listen and help you in any way possible. Let us help you…" He bends down and kisses my lips softly and I feel like my heart is about to explode with love. He sips at my lips before passing me off to Khal, who smiles, looking down at me.

"Precious, you have shown me that there's more than the cold, dark underbelly of this world. You are a radiant light in the darkness, guiding me in a new direction." The tips of his fingers lightly touch my forehead, sweeping my hair away from my face. "I will always be there for you however you need me to be." Khal kisses my lips softly before passing me next to Easton.

The aristocrat in the group adjusts his tie, then undoes it and throws it to the ground. "As much as I would love for everyone to believe I'm perfect, I'm not." His hands slide down my arms until he is able to grip my hands. "No one is perfect, no matter how hard we try to be. The only thing that matters is that you try." He plants a sweet kiss at the corner of my mouth before turning me to face Diaval.

He opens his arms to me in a silent request, and I go to him without hesitation, allowing him to envelope me in his arms. "I am going to give you two choices, Fer. Either choice is a good choice." His index finger comes up under my chin and tilts my head back so I can look him in his eyes.

"Okay?" I search his face for any hint as to what my choices are, and I find none.

"The first is we have a five almost six-hour drive to Vasserdell to make." He motions to the SUV. "Or..." He arches a brow and gets a mischievous look in his eyes.

"Or?" Butterflies flitter in my stomach as I stare up at him and see the flicker of his dragon in his eyes. My gut is screaming at me to run and hide from that look. On the other hand, my heart is content, excited to see what he's willing to offer us.

"Fly with me..." He turns his hand palm up, offering it to me. "Easton can fly with us without his feathers ignited if it makes you feel better." His eyes drop to his offered hand and my lungs constrict slightly.

This means so much more than just a flight. This is the point that D is finally ready to give me the D ... He wants to forge the bond the rest of the way. My hand trembles as I raise it to slide into his grip. A relieved breath escapes his lips, and a genuine smile graces his lips. "Just us ... I trust you and your drake."

Diaval's eyebrows shoot up when I choose to fly with him. He stiffly nods and then walks back to the SUV, gathering things up. "Are you sure this is what you want, little wolf?" Torben asks, glancing between Diaval and me.

"Yes, it's part of his customs and without everyone fully bonded to me, how do you expect to keep me safe? If he can't sense me like you can, is it fair?" My gentle giant nods and kisses me sweetly. "Be careful and do everything he tells you to do within reason." Torben boops me on the nose, then returns to the car to help Diaval.

I look over at Easton and Khal, who are in deep discussion, and they laugh. "What's so funny?" Both guys look like little children who got caught with their hands in the cookie jar.

"Diaval didn't think you would accept his offer." Easton says, stifling a laugh.

"He believed you would prefer to drive the five to six hours instead of the two hours flying. And if you accepted, you would want Easton with you, which then would eliminate sex." Khal offers between chuckles.

That caught me off guard. "Why would it eliminate sex? It's not like we all will end up in bed together at some point. Hell Khal, you've crawled in bed with Torben and I several times. You chose to leave when Torben got frisky." I pat his chest and smile before walking back over to where Diaval and Torben are, leaving Khal and Easton stunned.

"Are we ready to go?" I look between the guys and Torben holds out a pair of jeans, a tee shirt, and a jacket with a pair of my boots.

"You need to get changed first. A sundress will not keep you warm up there." He shoves the clothes in my hands, and I walk over to the front of the SUV and lay the clothing out and start changing.

"Are you sure this is what you want?" Diaval comes up alongside of me as I pull the tee-shirt over my head.

"Are you scared?" I fire back at him and smile sweetly.

"I can't be gentle, and I am very dominant." His voice takes on that deep growl that makes my core flutter in anticipation.

A soft laugh escapes my lips as I pull on my jacket. "If a wyrm dragon isn't dominant, he wouldn't be a wyrm dragon. Weakness is killed off with your species, especially with the males. The strong survive and the weak die. It's how it always has been and shall be. I did my reading at school. I am well aware of your society and its rules, Diaval." Stepping into his space, I place the bridge of my nose under his jaw in submission. "Make me yours..." I enunciate each word as I feel a shudder move through his body.

"Feray is ready to leave. You know the drill people!" Diaval shouts and my other three mates come up and kiss me goodbye and offer me words of encouragement. I watch my mates climb into the SUV and slowly pull away. I know it's killing Torben to leave me but he knows what needs to be done. Khal sticks his head out the window and waves one more time before climbing back inside.

"So, how do we do this? Where do I sit on your dragon?" I turn my gaze to Diaval. He steps away and grabs a stick and draws a basic outline of what his dragon's neck and head look like.

"There's a space here, just behind my horns on my neck where you can sit. You may have to clean out dead scales first, but this is the safest place. If another dragon attacks get under that ridge, it will protect you." He glances from the drawing, then back up at me, making sure I understand.

"Okay, so clean out under the ridge and take cover if we're attacked for whatever reason. Got it." I smile, trying to reassure him before he walks off. This time, I keep my eyes open as I watch him shift. It's almost like the fabric of reality opens and flexes several times before his dragon shimmers into existence. This time when I look at him, he appears twice the size he was the first time. *Can dragons control their size?* I'll have to ask Diaval about that later.

Diaval lays down and I walk over to his dragon looking it over. His claws are bigger than my wolf. Some of his scales are bigger than my wolf. *What the bloody hell was I thinking?* It's time to pull my big girl panties up and start climbing. Extending my claws, I start my climb up his neck. It feels like forever when I reach the top and I walk up his neck to his head and see the dead scales he warned me about.

Deftly I preen away all the dead scales, letting them roll off his neck and down to the ground. When I feel I have done a good enough job, I find a place to sit and pat his neck. "I'm ready." I shout, not sure how acute his dragon's hearing is. He rocks slightly as he rises to his feet, and it's now I truly take in how huge he really is. His head rises above the tree line and my heart pounds from the mix of fear and excitement.

His body shifts and he extends his wings and I hold on for dear life. With several flaps of his wings, we are airborne, and my stomach is somewhere down by my feet. It's now that I take the time to look around at the surrounding area. It's amazing the view from up here. Within moments we fly over the top of the SUV and I see Easton open the sunroof and shift to his phoenix and fly to catch up with us. He glides alongside me for a while, looking me over. I'm guessing making sure I'm alright before he heads back to the guys.

I watch him get back into the SUV and Diaval banks to the left, heading who knows where. The one thing I remember to do is take several photos and two videos and send them to Fi. Maybe she'll get them, maybe not. Only time will tell...

CHAPTER 17
DIAVAL

HAVING MY MATE ON MY BACK IS THE SINGLE MOST INTENSE THING I HAVE ever done in my life. She's so small and fragile compared to me in either form. I can hear her giggles as we ride the air currents, and I am enjoying her happiness. She's sitting perfectly still where she's at, and I can only hope she is enjoying the view.

It's been a little over an hour since we left the others and I have made a bold move and headed straight to the coast. I promised my mate she would get to see the ocean and I fully intend to keep that promise. Being the selfish bastard I am, I decided to not squander this moment.

When the first hints of salt air hit my senses, my dragon becomes excited. We're home. It's been over five hundred years since we last saw the ocean. Five hundred years, three months and seventeen days since the forced mating was announced. Some things you just never forget. I land within walking distance of the ocean, behind one of the higher sand dunes on the other side of the marsh trees that can survive the salt water.

Laying down, I extend a wing forward and Feray takes the hint and climbs on. Gently, I lower her to the ground and shift back immediately. "I have something I want to show you."

Feray arches a brow, and her eyes drop immediately to my crotch. "No, not that. Well, not at this present moment."

She giggles and steps closer. "So, what do you wish to show me?"

I pull my handkerchief out from my pocket and twirl it to make a blindfold. "Come here..." Tilting my head, I allow my dragon to surface. Again, I sense that untapped potential within my mate. Her wolf doesn't like to be told what to do. The fact her tiny wolf shows no fear amazes me. Perhaps it's because she knows I can't hurt her, or her wolf hasn't told her what she can do yet.

Tilting her head to the side, she mimics me. With a roll of her eyes, she spins so her back is facing me. "Oh, okay..." The minute her back is to me, I wrap the handkerchief head to cover her eyes.

"It will be worth it, I promise." Bending down, I scoop her up in my arms and begin the trek up the dune to the ocean on the other side.

"What's that sound?" The crashing of the ocean waves can finally be clearly heard.

"Your surprise." I trudge up the sandy dune, each step taking me closer to the top. The sun beats down on my back, and the sand feels scorching beneath my feet. I can hear the rhythmic, soothing sound of waves crashing against the beach, a constant lullaby in the background. My heart races with anticipation, and I hold my precious mate, Feray, securely in my arms.

The blindfold conceals her world, and I can feel her trembling with excitement. I've been looking forward to this moment for weeks, and now, at the crest of the dune, it's finally time. I gently remove the blindfold, revealing her eager, curious eyes.

Her breath catches as she takes in the panorama before her. The ocean stretches out endlessly, its shimmering blue expanse meeting the horizon, where the sky and water merge in a seamless union. Feray's eyes widen, reflecting the same deep blue as the sea. She sniffs the salty breeze, her nose twitching, and her ears perk up, trying to capture every sound.

The waves roll in, one after the other, a soothing symphony of nature's rhythm. Feray wriggles in my arms, wanting to get free, excited about seeing the ocean before her. She's never seen anything like this before, and it's a moment of pure wonder and amazement for both of us. I watch her closely, taking in her reaction, and I can't help but smile. This is a memory we'll treasure forever, the day Feray saw the ocean for the very first time.

"Welcome to the ocean…" Leaning down, I kiss her cheek before releasing her. Feray doesn't hesitate as I open my arms, letting her down onto the warm sand. With a burst of energy and excitement, she darts toward the ocean, her feet kicking up sand in her wake. Her long hair ruffles in the breeze, and her eager eyes are fixed on the shimmering horizon.

She stops just short of the water's edge, her tiny frame silhouetted against the backdrop of the vast, endless sea. The waves roll in, almost daring her to come closer, and she watches them with a mixture of curiosity and caution.

Then, she takes a step closer; she tilts her head, studying the sand's movement in the waves. The water washes over her feet for the first time, and she startles for a moment. But the cool sensation seems to intrigue her, and she ventures further in.

With a careful, almost deliberate movement, Feray bends down and picks up a seashell that the receding tide has left behind. She holds it in her hand, studying it with fascination. The intricate patterns and the textures of the shell seem to captivate her, and she carries her newfound treasure back towards me, her eyes filled with wonder.

I watch her in awe, grateful to share this precious moment with my mate as she explores the mysteries of the ocean's edge and discovers the treasures it has to offer. "Welcome to the ocean Feray." She holds up the empty shell and turns it around in her hand.

"What is this? I mean, I know it's a shell. What lived in it?" I watch her sniff the shell, trying to figure it out for herself.

"A saltwater snail lived in it. Then probably a hermit crab and then nothing." It's an ornate little snail shell that looks almost chromatic in this light.

"It looks like it was probably a very fancy snail when it was alive." She reaches forward and shoves the shell in the pocket of my expensive suit jacket. If it was anyone other than my mate, I would have fried them to a crisp on the spot.

Reaching out, I take hold of her hand and pull it to my chest. "There are things I need to warn you about in Vasserdell." I search her face, hoping she understands the importance of what I need to tell her.

"Okay? How bad can it be?" The way Feray looks up at me makes my heart swell with pride. Even with her having three other mates, she manages to make me feel like the king of the world.

"Females run the town." Feray's right eyebrow ticks up as she stares at me.

"Okay?" She shakes her head slightly as if to say so.

"A male's only value in Vasserdell is work and reproduction, and our mate's pleasure." I tilt my head, trying not to say that they force us into servitude if we ever want hatchlings of our own.

Feray, my beloved mate, had been listening attentively as I recounted the tales of the matriarchy ruling Vasserdell. I could see the gears turning in her intelligent, inquisitive mind. As the details sunk in, a moment came when the darker aspects of that town etched themselves into her understanding.

She had been absorbing the intricacies of that society, the hierarchy, and the dynamics of power. But within those tales lay a darker truth, a personal history that I hadn't shared entirely. Myra, my ex, had been a formidable figure in that matriarchy, almost holding me in a form of enslavement as her intended mate. As Feray pieced together the implications, I could see the change in her expression.

Her usual smooth, curious features contorted with a mix of emotions. First, confusion and then the dawning realization. But as comprehension gave way to a surge of rage, I saw a transformation in her. The power of her wolf heritage flared to life within her, visible in the intensity of her gaze and the sudden tensing of her muscles.

Feray's eyes, once brimming with curiosity, now blazed with a fierce determination. She turned those searing eyes towards me, and for a moment, it felt like the weight of her ancestors' strength and fury blazed through her. It was as if she could feel the injustice, the threat, and the history that had marred my life.

I swallowed hard, meeting her gaze with a mix of understanding and a hint of regret for unraveling this part of the past. In her eyes,

I saw not just anger but also a silent question, a need for assurance and explanation.

Quickly, I kneeled down, trying to calm the sudden storm brewing within her. "Feray, I know it's a lot to process. Myra's part of the past. Females have always ruled Vasserdell, not always well, but they have," I whispered, trying to convey both reassurance and a sense of security.

She held my gaze for a few more moments, her rage slowly giving way to a mixture of trust and a lingering wariness. I extended my hand cautiously, and after a heartbeat of consideration, Feray nuzzles against it, seeking comfort and reassurance in our bond.

The waves continue their rhythmic dance, whispering their story to the shore as Feray's gaze shifts away from me, fixed on the captivating expanse of the ocean. There's a solemn beauty in the way she watches the waves rolling in, almost as if seeking solace or finding a moment of reflection amidst the undulating waters.

When her eyes return to meet mine, a different intensity burns within them, a hunger, a fervor I haven't quite seen before. Her words cut through the gentle whispers of the sea, carrying a weight of urgency and an unexpected turn. "We need to complete our bond, Diaval."

I'm taken aback by the gravity in her tone, by the fervent desire mirrored in her eyes. She kneels beside me, her touch tender as she caresses my cheek. The warmth of her palm against my skin sends a shiver through me, a testament to the depth of her plea.

Her words hang heavy in the air, and I can feel the weight of their significance. They're not just spoken out of passion, but out of a longing for an unbreakable union. Feray seeks something more profound, something eternal in our connection.

"Make me yours eternally," she implores, her voice tinged with determination and a plea for a bond that transcends time.

I meet her gaze, searching her eyes for the depth of her commitment and the sincerity of her request. The idea of forever with Feray, an unbreakable bond that surpasses the confines of time, fills me with a mix of emotions—love, reverence, and a sense of responsibility to honor this moment. My fingertips dance over the edge of my scale that is implanted on her chest. It lives because she is meant for me, my perfect soul match.

Gently, I cup her cheek, mirroring the tenderness of her touch. "Feray, this bond, it's not just a simple vow. It's a connection that goes beyond words, beyond what we know. It's an unspoken promise etched in our souls," I express softly, trying to convey the weight of what she asks. "You will tap into the most primal parts of yourself when our bond completes." I nuzzle her cheek softly, hoping she understands what I am trying to convey.

With a deep breath, I meet her eyes, and in that shared gaze, I see the unwavering determination and the depth of our shared desire. As I lean in, our foreheads touching, the bond we share feels tangible, like an unspoken truth that binds us.

"Let our spirits intertwine and become one in all things," I whisper, affirming our connection as I gently press my forehead against hers. In this intimate moment, we affirm our eternal bond, sealing our commitment with a silent understanding that speaks volumes beyond the words we could ever articulate.

CHAPTER 18
FERAY

TIME TO TAKE THE BULL, OR SHOULD I SAY THE DRAKE BY THE HORNS. THE gravity of the moment isn't lost on me as I sit here, contemplating the significance of the choice I'm about to make. Diaval, an ancient wyrm dragon, a survivor of a matriarchy that values males so little, stands before me. My wolf stirs deep within, a simmering anger at the injustice of what this female tried to do to our mate.

Diaval may be an enigmatic, often vexing individual, but he's mine, undeniably and irrevocably mine. There's a unique bond between us, one that transcends his dragon nature, my wolf heritage, and any external expectations. It's a connection that defies logic, born of countless shared moments, understanding, and undeniable attraction.

As I draw in a deep breath, I muster the courage to take the first step toward this life altering choice. It's a decision that could bind us together in a way that nothing else could. With resolute determination, I unbutton his expensive suit jacket, my fingers navigating the intricate details of the fabric.

My movements are deliberate. Each button undone feels like a small victory, a step toward cementing our connection. The fabric peels away, revealing the strong, toned contours of his chest, a testament to his ancient lineage. I can feel the heat radiating from his body, and the power that lies within him resonates beneath my fingertips.

Diaval watches me with a mixture of surprise, curiosity, and a hint of vulnerability, a rare glimpse of the dragon beneath the grumpy exterior. His eyes lock with mine, and in that moment, the unspoken understanding between us deepens. We're on the precipice of a choice that will change everything.

With the last button released, the suit jacket slips off his shoulders and falls to the sand, forgotten. It's a symbolic act, shedding the trappings of society, revealing the truth beneath. Our connection, both primal and profound, becomes more evident with each passing second.

I run my hands gently across his chest, feeling the rhythm of his heartbeat, the heat of his skin through his shirt. Under it all, the promise of the uncharted territory we're about to explore together. As our eyes remain locked in silent agreement, the decision we're making goes beyond mere physical intimacy. It's a commitment to protect, honor, and cherish each other, no matter the challenges we face.

With the jacket now discarded, I take a moment to appreciate the craftsmanship of the tailored vest that clings to Diaval's form. The fabric, a refined slate gray, accentuates the hard lines of his body. My eyes trace the intricate embroidery of black silk thread that winds like a delicate vine adorned with blossoming flowers. The contrast between the rich, dark pattern, and the cool slate gray fabric is visually captivating.

For a moment, I'm lost in the details, the artistry woven into every stitch, and the elegance that this garment exudes. It's a stark juxtaposition to the wild, primal essence we both embody, a symbol of the different worlds we straddle.

But my focus quickly shifts, my hands guided by the unspoken desire between us. I slide my fingers over the firm planes of his chest, feeling the warmth of his skin beneath the layers of silk and fine fabric. Each touch elicits a response. A subtle shift in his breathing, a quiver of anticipation, and the intensity of our connection deepens.

With a gentle yet deliberate movement, my hands move to the buttons of his vest. They're small, delicate, and require a deft touch. One by one, I release them, the fabric yielding to my determined exploration. The vest slips from his shoulders, and I can see the definition of his muscles sculpted over centuries of existence.

His silk dress shirt, a stark contrast to the tailored vest, is a canvas for my fingers to glide over. The sensation of silk against my skin is luxurious, adding a layer of sensuality to this intimate moment. My touch is both an affirmation of our connection and a promise of what's to come.

"Enough teasing." Diaval's words cut through the air, his voice carrying an unmistakable undercurrent of lust. It's a tone that sends shivers down my spine, igniting the desire that has been building between us. I meet his gaze, and for a fleeting moment, I catch a glimpse of his dragon's primal instincts in his eyes. It's a reminder of the ancient power that resides within him, ready to emerge with our passion.

With a sensual urgency, he takes charge, his hands deftly undoing the top five buttons of his silk dress shirt. The fabric parts, revealing the chiseled contours of his chest and the definition of his torso. My heart races as the shirt is whipped over his head, revealing the magnificent sight of his bare, sculpted form.

Before I can fully take in the sight, he sweeps me off my feet with an effortless grace, and I find myself sprawled on my back, my body cushioned by the soft sand. Diaval moves with an unrelenting fervor, positioning himself above me, caging me in with his powerful body. The proximity of his heat, the sheer presence of his masculine form, makes it nearly impossible to focus on anything else but him.

Our eyes lock once more, a potent connection of desire and intimacy. His heated breath dances over my skin, sending a delicious shiver down my spine. In this moment, we're consumed by the magnetic pull between us, the raw, primal longing that has been building for so long.

The world around us fades into obscurity, the sound of the waves and the scent of the sea merging with the rhythm of our own desires. The sand beneath us molds to the contours of our entwined bodies, embracing us in a soft, sensuous cradle.

Desire courses through us, a flame that can no longer be denied, and our lips finally meet, setting off an explosion of passion that sweeps us into a realm where nothing else matters. His hands slide down to my waist and slide my shirt over my head. His eyes widen as he takes in the sight of me topless below him. My hands move down my body, heading to my jeans, and I unbutton them. *Why, of all days, did I have to wear something so complicated?* Diaval notices my struggle and reaches down and helps pull my pants down and he discards them over my head.

He rocks back on his heels and fights with his dress slacks. After several growling moments, he finally shoves his slacks down and his large proud cock juts out free from its prison. Diaval nestles himself between my legs and he looks at me with a hunger that

I've never seen from him before. His dragon is seconds from breaking free of its master's bonds. Rocking forward, his hips ghost his cock over my wet folds and he groans, feeling how ready I am for him.

His hands move to my arms as he drags them up and over my head. A feral grin crosses his lips as he holds my hands with one of his. Then he thrusts his hips forward, seating himself deep within me. A gasp escapes my lips from the unexpected intrusion. He lowers his head and nuzzles my cheek before thrusting slowly, dragging his length through my core, teasing the hell out of me. Teeth find their way to my throat and I arch up into it, enjoying his level of possession. Diaval's grip on my hands tightens as he picks up the pace, burying us deeper into the sand.

His mouth paints a scorching path up my throat to my ear and his lips tease my lobe before he bites it. "Come for me, my mate. Bite me and make me yours." As if on command, my body obeys his wishes. My core crushes down on him, pulsing along his length, dragging him over the edge with me.

The minute I feel him come with me; I strike. Curling up the best I can, I sink my teeth into his chest. The eruption of his blood on my tongue sends a searing shockwave through my entire being. It's an intense burst of heat, as if liquid fire has ignited within me. I hastily release him, but the aftermath leaves me in a state of convulsion. My body quivers uncontrollably, and I'm powerless to rein in the tumultuous sensations coursing through me.

"Shh ... it's okay. It's just the scale and good dose of my blood strengthening you." Diaval restrains me, keeping me from harming myself. "Breathe with me, in through your nose, out through your mouth." I can feel the deep rumbling purr of his dragon through his chest and into what feels like my soul.

My muscles spasm as I feel my wolf as if she is fighting against something. As if she is fighting against physical restraints. "My wolf ... She's trapped... Fighting..." Through gritted teeth, I try to tell Diaval what I am feeling.

"It's to be expected. Whatever magic was used to suppress your wolf has lingering effects. My blood combined with Easton's blood is cleansing your body of the magic that bound you." He gently strokes my hair as my body moves of its own volition.

Something feels as if it's moving in my stomach and suddenly, I start feeling as if I am going to get sick. "Diaval ... I'm gonna..." He releases my hands and rolls me to my side. I heave my guts out and it feels like a slithering slime is moving up my throat.

A black inky mass splats upon the earth and tastes like black licorice. Cough after cough, splat after splat, I start feeling lighter, almost freer if that's possible. When the last of the junk escapes my mouth, I draw in a deep breath, staring at the undulating mass. "What is that?" I point at the moving inky mass.

"That is the last of the magic that was holding you back." He kisses my temple and pulls me into his lap, holding me tightly.

"Why would they do that to me? Or better yet, who did it to me?" I curl against Diaval, staring at the mass as it moves.

"I feel your power clearly now. Whoever or whatever was hunting you will sense you as well. As to why they did it, I can only assume it was to protect you." He presses his lips to my temple and sighs softly against my skin.

"What can we do?" I hug him tighter.

"We get you to Vasserdell and figure out when it will be safe to move on to Blackmoor." He threads his fingers through my hair, removing the knots we just put there. Somehow, my grumpy dragon knows just what to do to soothe me.

I look out across the water as Diaval gathers our clothing and helps me get redressed. "Do you think the guys have made it to Vasserdell yet?"

Diaval pulls out his phone from his pocket and stares at it for several moments. "According to where my smart watch says it is, they will be there in the next twenty minutes. We should probably prepare to leave." He offers me his hand and helps me to stand up and dusts me off. "Ready to fly again?"

Looking around, I make sure we're not forgetting anything. "Yes, let's get going." Glancing up and down the beach, I'm not exactly sure where to stand.

Diaval sees me searching the shoreline and moves me back by the dune, and winks at me before moving away. His shift still amazes me. How such an enormous beast can fit within his chest is beyond a miracle.

Diaval strides back, distancing himself from where I am. In a mesmerizing transformation, he undergoes a metamorphosis into his magnificent skull dragon form. The tactile reality of his change resonates as the ground trembles beneath the sheer power of the shift.

As the enormous creature takes shape, its obsidian scales absorb the surrounding light, rendering them a surreal, almost unreal, depth of blackness. My fingertips, drawn by an irresistible curiosity, graze the cool, rough surface of those scales. They feel solid and unyielding, a testament to the strength embodied in every inch of the dragon's formidable frame.

With a low, resonant growl, the massive beast gracefully lowers itself to the ground, inviting me to climb aboard. The heat emanating from its colossal form creates a palpable aura. As I step closer, the warmth washes over me like a comforting wave.

The proximity to such a majestic creature is awe-inspiring. I can feel the subtle vibrations of its deep breaths and the power that lies dormant within its stillness. Determination surges through me as I mount the dragon, ready to take flight toward the distant town of Vasserdell. The anticipation tingles in my fingertips, echoing the pulsating energy that radiates from the dragon beneath me. Without warning, Diaval launches up into the air. The whoosh of his wings as they beat furiously gaining altitude tells me something was there, and he was getting us to safety. Looking back, small dots of four beings move around. I'm not sure what we are running from, but whatever it is, my mate kept me safe.

CHAPTER 19

TORBEN

THE WEIGHT OF ANTICIPATION HANGS THICK IN THE AIR, EACH PASSING second stretching into an eternity as I cast a furtive glance at my watch. The hands seem to move with maddening slowness, as if time itself is reluctant to release its grip. I can't help but wonder if Diaval's transformation has encountered unforeseen challenges, or if the journey on the way to Vasserdell is proving more treacherous than expected.

My gaze instinctively shifts upward, scanning the vast expanse of the sky for any sign of the colossal skull dragon that heralds Diaval's return. The heavens stretch out in an endless canvas of blue, wisps of clouds drifting lazily as if unaffected by the urgency that grips my every thought. The air holds a subtle tension, a silent echo of the impending reunion with Feray and Diaval.

The bond we share, a delicate web woven through time and circumstance, sends ripples through my senses. I felt the shift, an imperceptible alteration in the threads that bind us. Feray's bite, a symbolic gesture that transcends mere physical contact, marked

Diaval's full acceptance into our unique family. It's connection forged a bond that now courses with a new vitality.

Beyond the immediate impact, an undercurrent of power pulses through the air, a force that transcends the physical and resonates with the very essence of our beings. I feel it, a tingling awareness that dances across my skin like the whisper of unseen energies. It's as if the fabric of reality itself has acknowledged the transformation, sending out a pulse that touches each of us, an acknowledgment of the profound shift taking place.

Turning my gaze from the skies, I glance over at Khal and Easton. They're huddled around the map spread out on the hood of the SUV, their expressions a mix of concentration and anticipation. The map, a labyrinth of intricate lines and symbols, charts the path through the rugged terrain leading to the forest entrance of Vasserdell. The journey ahead demands not just navigation but a keen understanding of the interspecies currents that weave through the city's population.

The SUV, stands as a sturdy sentinel against the backdrop of the wilderness, is parked strategically about five miles from the mountain entrance. The decision to wait here, grounded in both strategy and caution, reflects our awareness of the unpredictable nature of Vasserdell. It's a tight-knit town where time dances to its own rhythm, and the landscape shifts with a capricious whimsy that defies logic.

The surroundings, though seemingly still, vibrate with an unspoken energy. The rustle of leaves, the distant murmur of a concealed stream, and the occasional call of a bird create a symphony of nature's whispers.

As I wait, a mixture of emotions swirls within me. There's the apprehension of the unknown, the unpredictable nature of Vasserdell, and the concern for Feray and Diaval. Yet, intertwined with the anxiety is an undercurrent of excitement, a sense of purpose that propels us forward into the unknown.

In this suspended moment, time seems to hang in delicate balance. The SUV stands as a temporal anchor, tethering us to the familiar world we know. Yet, with each passing second, the invisible threads of destiny draw us closer to the forest entrance, where the gates to Vasserdell await, and where Feray may finally get more answers to where her true lineage lies.

Diaval's ex is apparently the leader of the main nest in Vasserdell, and I am unsure how she is going to take Diaval being mated to a wolf. While we wait for their return, we've come up with several contingency plans just in case the entire visit goes left.

"There they are!" Easton shouts as he comes up alongside of me, pointing out over the ocean.

My eyesight is not as keen as Easton's strains against the canvas of the horizon. While his sharp vision dissects the distance, mine remains locked on the expansive panorama before me. Out over the undulating expanse of the ocean, a silhouette materializes against the canvas of the setting sun.

A vast, black mass takes shape in the distance, suspended between the sky and sea. The contrast against the vivid hues of the twilight sky paints an otherworldly picture. The sun, a molten orb on the cusp of the horizon, casts a golden glow over the approaching dragon, infusing it with an ethereal radiance.

As the mass draws nearer, details emerge—the rhythmic beat of enormous wings, the rough curvature of obsidian scales catching the last rays of daylight. It's Diaval, in his colossal skull dragon form, a majestic entity that defies the limits of imagination. The wind carries the distant echo of his wingbeats, a subtle percussion that resonates through the air.

The setting sun, now a fiery halo behind the advancing dragon, lends an almost mythical quality to the scene. It's a convergence of natural elements and magical forces, a moment suspended in the delicate balance between day and night. The air, tinged with the scent of sea salt and the subtle undertones of the local wild-flowers.

I fumble for my phone, hands trembling with a mixture of awe and excitement. I draw the device from my pocket, and with quick, eager motions, I activate the camera. Framing the majestic sight before me, I snap several pictures, each click capturing a fraction of the magic unfolding over the ocean.

The photographs, mere frozen moments in time, become a tangible record of one of Feray's first flights. I can already envision sharing them with Feray, a testament to the incredible journey that she has embarked upon. The phone's camera captures the play of light on Diaval's scales, the dynamic sweep of his wings, and the expansive canvas of the sky that frames this airborne spectacle.

As each image is captured, I am acutely aware of the significance of this moment. It's not just about witnessing Diaval's return; it's about taking yet another step closer to finding out who Feray's people are.

We watch in awe as Diaval's dragon circles overhead and then lands in the field nearby. He lowers his head slowly and brings his wing forward and Feray steps onto it like a seasoned pro. Diaval lowers his wing to the ground and Feray steps off and looks back over her shoulder at him. Within seconds he shifts back to his human form and takes ahold of Feray's hand, walking towards us.

"We need to get inside the town." He states as he blows past us and shuffles Feray into the back of the SUV. Without another word, he runs to the driver's side and gets in, starting the vehicle.

"What happened?" I climb in the back with Feray and kiss her lips softly.

"Creatures found us as we took off." His answer is clipped as he pulls onto the road, driving quickly.

"Shit, okay … Will we be safe in Vasserdell?" I look at Diaval, then over at Easton in the passenger seat up front.

"I will burn the world to ash if I have to." The fire ignites in Easton's eyes as he looks back at me, then over to Feray.

She tilts her head to the side, looking at him, feeling the anger radiating off of him, and reaches out to touch him. The moment her hand makes contact with him, he visibly calms immediately.

There's a soothing feeling that moves through the cabin of the vehicle, and any anxiety I was feeling over the impending danger is gone. "We'll be okay…" Feray says as she pulls her hand back.

Diaval sits up from with a cheshire cat grin on his lips. "We've managed to purge the last of the magic that was restraining Feray's wolf."

"Our blood worked?" Easton questions as he moves to look between Diaval and Feray.

"What do you mean, your blood worked?" Glancing between the two mythics, I am beyond puzzled.

"Whatever was done to me as a baby for my safety has finally been removed. I feel a deeper connection to my wolf and the earth as a whole. Like I'm finally where I need to be. If that makes sense." Feray shrugs her shoulders as she climbs up onto my lap and curls up with a yawn.

Running my fingers through her hair, she seems to drift off to sleep quickly. Khal is falling asleep as well, even though he's trying to fight to stay awake at least until we get to Vasserdell.

"She vomited a mass of black viscus material before we came here. She may be tired for a while. When we reach the inn, I'll order us room service. I don't want to expose her to anyone if I can help it." Diaval says as he looks at Feray in the review.

The SUV rumbles along the winding dirt road, flanked on either side by the towering sentinels of an old-growth forest. Ancient trees, their gnarled branches reaching towards the heavens, cast intricate patterns of light and shadow on the uneven path beneath our wheels. The air is thick with the scent of moss and damp earth, a heady reminder of the untamed wilderness that envelops us.

As we venture deeper into the heart of this ancient forest, the remnants of a bygone era become increasingly evident. The forest floor, once a carpet of verdant foliage, now bears witness to the bones of fallen dragons and other mythical creatures. The scattered remains tell a haunting tale, an echo of the dark past that shadows the city of Vasserdell.

My eyes trace the skeletal fragments, each bone a silent testament to the ancient struggles and the formidable creatures that once roamed these enchanted woods. I'm thanking the Gods above that Feray is sleeping through this leg of the trip. I would almost be afraid to see her reaction to this vast graveyard.

Diaval's grip on the steering wheel tightens audibly, the leather creaking in protest. The tension in the air is palpable, and if the dragon shifter at the helm is on edge, the gravity of the situation weighs heavily on the rest of us. The forest seems to close in around us, a living tapestry of secrets and forgotten lore.

"It seems like we are walking into the gates of hell, Diaval." I state, watching the occasional bone or skull catch my attention.

"Vasserdell doesn't take kindly to invaders. Which is exactly why we will be safe there for the night or the next few days. Whatever Feray wants." Diaval refocuses on the road ahead. I'm not sure if his words were meant to provide comfort or add to my concern.

I steal a glance at Easton, his head on a constant swivel as he scans the forest, his eyes probing the shadows for any sign of movement. The steady hum of the engine is punctuated by the occasional snap of a twig beneath the SUV's tires. It's an uneventful drive through the heart of this mystical woodland, yet the anticipation of what lies ahead hangs like an invisible veil.

Emerging from the dense thicket, the landscape transforms. The imposing mountains that guard Vasserdell to the north loom into view, their jagged peaks reaching towards the sky. The sight is awe-inspiring, a stark contrast to the serene beauty of the forest. Bones, as numerous as the leaves on a forest floor, scatter the mountainside, a silent testimony to the years of war and the successful defense of the hidden city.

The SUV navigates the forest pass, and the air grows heavier as we approach the entrance to Vasserdell. The terrain shifts beneath us, becoming steeper and more rugged. Remnants of fortifications, now weathered and worn, stand as silent sentinels, guardians of a city veiled in secrecy.

My imagination dances with images of the dangers that may lurk within the ocean city. Shadows seem to writhe in the corners of my vision, and the tales of mythical creatures, once dismissed as mere folklore, take on a tangible presence. The forest, cloaked in a mysterious aura, cast an imposing silhouette against the darkening sky.

Diaval's gaze remains fixed on the path ahead, his expression unreadable. The SUV moves steadily, navigating the twists and turns of the forest pass with a practiced ease that belies the treacherous nature of the terrain. The distant calls of unseen creatures and the rumble of the engine broke the collective silence within the vehicle.

As we near the entrance, a formidable gate comes into view. It's a massive structure, adorned with intricate carvings that depict the city's rich history. The gate swings open slowly, a reluctant admission to those deemed worthy of entry. Beyond the threshold lies Vasserdell, a city veiled in magic and shrouded in the echoes of a past that intertwine with the present. The journey through the forest, the bones scattered on the roadside, and the imposing gate—all serve as a prelude to the mysteries that await within the city of Vasserdell.

CHAPTER 20

FERAY

In the ethereal landscape of my dream, I am liberated from the constraints of humanity, my spirit running wild as my wolf across a pristine field of snow. Each paw print leaves an ephemeral mark on the frozen canvas, a testament to the freedom inherent in my lupine form. My breath forms clouds in the frigid air, signaling a temperature that should sear through my skin, yet I remain impervious to the biting cold. Apparently, I am built for this weather. The world is a monochrome symphony of whites and blues; the tundra stretching endlessly under the vast expanse of an azure sky.

"We're home," my wolf's voice resonates in my mind, a gentle whisper carried on the crisp breeze. *We must come from a region that is blanketed in snow most of the year.* The words hold a profound resonance, awakening a sense of belonging that transcends the physical world. As we traverse the snow-covered expanse, my wolf imparts knowledge, a sacred understanding of the luna gifts that course through my veins. *I'm stronger than I ever thought I could be.*

In the dream, my wolf becomes my guide, unveiling the mysteries of these innate abilities. Luna gifts, bestowed upon me by the mystical connection with the moon and my bloodline, unfold like a celestial tapestry. Most are gentle, designed to heal and soothe the wounds of both body and spirit.

But there are others, gifts that shift the balance towards defense and attack. The dream becomes a canvas upon which my wolf paints vivid images of these abilities. A shimmering barrier of protective energy, a cascade of ethereal light that can mend the deepest wounds, and a controlled surge of force that can repel any threat. I am not just a creature of the night; I am a guardian, a force to be reckoned with.

As the dream unfolds, my wolf's teachings echo in my consciousness. For the first time in my waking or dreaming life, I realize I am not defenseless. I possess the means to shield those I hold dear, to stand as a bastion against the shadows that seek to encroach upon our existence. The awareness dawns like the sun rising over a snow-covered horizon, casting its golden glow on the landscape of my newfound understanding.

"Feray!" The distant call breaks through the dream, a faint echo reaching me from a different reality. It's Easton's voice, his tone filled with urgency and concern. *I wonder what's wrong.* The dreamworld wavers, the snowy field, and the comforting presence of my wolf dissipating like mist in the morning sun. Reluctantly, I relinquish the lupine freedom and emerge from the dreamscape.

My eyes flutter open to a room suffused with soft light. The transition from the dream realm to reality is seamless. I find myself lying on a plush bed, the comforting weight of blankets cocooning me. Surrounding the bed are the four men who have become the pillars of my life, their eyes reflecting a mix of relief and affection.

Easton's voice, no longer a distant echo but a tangible presence, calls my name once more. The dream lingers in the recesses of my mind, a lingering warmth and a sense of empowerment seared into my consciousness. The boundaries between the dream and waking worlds blur momentarily, the residue of the lupine revelations lingering in my waking thoughts.

I meet the gaze of the men who love me, each of them a testament to the bonds forged through shared struggles and unspoken connections. Their concern, etched in the lines of their faces, is met with a reassuring smile. In that moment, I carry with me not just the memories of the dream but a newfound conviction—a belief in myself and the strength that lies within the harmony of luna gifts and the love that surrounds me.

"I had a dream…" Furrowing my brows, I make eye contact with each of them. It's Diaval that sits on the bed closest to me and takes my hand openly, showing affection.

"What was your dream about? We felt a profound peace move through us and happiness." He strokes the back of my hand as Khal comes and sits on the opposite side. Easton and Torben move to stand where they can see me easily.

"My wolf…" Shaking my head, I try to parse the information together.

"Take your time, Precious." Khal offers as he gives my hand a squeeze.

Torben moves closer and sits on the end of the bed and rests his hand on my leg, giving it a squeeze. "Where did your wolf take you?" He tilts his head to the side, watching me. I feel as if he's studying every little movement I make.

"I think the tundra. It seemed like it was below freezing, but it didn't bother us." I close my eyes, reliving the dream in vivid detail.

"Go on, my eternal. What else did you see?" Diaval's voice hits that hypnotic tone where I feel like I need to tell him everything. My wolf wants to please him, to anything to make him happy. She acknowledges him as the bigger predator, and she feels safe with him.

"She told me what it is to be a luna. What I can do in time." Slowly, I open my eyes and I know my wolf is at the forefront. My vision is all hers and the room's colors are muted like my wolfs.

"What did she tell you, my flame?" Easton sits on the other side of the bed at the foot. His strong hands take my foot from under the covers and start massaging the arch.

Swallowing hard, I take a deep breath and pull both hands into my lap. "I am a healer, but I am also a weapon and a shield." Slowly, I look up at each of my mates. "I'm not a fighter. I don't like violence." Shaking my head, I sigh. I have mixed feelings about what my wolf told me in my dream. *Can I fight?* Better yet, will I fight or run like I usually do? Fi is the fighter, not me.

"You're fretting again. What is on your mind, little wolf?" Torben asks as he gives my leg another squeeze.

"Fi is the fighter and not me. I don't fight, I run. I run like I've always been told to do. Run and don't look back." A single tear rolls down my cheek and I swipe it away quickly. "Ever since my wolf has been free, I don't want to run, and it scares me."

Khal pulls me closer to him. "Trust your wolf. She has spent her entire existence with the knowledge of what to do." His fingertip traces the ridge above my eye, just above my eyebrow. It's soothing and my eyes are close of their own volition. "Listen to my voice Feray." My body goes lax in his arms, and he lays me back down.

"Deep breath and let it out slowly. Your wolf knows what to do. Trust her." His fingers keep tracing my eyebrows, lulling me into a deep sense of relaxation.

"Are you doing what I think you're doing?" Diaval's voice almost breaks through the haze.

"Yes, I am. She fights herself daily because of all the fear and need to hide all of her life. She will never live up to her potential if she remains afraid of who she is. Subspace lets her work through everything where she feels safe. No barriers." He keeps running his fingers along my brow, keeping me under.

"Diaval, you are the strongest shifter in this room. Besides Torben she was immediately drawn to you. Her wolf knows your dragon will protect them. Talk to her." I hear him urging Diaval.

"My eternal." His voice resonates in my very soul.

"Little wolf..." Torben follows shortly after.

"You have no reason to be afraid anymore. We will protect you." Diaval strokes my cheek, and his words feel like a warm hug.

"In all reality, little wolf, you are strong enough to protect yourself. You just need to believe in yourself." I feel the bed shift and then the press of his lips on my forehead before his heat vanishes.

I told you ... My wolf says after Torben leaves.

Khal leans down and whispers near my ear. "Time to rise, my queen." His words infuse me with an energy I haven't felt before and when my eyes open, I feel as if they took a great weight off my shoulders.

Shaking my head, I look back at the guys and then down at my hands. "I'm tired of running and being afraid." I squeeze Diaval's and Khal's hands as I look at Easton and Torben, trying to push how much I love them to them.

"Then don't be. As it sits right now, you are probably one of the strongest Lunas in existence. Perhaps even history." Diaval says before the others have a chance to speak.

"How do you figure? I don't have a pack." Shaking my head, I look at him, puzzled.

"You don't?" Torben smirks and shoves Khal out of the way to sit next to me. "A pack is a wolf's family." He arches a brow, looking at me. "We are your family, your sleuth, your nest, your pack. We are whatever you need us to be." He motions to the others. "How many Lunas can say they have a dragon and a phoenix in their pack? A basilisk and a Kodiak?"

At the mention of our family, I look at each man and then it clicks. "Oh, shit ... A luna gets her power from her pack." I stare at my hands, trying to will something to happen.

"What are you trying to do, my flame? It looks like you are straining." Easton tilts his head left, then right, as he studies me.

"Trying to get something to happen besides my claws?" I state more as a question than as a statement. To be perfectly honest, I'm not sure what the hell I'm trying to do. But I'm trying to do something.

"That will take time and patience. Once we find your pack or a pack with a good Luna, she can teach you." Khal offers before he smiles as he walks off.

"Finding a pack would be nice." I look down, hearing the whine of my wolf in my head.

Torben runs his fingers through my hair and pulls me to him. "It's important for a wolf to have a pack. We can do the best we can to be a pack for you. I'm the only one that can really hunt with you, but I can't keep up." He sighs and hugs me tighter. "We will do everything we can to get you to your people." Just as Torben hugs me, Diaval's phone pings.

A deep rumbling growl escapes his lips as he glares daggers at his phone. "Fucking Myra…" When he looks up at me, his dragon is on the surface and looks like he's ready to go on a rampage.

I do the only thing I can think of doing. I launch myself at him and wrap my arms and legs around him tightly, as if trying to hold the dragon in his body. Softly I hum and push as much calming energy as I can towards him through the bond. Eventually, his ridged frame relaxes under me and his arms band gently around me as he carries me over to the couch. Diaval sits down and I move to straddle him, still refusing to release him.

"What was that all about?" Easton asks as he comes to sit beside us.

"My ex, Myra, the queen of Vasserdell, wants us to come to her nest for dinner tonight." Diaval mutters against my throat as he presses his lips there.

"Oh, that can't be good." I sigh and make eye contact with Easton. "What am I supposed to wear? All I have are my sundresses and several sets of leggings and baggy shirts." I stare at him, praying for an answer.

"You're in luck. Diaval and I already planned for this possibility. We have an elvish gown for you that compliments your skin tone and hair." Easton moves to the odd small suitcase that they have with them and opens it. Khal moves over to assist Easton as he pulls the flowing gown from the suitcase. It's white as snow and sparkles like fresh powder on a winter morning when the sun first comes up. The bodice is cinched with silk ribbons that are intricately woven from the top to the waistline. Khal moves forward with an elvish tiara. Instead of a jewel adorning the teardrop, a single black scale dangles in its place.

"Before you ask, it's one of mine." Diaval says softly as he lifts his head and releases me. "It's a mating present, an adornment that a drake gives his mate. It's a visual statement of belonging." Khal offers me the tiara and I look it over carefully.

"When did you have it made?" I continue to stare at the intricate craftsmanship. Whoever made this tiara is an extremely skilled artisan.

"The next morning, after you gave me the mug. When you chose me until death." He reaches out and takes the tiara from me and rests it on my head. Carefully, he moves some of my hair around, then ties the ribbons underneath. A soft smile graces his lips as he adjusts the pendant with his scale to rest against my forehead. "Perfect, just like its owner."

Diaval leaves me speechless as he heads to the door to the room we are staying in. "I need to make several arrangements before we leave. Please continue to get ready. We leave as soon as I return." With that, he leaves the room swiftly, setting everyone into motion. I sit there stupefied, staring at the dress and then the door.

What am I about to walk into?

CHAPTER 21

EASTON

If my bird squawks any louder in my head, I swear the others will hear him soon enough. He's warning me of the danger we're about to walk into. If I am being honest with myself, I am ready to ignite at the first sign of danger and torch anything that stands in my way.

The open four-horse drawn carriage glides through the cobbled streets, an imposing spectacle that demands the attention of every onlooker. The queen is doing this on purpose. Feray, poised in the center, sits between Diaval and Khal, an ethereal vision in her white elvish gown that occasionally flutters with the whims of the breeze. The three-piece gunmetal gray suits worn by the dragon kin duo lend an air of formality to the entourage, a visual testament to the significance of the occasion.

Torben, despite the discomfort etched on his face, navigates his own three-piece suit with a sense of reluctant elegance. It's a humorous sight, seeing him squirm within the confines of formal wear, a stark contrast to the accustomed ruggedness of his usual attire. The mystery of how Diaval found a suit accommodating his formidable, muscular frame remains unsolved. Somehow, the ensemble adds a layer of refinement to the otherwise imposing figure.

Seated in my slightly lighter shade of gray suit, I find a sense of camaraderie in our matching attire. The carriage, a mobile stage for this regal procession, glides beneath the rhythmic clopping of the horses' hooves. The sound reverberates against the cobble-stone streets, creating a steady cadence that echoes through the air.

Townspeople, alerted to the approaching spectacle, emerge from their residences, curious faces peering out from behind half-closed shutters. As the carriage progresses, the streets seem to come alive with the hushed whispers of the curious and the wide-eyed gazes of the intrigued. The eyes of the townspeople follow us, their collective attention transforming the carriage into a moving centerpiece, drawing the focus of the entire town.

The atmosphere is charged with a palpable awareness. The weight of scrutiny presses upon us, and the gaze of the towns-people becomes an almost tangible force. It's as if the very air is charged with a silent acknowledgment of the significance of our journey to the Dragon Queen's court. The sight of so many eyes fixed upon us sends a shiver down my spine, the hair on the back of my neck standing on end.

Feray, a vision of grace in her elvish gown, maintains a regal composure. Her gaze, unwavering, seems to meet the eyes of those who dare to stare. Diaval and Khal, flanking her on either side, exude an air of protective authority. The gunmetal gray suits, tailored to perfection, accentuate their presence, the sharp lines mirroring the strength that lies within.

Torben, despite the discomfort etched on his face, manages a wry smile. His presence, a testament to the diverse tapestry of our group, adds a touch of authenticity to the otherwise formal procession. The clatter of the horses' hooves persists, a steady rhythm that propels us forward through the heart of the town. The architecture, a blend of medieval charm and fantastical elements, serves as a backdrop to our journey. The buildings, adorned with intricate carvings and mystical symbols, stand witness to the centuries that have shaped this mystical realm.

As the carriage moves through the town, I catch glimpses of faces in the crowd—wide-eyed children, elders with weathered faces, and curious shopkeepers who pause their activities to witness our passing. The collective gaze follows us like an invisible thread, connecting us to the heartbeat of the town.

In this moment, the carriage becomes a vessel, carrying not just individuals but the hopes and fears of those who catch a glimpse of our passage. The air is charged with a sense of expectation, the unspoken understanding that our arrival heralds a momentous event. The Dragon Queen's court awaits, and our journey through the town becomes a symbolic prelude to the mysteries that lie within the hidden heart of Vasserdell.

The medieval castle, with its brooding architecture carved into the face of the mountains, looms ahead, a silhouette against the backdrop of the darkening sky. It's a fortress that seems torn from the pages of a Bram Stoker novel, its towering spires and imposing walls exuding an air of ancient mystery. As the carriage approaches, the castle becomes a daunting presence, casting shadows that dance across its stone facade.

The surrounding atmosphere vibrates with an undercurrent of anxiety, a palpable tension that seems to seep from the very stones of the castle. The closer we get, the more the fear intensifies. It reaches a fevered pitch, a crescendo of collective unease that threatens to engulf us all. Feray, seated between Diaval and

Khal in the open carriage, senses the mounting tension. The sleeves of her ethereal gown billow weightlessly in the breeze as she rises, a figure bathed in the soft glow of twilight.

In a moment that freezes time itself, Feray raises her hands, her eyes shifting to the brilliant yellow glow of her wolf form. The air stills, as if she has harnessed the very essence of the atmosphere. The oppressive weight of anxiety that had gripped the townspeople, and us dissipates. It's a soothing balm, a Luna gift woven into the fabric of her being.

The transformation is both visual and visceral. Furrowed brows of worried onlookers smooth, and the lines etched with fear soften. The air, once thick with tension, becomes lighter, and the collective breath of the townspeople releases in a sigh of relief. It's a testament to Feray's Luna power, a force that transcends the physical realm and reaches into the hearts of those around her.

I watch in awe as the older residents, some with tears in their eyes, gaze upon Feray with a mixture of gratitude and wonder. In this moment, she stands not just as my beloved, but as a beacon of solace for the town. Her ethereal glory is a sight to behold, a radiant presence against the darkening backdrop of the castle. I see her as my beautiful flame, embracing her birthright with a grace that resonates with the ancient power flowing through her veins.

As the Luna gift of soothing envelops the town, Feray becomes a conduit of peace. It's a profound and important step in our journey, a moment where she not only accepts her own power but harnesses it for the greater good. The collective anxiety, like dissipating storm clouds, disperses, leaving behind a calm that settles over the town like a gentle caress.

Feray, her task accomplished, gracefully takes her seat once more. I watch her in silent admiration, my heart swelling with pride for the strength she has displayed. She has not only brought peace to the town but has demonstrated the potential of her Luna gifts. In this quiet moment, as the carriage continues its journey toward the foreboding castle, I reflect on the significance of what Feray has just done. She has not only quelled the immediate fears but has sown the seeds of trust and understanding between us and the townspeople.

The castle, with its ominous presence, seems less foreboding now. The journey ahead, though fraught with unknown challenges, carries with it the assurance that we are not alone. In the glow of twilight, the castle stands as a symbol of our collective destiny, and Feray's act of soothing becomes a beacon of hope that will guide us through the shadows that lie ahead.

"When we enter the castle gates, we need to present a unified front." Diaval says as he looks at each of us before continuing on. "Myra will use her gift of intimidation on you. She will try to drive you into submission. Hopefully, now that Feray has bonded with me, my protection will extend to each of you."

"What do you mean, your protection?" Torben looks puzzled between all of us.

"My scale will negate the effects of her intimidation." He arches a brow and smirks. "Then again, Feray can probably shield you." He shrugs and goes back to watching the road ahead of us.

"My wolf said something about being able to shield." Feray does that head tilt that indicates she truly wants the answer.

"It's a common luna gift for the ones that have the larger packs or the more powerful packs." He cocks his head to the side, looking at her, waiting to see if he answered her silent question.

Feray bites her bottom lip as her brow furrows. Her eyes lower to her hands and then she looks up at me. "Do you think I can do it?"

Her question catches me off guard and I really have to put some thought into how I am going to answer her. "At this exact moment. No." I raise my hand to stop the others from chiming in. "I believe that when you need it, you will do it without realizing you did it. It should be more of a defensive reaction." I pull out my pocket watch and glance at it for a moment before looking back at her.

"I hope you're right." Feray leans forward and grasps my hand briefly before sitting back again.

Passing through the towering gates of the ominous castle, Feray's gaze sweeps across the imposing surroundings. I sense the internal battle raging within her, a silent struggle between the instinct to flee and the readiness to confront whatever challenges lie ahead. Her ethereal gown, touched by the evening breeze, seems to ripple like a flag torn between opposing winds.

Across from me, Feray sits in the open carriage, her posture a reflection of the dichotomy within. One half of her yearns to escape, to run into the embrace of the unknown and hide from the looming shadows. The other half, emboldened by the whispered counsel of her wolf. Feray stands ready for battle, shoulders squared and eyes fixed on the foreboding castle.

I watch as Feray engages in a silent conversation with her wolf. There's a nod, a subtle affirmation that whatever counsel has been exchanged has left her determined. The look in her eyes shifts, a spark of resolve igniting within. It's a fire that catches on the feather I gifted her, flames dancing in the gentle breeze. Her determination is palpable, and the flame in her eyes reflects the inner fire that fuels her strength.

"Settle down, sparky," I tease, breaking the tension with a playful tone. Her blush, a subtle bloom of warmth against her fair skin, speaks of the connection we share. "A wolf with a flaming feather in her hair may spook everyone a bit."

She chuckles, a musical sound that dances in the air. "It may be a good thing?" she muses, her words carrying a note of mischief. Diaval, ever the protector, takes her hand and tucks her under his arm. The gesture is both reassuring and possessive, a silent declaration of solidarity. Together, they move towards the foreboding castle doors.

The doors swing open with an eerie creak, revealing the dark expanse within. A blast of warm air, laden with an ancient scent, hits us in the face. Diaval takes the lead, Feray at his side, their figures silhouetted against the dimly lit grandeur of the castle's interior. The clicking of our dress shoes on the polished marble floor echoes through the vast hallways, a stark contrast to the silence that seems to wrap around us like a shroud.

Despite the opulence of the surroundings, an unsettling chill runs down my spine. It's a sensation that screams of danger, an instinctive warning that we are not as safe as the grandeur of the castle might suggest. My gaze remains fixed on Feray, a silent promise echoing within me. If it comes to it, I would burn this place to the ground to ensure her safety.

The grand hallways unfold before us, adorned with intricate tapestries that seem to whisper tales of forgotten histories. The air is heavy with the weight of the past, and the shadows that dance along the walls carry a sense of ancient secrets. Diaval's grip on Feray's hand tightens, a silent reassurance that resonates in the otherwise silent corridors.

As we traverse the echoing halls, I catch glimpses of towering statues and paintings that watch our progress with eyes that seem to follow our every move. The castle, with its grandiosity, becomes a labyrinth of mystery, and every step feels like a deliberate dance through an unseen tapestry of power.

Feray's determination remains unwavering, her gaze fixed ahead as if ready to face whatever awaits us. The flame on the feather in her hair flickers in response to the air currents, a symbolic beacon of her resilience. I find comfort in the sight. Knowing that her strength, paired with the unity of our group, is a formidable force against the shadows that threaten.

As we approach the heart of the castle, I can't shake the feeling that the true test lies ahead. The echoes of our footsteps seem to be swallowed by the ancient stone walls, and the anticipation tightens in the air like a taut bowstring. I steal a glance at Feray, her profile etched in determination, and I brace myself for the challenges that await beyond the looming doors.

The herald's voice reverberates through the grand hall, announcing each of us by name with a formality that underscores the weight of our presence. The echoes of our names seem to linger in the air as we await permission to enter the throne room, the anticipation humming beneath the surface.

At the far end of the hall, a regal figure sits upon an alabaster throne, a stark silhouette against the ornate backdrop. Raven hair cascades over bare shoulders, falling in a sleek river that mirrors the rich ruby of her gown. The queen's ample curves are accentuated by the form-fitting fabric, and her stony gaze pierces down the carpeted aisle, scrutinizing our approach.

Diaval, ever the stalwart protector, gives Feray's hand a reassuring pat, a silent gesture of support. With a nod, he takes the lead, guiding Feray down the aisle. Khal remains at her other side, a steadfast presence, while Torben and I bring up the rear. The atmosphere is charged, a palpable tension that hangs in the air like a veil of anticipation.

The queen's voice slices through the silence as we traverse the aisle, a sound that carries a hiss of disdain. "Brought me a snack, handsome," she remarks, the words dripping with a venomous edge. Feray's back stiffens at the queen's comment, and I catch the muscles bunching beneath the delicate fabric of her gown.

"No, this is my mate, Feray," Diaval declares with unwavering conviction. The weight of his words is underscored by a tender kiss pressed to Feray's temple, a display of affection that seems to irk the queen. His gaze, adoring and resolute, never wavers from Feray, a declaration that ripples through the air.

"My eternal," he affectionately addresses Feray, a term of endearment that carries a significance beyond the throne room's understanding. The queen, Myra, regards them with an icy stare, and the tension in the room tightens like a coiled spring. Feray's presence, her connection with Diaval, is a challenge to the established order, and Myra does not take kindly to it.

"What is this blasphemy?" Myra abruptly stands, her regal stature commanding attention. Feray's gaze turns to her, a steely determination in her eyes that seems to give the queen pause. Despite the regality of Myra's presence, something in Feray's stare makes her hesitate. She sits back down, a move that carries a hint of uncertainty.

"Dragons don't mate with her kind," Myra states, her words cutting through the air with an icy precision. The discriminatory declaration hangs heavy in the room, a proclamation of the rigid hierarchy that governs their society. Feray, however, doesn't flinch.

"My kind is exactly what his drake wanted, not some overgrown, self-righteous lizard," Feray fires back, her voice carrying the weight of defiance. The flame on the feather adorning her head blazes to life, a visual manifestation of her anger. I catch a glimpse of the fiery intensity in her eyes, and a knot forms in my stomach. Now is not the time for her to challenge the queen openly. The throne room, with its aura of power and hostility, is no place for insubordination.

The air crackles with tension, and I exchange a wary glance with Torben. The delicate balance of the situation is teetering on the edge, and I can't shake the feeling that one wrong move could set off a chain reaction. Myra, angered by Feray's defiance, eyes her with a mix of disdain and calculation. In this moment, surrounded by the grandeur of the throne room and the weight of centuries-old traditions, we stand on the precipice of a dangerous confrontation. Feray's courage is commendable, but I fear that her boldness may be met with a fire far more perilous than the flames dancing on the feather in her hair.

CHAPTER 22
FERAY

Diaval's warning about the cold and calculating nature of his ex, Myra, proves to be more than just cautionary words. As we stand in the grand throne room, the atmosphere is thick with tension, and Myra's presence exudes a serpentine aura. The strong angles of her face give her a regal yet menacing appearance, and her stance radiates defiance, a queen unyielding in the face of perceived threats.

The hostility directed towards me is palpable, evident in the sharp glint in her eyes and the curl of her lip. Myra's disdain is laid bare for all to see, and it stings despite my attempts to remain composed. The cold reception is expected, given the intricacies of dragon society and the disdain for intermingling with other beings.

"The mutt doesn't deserve a dragon's scale," she sneers, her words laced with venom. In a swift motion, her hand shoots out, attempting to snatch the pendant containing the scale Diaval gave me. I instinctively jerk back, evading her reach. The tension in the room ratchets up, and I can feel the collective gaze of the court on us.

"I may be a mutt to you," I declare, my voice steady despite the roiling emotions within me, "but I am his mate, as he is mine. He bears my mark, and I bear his."

With a deliberate movement, I sweep my red hair aside, revealing the obsidian scale on my chest—the tangible proof of our bond. The pendant and the scale harmonize, twin symbols of a connection that transcends the rigid boundaries of dragon society. Myra's eyes narrow as she takes in the display, a flicker of uncertainty momentarily crossing her features.

Diaval, standing at my side, places a protective hand on my shoulder, a silent gesture of solidarity. The tension in the room becomes a palpable force, a current that courses through the air like a storm gathering on the horizon. The court is a silent witness to this confrontation, watching with a mix of curiosity and apprehension.

"I see you've chosen a companion far beneath your station," Myra retorts, her voice dripping with disdain. The words are a deliberate provocation, an attempt to undermine the legitimacy of our connection. I take a steadying breath, refusing to let her words pierce the armor I've built around my emotions.

"Love knows no station," I respond, the words a quiet but resolute declaration. The grandeur of the throne room seems to shrink, and for a moment, it's just Diaval and me against the scrutiny of the court.

Myra, however, remains undeterred. Her gaze flickers to Diaval, a silent challenge in her eyes. "Is this what you've become, Diaval? Lowering yourself to the level of a mutt?"

Diaval's jaw tightens, and the muscle in his cheek twitches as he reigns in his anger. "I've found happiness where you only found power games, Myra," he replies, his tone measured but firm. The exchange between them is layered with history, a past that I am only beginning to understand.

The court, caught in the crossfire of this emotional battlefield, watches the scene unfold with bated breath. The throne room, once a symbol of regal authority, becomes a stage for the clash of emotions and the collision of past and present.

Myra's eyes narrow further, and a dangerous glint surfaces. "You'll regret this," she hisses, her words a veiled threat that hangs in the air like a dark omen. The courtiers shift uncomfortably, sensing the rising storm in the room.

Diaval's grip on my shoulder tightens, a silent reassurance that we face whatever comes next together. The emotions swirling within me—anger, defiance, and a touch of fear—remain beneath the surface, held in check by the armor of determination. Within the throne room, with its lofty ceiling and opulent decor, becomes a crucible, and I stand ready to face whatever trials may arise. The confrontation with Myra is a storm on the horizon, and I can feel the first gusts of its impending arrival.

As Khal steps forward, a formidable presence that shields me from the cutting gaze of Myra, I feel a mixture of gratitude and an undercurrent of tension. His hand rises to his sunglasses, an unexpected detail that adds a layer of mystique to the situation. I watch, my breath caught in my throat, as he addresses Myra with a calm but assertive tone.

"Do you know what I am?" Khal questions, his voice carrying the weight of ancient power. His hand presses me protectively behind him, creating a barrier that shields me from the hostile energy emanating from Myra. I feel a reassurance in his presence, a silent acknowledgment that he stands between me and the storm brewing in the throne room.

"A basilisk," Myra responds, her voice a hiss that echoes through the grand hall. Khal's fight, it seems, is not with her, and his posture reflects a readiness for the impending confrontation. The dynamics shift as he presses a kiss to my cheek, a brief touch that carries a multitude of unspoken emotions. His free hand rests on my hip, a grounding touch that anchors me amidst the brewing turmoil.

"My fight isn't with you," Myra asserts, redirecting her attention past Khal to Diaval. The tension in the room is thick, and I sense the invisible threads of conflict weaving through the air. My gaze remains fixed on Diaval, his face a stoic mask that belies the turbulence within. My wolf stirs, a low growl building in the depths of my consciousness—a primal reaction to the perceived threat.

"I want what is owed to me," Myra declares, her focus squarely on Diaval. The intensity of her gaze sends a shudder through him, a reaction that doesn't go unnoticed by my heightened senses. Anger simmers beneath the surface, and my wolf, always fiercely protective of its pack, stirs with a readiness to defend.

"I don't owe you anything, Myra," Diaval states with a firmness that cuts through the tension. He angles his body, pulling me closer to him, a silent declaration that he stands resolute against whatever claims she may assert. The atmosphere crackles with unspoken conflict, the throne room a battleground for emotions and unresolved history.

"You owe me a clutch, just like any male I choose to be worthy," Myra hisses through gritted teeth, her words carrying a demand rooted in the rigid traditions of dragon society. The weight of expectation and obligation hangs in the air, a tangible force that threatens to engulf us all.

Diaval's jaw tightens, and I can feel the conflict radiating from him. The bond between us pulses with shared determination, a unity that stands against the antiquated expectations of the dragon hierarchy. Myra's claim is a challenge to the very core of our connection, and my wolf stirs with a fierce loyalty that transcends the boundaries of tradition.

Courtiers, mere spectators of this familial drama, watch the scene unfold with a mix of fascination and trepidation. The throne room, once a symbol of authority, becomes a crucible for emotions and unresolved conflicts. The air becomes charged with the weight of expectation, and the silence that follows Myra's demand is a pregnant pause before the storm.

Diaval's gaze remains fixed on Myra, a silent defiance in the set of his shoulders and the unwavering determination in his eyes. The bond we share, strengthened by trials and tribulations, becomes a shield against the demands of tradition. Myra is a figure of authority and a relic of a bygone era, stands as a formidable adversary, but we face her together as a pack and most importantly as a family.

As the echoes of Myra's demand linger in the air, I brace myself for the storm that threatens to break. The throne room, with its opulent decor and imposing grandeur, becomes a battleground for the clash of tradition and the resilience of love. The emotional currents in the room swirl with intensity, and I stand alongside Diaval and Khal, ready to face whatever challenges may arise in the wake of Myra's claim.

As the tension in the throne room escalates, an elder, draped in flowing blue robes, steps forward. His kind smile is a balm to the charged atmosphere, and a sense of reassurance settles within me. I lean my head on Diaval's shoulder, seeking solace in his presence. The elder, a figure of wisdom and authority, addresses Myra with a respect that carries the weight of tradition.

"My queen, a true mate claim supersedes any claim you may have had on him," the elder declares with a deep bow, his words resonating through the hushed silence. The significance of the statement ripples through the court, challenging the authority Myra seeks to assert. There's a moment of tense anticipation as the elder gracefully retreats, leaving the air heavy with the unresolved conflict.

"Nonsense. My claim trumps everything. You will give me what is owed," Myra growls, her voice taking on a feral edge. The transformation begins, and her fingernails morph into talons, bone plates shifting beneath her face. The ancient power she wields becomes more evident, a display of the formidable force she represents.

Something within me snaps as she advances, a surge of instinctive protectiveness that surges through my veins. It feels like time slows as I raise my hand toward her. In that moment, an unseen force emanates from my outstretched hand, knocking Myra back with an unexpected strength. The court gasps in collective astonishment, and I stare at my hand in wonder, a mix of confusion and awe coursing through me.

"Did I do that?" I whisper to Diaval, seeking confirmation in his eyes. He nods proudly, his gaze filled with a mixture of admiration and love.

"There's my little luna," he says affectionately, the term of endearment resonating with a depth of meaning. In that instant, I realize the power that lies within me, a force connected to the celestial bond we share.

Myra, now regaining her composure, glares at me with a mix of surprise and indignation. The courtiers murmur amongst themselves, the once silent spectators now caught in the unfolding drama. The throne room, with its towering pillars and ornate decor, becomes the stage for a clash of ancient power and the unexpected emergence of a force that defies convention.

Diaval stands beside me, his protective stance unwavering. The emotional currents in the room swirl with a heady mix of defiance and uncertainty. Myra, her gaze fixed on me, attempts to regain control of the situation. "This changes nothing. The claim is still valid," she declares, her words carrying a weight that threatens to smother the burgeoning sense of empowerment.

The elder, who had stepped back, watches the scene unfold with a contemplative expression. His eyes, filled with a depth of understanding, meet mine briefly before he fades into the background. The courtiers, caught between allegiance to tradition and the unexpected twist of fate, exchange uneasy glances. The throne room, once a symbol of unwavering authority, now teeters on the edge of an unforeseen shift in power dynamics.

Diaval, sensing the ripple of uncertainty, tightens his grip on my hand. His eyes, a reflection of shared determination, convey a silent message of solidarity. Whatever challenges may lie ahead, we face them together.

Myra, undeterred by the unexpected display of power, narrows her eyes at me. "You may have a few tricks, but the true claim cannot be undone. You will give me what is owed," she asserts, her voice a low growl that reverberates through the room.

I stand my ground, the newfound strength within me pulsing with a quiet but resolute energy. The courtiers are uncertain of the outcome, hold their breath, awaiting the next move in this unexpected confrontation.

Diaval, unwavering in his support, stands at my side. The elder, having observed the unfolding events, reappears with a knowing smile. The atmosphere crackles with tension, and I prepare for the uncertain path that stretches before us. In this moment, I am not just a pawn in the ancient game of dragons. I am a force that defies expectation, a luna who has discovered the strength that lies within.

CHAPTER 23
DIAVAL

Pride surges within me as I witness Feray, my sweet mate, finally taking a stand for herself. The mythical bond we share pulses with the echo of her newfound strength, and I marvel at the defensive power revealed by her Luna gifts. The throne room, once a battleground of conflicting claims, now bears witness to the emergence of a force that defies the rigid expectations of dragon society.

"Let's go... It's obvious we are not welcome here," I declare, positioning myself protectively behind Feray, ready to shield her from any potential attack. My gaze, filled with a mix of determination and concern, meets hers and I see a flicker of gratitude in her eyes. The court seems to hold its breath, uncertain of how the unfolding drama will conclude.

"You can't leave. I haven't given you permission," Myra bellows from her imposing throne, her authoritative voice cutting through the air. The weight of her words echoes with the centuries-old traditions that have governed dragon society. However, the resonance of tradition now clashes with the emergence of a force that refuses to be confined by the expectations of the past.

"By age and right, it should be me on the throne," I proclaim, challenging the very foundation of the hierarchy that has dictated the rule of dragons for generations. The room vibrates with tension, and I pass Feray over to Khal and Easton, a silent directive to guard her with their lives. The urgency in my words lingers in the air as they hurry out of the throne room, leaving me to face the storm brewing before the alabaster throne.

"Males are breeders, not leaders... It's how it's always been and shall always be done," Myra asserts, her frustration palpable as she stomps her foot on the ground. The tantrum she throws is a manifestation of the clash between tradition and the unexpected defiance embodied by Feray.

As the door closes behind my family, the throne room becomes a stage for the confrontation that reaches a critical juncture. Myra, her regal facade momentarily shattered, glares at me with a mix of anger and indignation. The courtiers, caught between allegiance to tradition and the winds of change, exchange uncertain glances.

I stand firm, my gaze unwavering as I meet the challenge presented by Myra. The elder, still observing from the shadows, watches the scene unfold with a contemplative expression. The air crackles with the weight of history, and I brace myself for the verbal sparring that is about to ensue.

"Your mate may have displayed a parlor trick, but it changes nothing," Myra declares, her voice carrying a dismissive tone. "You cannot escape the ancient traditions that have governed us for centuries. The true hierarchy will always prevail."

"Times change, Myra," I respond, my words laced with a quiet but unyielding strength. "The true hierarchy is not bound by outdated notions. I have the right to choose my destiny, and I stand with my true mate." Arching a brow I watch her reaction closely.

Myra's eyes narrow, and the bone plates beneath her face shift with the tension that courses through her. "You stand against your queen, against tradition. There will be consequences."

I feel the weight of those words, the threat of consequences that echo through the centuries of Draconic history. The courtiers, silent witnesses to this clash of wills, wait with bated breath. Even they are uncertain of how the scales will tip in this power struggle.

"Feray is my mate, and I will not bow to traditions that seek to suppress our true potential," I declare, my voice carrying across the throne room with a resonance that reverberates through the ancient stone walls.

Myra's fury intensifies, her gaze locking onto mine with a searing intensity. "You will regret this defiance. The true order will be restored, and you will kneel before your queen."

I stand resolute, the echo of Feray's newfound power still resonating within me. The elder, having reemerged from the shadows, watches the unfolding confrontation with an inscrutable expression.

"You may have power, but true strength lies in embracing change," I retort, my words a challenge that hangs in the air like a gauntlet thrown. The courtiers, sensing the shifting currents, exchange uneasy glances.

Myra, undeterred, rises from her throne. Her form towering over the masses as she tries to regain control of the room. The air thickens with anticipation as she steps down, her eyes locked onto mine. The elder, recognizing the gravity of the moment, remains a silent observer to the ebb and flow of Draconic history.

The confrontation reaches a critical juncture, and I brace myself for whatever consequences may follow. The throne room is a witness to the clash of tradition and change. Collectively the masses holds its breath in the face of the uncertain path that stretches before us. Feray's courageous stand has set in motion a chain of events that will redefine the course of Draconic history.

Myra's glare hardens, and she crosses her arms beneath her chest, a clear declaration of her displeasure. "If you choose the mutt, you are no longer welcome within the mountains of Vasserdell," she declares, the weight of her words hanging in the air. Within the court, a sea of dragon eyes fixed on the unfolding drama, awaits the resolution of this power struggle.

Arching a manicured brow, Myra's Draconic eyes glow in the dim light of the throne room as she watches the reactions of the courtiers. The tension is palpable, and I feel the collective gaze of the court weighing on me.

With a measured nod, I acknowledge her ultimatum. "So be it."

I turn away, giving her my back—a deliberate act of ultimate defiance. I do not wait for her dismissal, nor do I allow her the satisfaction of having the last word. My departure is a silent proclamation that I will not be bound by the expectations of the past.

"You can never return, Diaval. You are a dragon without a flight from this day forward," Myra bellows, her voice echoing through the throne room. My dragon cringes internally at the proclamation, and I draw in a deep breath to steady myself.

"I may be without a flight," I declare, turning back to face her with a resolute gaze, "but I have a pack that has my back one hundred percent of the time. I am respected and treated as more than just a mere toy. Freedom is a beautiful thing."

I glance over my shoulder, watching her fume on her imposing throne. The courtiers, caught in the midst of this dramatic departure, exchange whispers that increase in intensity to a fevered pitch. The chaos left in my wake should keep Myra busy for several hours. The chaos I caused should me the time needed to distance myself from the confines of Vasserdell.

As I make my way through the grand hallways, the opulence of the surroundings serves as a stark contrast to the weight of the decision I've just made. The stone walls, adorned with intricate carvings, bear witness to the history of Vasserdell. A history that now includes my defiance of tradition.

The echoes of Myra's bellowed decree reverberate within me. The solidarity and strength of my pack remains a source of strength. Khal, Easton, Torben, and Feray are waiting beyond the confines of the castle, their support unwavering. The choice to stand against tradition and choose love over the constraints of Draconic hierarchy is a path fraught with challenges, but it is a path I willingly embrace.

Exiting the castle, I step into the crisp mountain air, the scent of pine mingling with the lingering tension. The distant peaks, shrouded in mist, stand as silent witnesses to the unfolding events. I make my way to where my pack waits, their expressions a mix of concern and determination.

"You did what needed to be done," Khal affirms, his tone carrying the weight of experience. Easton nods in agreement, a silent acknowledgment of the complexity of the choices we face. Torben holds Feray as she watches me anxiously. She breaks free of his grip once I get close.

Feray, her gaze meeting mine, takes a step forward. "I chose you, Diaval, and I stand by that choice. No matter what comes next, we face it together."

The bonds of our pack strengthen in that moment a shared commitment to navigate the challenges that lie ahead. The mountains of Vasserdell, once a symbol of tradition and hierarchy, now fade into the background as we embark on a new journey. A journey defined by love, freedom, and the unbreakable ties that bind us as a pack.

-SEVERAL HOURS LATER.

I move to the driver's side of the SUV, the cool leather of the seat welcoming me as I settle in behind the wheel. Glancing at the rearview mirror, I see Khal and Torben taking the back seats, their expressions a mix of vigilance and readiness. Easton, his healer's instincts always at the forefront, sits beside Torben, his piercing gaze scanning the surroundings for any potential threats.

Oddly, Feray joins me up front, her decision unspoken but deliberate. As she reaches over, her hand rests on my thigh in a silent gesture of support. Her eyes, filled with a mix of determination and concern, never leave me as I navigate us through the oldest part of Vasserdell. The ancient buildings loom on either side, silent witnesses to the upheaval left in our wake.

The guys engage in a discussion about the different routes we need to take and the perils along the way. Feray turns in her seat to watch me, her eyes a steady presence. "I'm sorry you lost your flight over me," she confesses, her earlier strength replaced by regret.

"I didn't lose them over you. I lost my flight the minute Myra became the leader," I assure her, forcing a smile as I steal a glance in her direction. "Besides, you gave me a pack, and I'm finding it to be much more palatable than a flight."

I chuckle to myself, shaking my head. "Look at the big picture. Each of us has something we're very good at." I gesture to the back seat. "Khal, when he's awake, can gain intel for us, keeping us one step ahead of whatever is after you. His toxic bite and stone gaze are nothing to laugh at either." Khal grunts, acknowledging my words before turning towards the window, settling in for a nap.

"Torben has immense strength in both his human and bear forms. His sense of smell is almost as keen as yours, so it's extremely helpful." In the rearview mirror, I see Torben nod in agreement. "Easton is not only a healer but a massive force of destruction, if need be. His eyesight is unrivaled in the group." Easton dips his head slightly in acknowledgment.

"That brings us to the grumpy dragon," Easton says, and his teasing earns him a giggle from Feray. "Not only is he incredibly rich, but his dragon's acid breath can kill anything it comes in contact with. Most importantly, if we need to evacuate you out of an area, Diaval is the only one able to do it swiftly." There's a pain in Easton's eyes as he speaks, and I understand the weight of the responsibility he feels. This part of the discussion is clearly bothering him.

"My eternal, there's nothing to fret over from this day forward. In a few hours, we'll arrive in Blackmoor and play hide and go seek for your answers." I rest my hand on hers and giving it a reassuring squeeze. I can only hope our little talk helped alleviate some of her worries.

The journey continues through the winding roads; the landscape changing as we approach the northern pass that leads to the mountains of Blackmoor. The tension in the air is palpable, a mixture of uncertainty and determination. Feray, her hand still on my thigh, glances at me with a silent reassurance.

As we navigate through the mountain pass, the towering peaks of Blackmoor come into view, their rugged beauty a stark contrast to the political intricacies left behind in Vasserdell. The SUV moves steadily along the winding road, and I can sense the anticipation building within the group.

The sun begins its descent, casting a warm glow on the mountainous terrain. In the quiet moments between discussions about the journey ahead, I steal glances at Feray. Her eyes, a reflection of the trust she places in me, convey a mixture of emotions. The road ahead may be fraught with challenges, but with the strength of our pack and the unwavering support of my eternal we face it with a unity that transcends the uncertainties of the unknown.

As we approach the entrance to Blackmoor, the landscape becomes increasingly untamed. The SUV moves through the outskirts of the small town that guards the secrets of the mountains. The air is charged with an energy that hints at the mysteries awaiting us.

The road winds higher, and the SUV climbs with determined resilience. The mountains, their peaks shrouded in mist, stand as sentinels guarding the secrets Feray seeks. Slowly, the discussion in the car becomes hushed as we draw closer to our destination, a shared understanding settling over the group.

In the last stretch, as Blackmoor unfolds before us, I steal a glance at Feray. Her eyes meet mine, and a silent exchange passes between us. The mountains, with their ancient secrets loom ahead. The journey has brought us to this pivotal moment, and with each passing mile, the weight of the unknown lessens. Together, we face the challenges that await in the heart of Blackmoor. Above all else, we protect Feray.

CHAPTER 24

KHAL

The dirt road winds its way up the mountain toward Blackmoor, offering both a scenic view and a reminder of the dangers that lie ahead. My thoughts linger on the recent encounter with Myra, a dragoness who seemed to redefine the term "crazy ex-almost baby momma" by demanding breeding rights after centuries of exile. A shiver runs down my spine as I reflect on the narrow escape Diaval had from that fate. It could have been disastrous if not for finding Feray.

As we ascend, I check my phone for the umpteenth time, only to find I still have no signal. The realization that I'm cut off not only from my twin but also my informants settles heavily in my chest. "Anyone have reception up here?" I inquire, the chorus of negative responses confirming my fears. The lack of communication leaves a void, a blind spot in our information network.

"The entrance to the town is just ahead," Diaval announces, bringing the SUV to a stop. Feray turns her attention to him, awaiting instructions. "Feray, this is a wolf stronghold. You will need to secure the suite for us," he instructs. Her gaze shifts between each of us before returning to Diaval, confusion evident in her eyes.

"Why?" She questions, seeking clarification.

Diaval, running his hand down his face, appears burdened by the weight of the explanation. Sensing the need to intervene, I offer insight. "Because wolves rarely trust other species. Because you weren't raised as a wolf, you don't have that thought process ingrained in you."

Reaching forward, I rub her shoulder in a reassuring manner, hoping she understands the necessity of the arrangement. "Oh, okay," she responds, her eyes widening as she looks down into her lap. The discomfort she feels is palpable, and I offer a supportive smile to settle her unease.

"They will accept Torben with you, so he can go in with you. Hopefully, they have cottages we can rent," I suggest, looking to Diaval for confirmation. He reaches into his suit jacket and hands Feray a bag that jingles with the sound of coins.

"Use this to pay for us," Diaval says with a smile, and she reluctantly takes the coin purse.

Once inside the town limits, we exit the SUV. We gather outside, the mountain air is crisp and invigorating. The town of Blackmoor lies before us, concealed within the embrace of the mountains. Feray, accompanied by Torben, leads the way through the wolf stronghold, her unease masked by determination. The dirt road beneath our feet gives way to cobblestone as we approach the main part of the town.

The scent of pine and earth fills the air as we enter the town. The architecture, a blend of rustic charm and practicality, reflects the nature of the wolf stronghold. Wooden cottages with sturdy shutters line the streets, and the inhabitants, clad in fur and leather, cast curious glances our way.

Feray, guided by Torben, navigates the unfamiliar terrain. The wolf stronghold, with its tight-knit community, radiates a sense of unity and shared purpose. We follow at a respectful distance, Diaval leading me aside for a brief conversation.

"Keep an eye on Feray. This is all new to her, and wolves can be territorial," he advises, his concern evident in his eyes. I nod in acknowledgment, understanding the delicate nature of our entry into the wolf stronghold.

As we approach the center of town, Feray and Torben secure a suite for us. The wolf's den, as they call it, is a spacious lodging that can accommodate our group. Feray, guided by the unfamiliar intricacies of wolf etiquette, manages the transaction with a blend of hesitance and determination.

Inside the den, the rustic charm continues, with wooden furniture and furs creating a cozy atmosphere. We settle in, each finding a place to rest and regroup. Feray, visibly relieved to be indoors, looks around with a mix of curiosity and trepidation.

"Thank you for doing this," I say to Diaval, expressing gratitude for his foresight in preparing Feray for the unique challenges we face within the wolf stronghold.

He smiles, a mixture of reassurance and affection in his gaze. "We're in this together. Always."

As the sun sets over Blackmoor, casting a warm glow through the den's windows, I can't help but feel a sense of anticipation. The mountains, with their hidden secrets, loom outside, and our journey to uncover Feray's past is just beginning. Torben receives word that the dinner we were supposed to have with the alpha has been put off because of unforeseen reasons. Diaval nods acknowledging the earlier information that others have been trying to take over as alpha. More than likely, that is the business that the Alpha has to attend to.

Feray paces anxiously around the interior of the den. Even in her human form, I watch her nose working overtime as she sniffs everything. "You need to relax." I state, and Easton slides up behind her, his eyes glowing.

"Yes, you definitely need to relax." Torben hears the change in Easton's tone and shoves a tonic in Feray's hand.

She glances down at it and nods before popping the cork and swallowing the elixir in one gulp. "Sorry, with everything going on, I almost forgot to take my tonic." She shrugs her shoulders and mouths *thanks* to Torben.

"What's in that tonic?" I take the bottle from her and look it over.

"Its birth control, well it stops me from going into heat." She rolls her eyes and sighs. "I want a family." She makes sure to make eye contact with each of us. "Until we know who I really am and where I came from. Most importantly of all why I was hidden, it's not safe for me to be pregnant." We fall silent as a group and nod. Her logic is flawless. It would be damn near impossible to keep her and a newborn safe.

There's a knock at the door and Feray goes to answer it. Several tilts of her head, she reaches over to the side table and scrolls a quick note and passes it to whomever is on the other side. She closes the door and turns around, looking at us. "Alpha Roman heard of our arrival and has invited us to meet with him and the council." Her tone is cold and calculating. It's very clinical in the way she provides the information.

"You don't like something about it?" I tilt my head like she does and wait for her to answer.

"Last I heard, Roman was still in the archive." She paces the room and I know that's a clear sign something is bothering her.

"So why is he here? Maybe it's just because of the young alphas trying to take over?" Diaval questions as he moves to look out the den window closest to him.

"Perhaps the sphinx told him what we revealed in the archives." Feray stops and stares at me openly and I see the pulsing of her wolfs eyes behind her human ones.

"Feray, I can feel your wolf over here. It's almost as if she's gained your intimidation power, Diaval." Easton mentions and that, makes the dragon take notice and turn to face her fully.

Diaval closes the distance between him and Feray, and he gently grips her jaw and looks into her eyes. "Oh, this is going to be fun." A sadistic grin crosses his lips as he turns to face the group. The dark version of Diaval that I had heard stories of is standing before me. There's a hard edge to him now that I notice it. His features seem sharper, and his eyes hold the slitted pupils of his dragon.

"What's going to be fun?" Feray looks up at him innocently. Her fiery mane flowing in gentle curls down the length of her back.

A deep chuckle escapes Diaval's lips and you can see his canines had shifted to that of his dragons. "Watching you, my eternal, stand toe to toe with the elder Alpha." A serene smile slips across his lips, and it makes the hair on the back of my neck stand on end. "You are no longer the delicate flower he met a few months ago. Dare I say, you've become a force to be reckoned with. All you have to do is believe in yourself. Be the Luna you were always meant to be." He presses a kiss to her forehead and looks over at me. "Trust no one. We may be in the middle of a pack, but there are always snakes in the grass."

Diaval speaks of the secret contingent of mercenaries that my people are famous for. They are fangs for hire and will kill for a price at a moment's notice. I don't have the stomach for violence like my brother does. But when it comes to Feray … I pause, staring at my precious mate, and I know deep in my black heart I would turn the world to stone to secure her safety. "I'm well aware…" I state plainly as I watch Diaval for a few moments.

"Let's makes sure you're dressed for the occasion, little wolf." Torben scoops Feray up and ushers her into the bathroom.

Once she's out of the way, I look back towards the door and stare at it for several moments. "The alpha being here is very interesting, don't you think? I mean, he offered to host us for dinner." I say to both mythics, not really directing my question, to either one in particular.

"Indeed…" Easton states as he pulls out a suit and starts getting changed. His entire demeanor has changed since the mention of the dinner invitation.

"What do you mean, indeed?" I move to stand closer to him as I watch him prepare for the dinner.

"That's easy. We've suspected that there is corruption on the council." He motions between himself and Diaval.

"The council and the witch council have had an understanding for the last several hundred years." Diaval arches a brow, looking at me, and suddenly the picture is crystal clear. The arranged matings, the way the girls were singled out. Everything makes sense now.

"He wants to see if she took a mate beyond Torben and I." I pace as I ponder the meaning of all of this. "A luna is only as strong as her pack. He knew we needed to come here." My head whips up and I stare at Diaval and then Easton and they nod at me.

"Either he's going to mislead us or help us." Diaval states as he stares at me. "I don't trust him as far as you can throw my dragon." Diaval says off handedly as he changes his tie and tie tack.

"I'll be ready for it." Feray says as she steps out of the bathroom wearing a strapless black dress, allowing her bites and Diaval's scale to be on display. There's a fresh hickey on her neck and we all know what Torben did to settle her nerves about dinner.

"Are you sure? He's another wolf..." Easton states and moves closer to her and looks her over. He runs his fingers through her hair, freeing his feather from her hair. Gently he moves it to lie in front, taking a prominent place. He leans in and kisses her cheek and then passes her off to me.

"Do you know where we are going, precious?" I press my lips to her temple and breathe in her scent deeply. Even though my sense of smell is muted compared to hers, I love her scent.

"We need to head to the alpha house." She heads towards the door and we walk out into the street. Turning her nose to the wind, she turns left, heading up the street. "It feels strange to be in the middle of a pack and not see any wolves." She muses to herself as she grips my hand tighter.

"What do you mean?" I give her hand a squeeze to encourage her to answer.

"They're scared." She glances at me and smiles. "They're scared and I feel it." An easy, confident smile crosses her lips as she turns slightly to face me. "Once the prey, now the predator..." She arches a brow, then glances over at Diaval for approval. He gives her a smile and a nod before looking back at me.

"Does their fear please you?" My curiosity has been piqued as I stare at a more confident version of my mate.

"No, but I'm not concerned that they may attack me." She smiles and kisses my cheek. "We're going to be late if we don't pick up the pace." Feray gives my hand a squeeze before she looks over her shoulder at Diaval.

What is my feisty little minx up to?

CHAPTER 25

FERAY

W̲HEN̲ I̲ ̲SLEEP̲ ̲MY̲ ̲WOLF̲ ̲HAS̲ ̲BEEN̲ ̲TEACHING̲ ̲ME̲ ̲ABOUT̲ ̲WOLVEN̲ politics. She told me that through the Luna line knowledge is passed down generation to generation. Roman is of the old school of thought where the females are meant to be seen and not heard. He already tried to dominate me once and failed.

"Diaval, I need you…" I extend my hand out and take a hold of his hand when he approaches.

"I sense a wicked plan my eternal." He arches a brow with a twisted grin on his lips.

"I will not bow or break. I smell the scent of several elders from the pack in that house. They will try to get me to submit. They will fail." My wolf bolsters my self-confidence and for once I don't feel like a frightened little girl anymore.

"There's the luna I have been waiting to see." Diaval caresses my cheek and releases my hand. "You need to walk these last steps alone."

I understand what he means, to lean on him and his ancient power will only make me look weak. Kissing his cheek, I step away and walk towards the front steps of the alpha house.

The slate stairs leading to the grand log cabin alpha house are an impressive sight, each step resonating with the weight of history. As I ascend, the sheer magnitude of the building becomes apparent—the embodiment of generations of Alphas and Lunas who have governed over our people. The grandeur of the structure is matched only by the sense of responsibility that permeates the air.

The rich mahogany doors stand tall before me, bearing witness to the secrets and legacies of countless eons. I extend my hand and touch the cold brass handle, the chill a reminder of the protective embrace of the mountains. Strangely, the cold doesn't bother me. With a firm push, the doors swing open, revealing the heart of the alpha house.

The scent of pine, earth, and wolf fills my senses as I step into the expansive foyer. My eyes instinctively shift, adapting to the dim lighting within. My mates—Khal, Diaval, Easton, and Torben— follow closely behind as we traverse the halls, heading toward the grand banquet hall. The walls seem to echo with the whispered conversations of those who came before us.

My senses remain on high alert, attuned to every subtle sound. The familiarity of the surroundings is both comforting and daunting all alpha houses look the same. I lead the way down the hall, each step measured, the anticipation of the encounter with Alpha Roman and the gathered elders palpable.

Raising my hand, I bring our group to a halt about ten feet from the towering pine doors that separate us from the grand banquet hall. The scent of aged wood and the resonance of distant conversations seep through the gaps, signaling the importance of the assembly on the other side.

The doors are adorned with intricate carvings depicting the history of the Blackmoor pack, stand as a symbolic barrier between us and the pivotal meeting that awaits. I exchange glances with my mates, a silent acknowledgment of the weight of the moment. Khal's steady presence, Diaval's unwavering support, Easton's calm assurance, and Torben's quiet strength—all crucial pillars in the foundation of our family.

As the doors creak open, revealing the grand banquet hall bathed in warm flickering candlelight, the atmosphere shifts. The room, with its polished wooden floors and ornate chandeliers, exudes a timeless elegance. Alpha Roman, seated at the head of a long, intricately carved table gazes at us with a mix of curiosity and authority.

The elders, flanking him on either side, regard us with measured expressions. I lead our group forward, navigating the space between the long tables. The air is thick with tension, and the eyes of the assembled elders, each carrying the weight of centuries, follow our every move.

"Alpha Roman," I greet, my tone respectful yet assertive. "We come seeking guidance. I seek the knowledge of my family and those that remain within this mountain pack." Alpha Roman acknowledges our presence with a nod, his gaze lingering on each member of our group. The elders remain silent, their expressions guarded.

"We have information that leads us here to your pack," I continue, choosing my words carefully. "We seek your counsel and the wisdom of the elders in locating my last surviving relatives that live here."

As the words hang in the air, the room falls into a heavy silence. Alpha Roman, his gaze unwavering, finally speaks, his voice carrying the weight of authority. "Share your information, and we will consider its relevance to the pack. But know this—the decisions we make today will be to protect our people first and foremost."

With a nod, I signal to Khal, who steps forward with a map detailing the information we've gathered. The flickering candlelight casts dancing shadows on the faces of those gathered, heightening the intensity of the moment.

As we unfurl my family tree on the long table, the eyes of the alpha and elders scrutinize the details. The room is charged with an unspoken understanding—the delicate balance between tradition and maintaining safety.

Alpha Roman and the elders scrutinize the list of names we've uncovered, their collective knowledge attempting to make sense of the puzzle before them. The grand banquet hall is now charged with an undercurrent of tension as the fate of our pack hangs in the balance.

"I know the Havardr family and the Torsten family. The rest of these names, I do not know who they are," declares the elder and advisor to Alpha Roman. His gaze moves across the parchment, his furrowed brow revealing the weight of his contemplation. I take note of the familiarity in his expression, a recognition of certain names that brings forth memories of Blackmoor's extensive history.

"I am Clem, advisor to Alpha Roman. I can take you to meet with the families tomorrow," he offers, providing a potential solution to the mystery that shrouds these enigmatic names.

Roman, however, interrupts with a forceful gesture that echoes through the hall. "I didn't give permission," he growls, directing his glare at Clem.

The sudden outburst draws my attention back to Roman, and I feel a subtle nudge within me—an instinctual response to assert dominance. Before Roman can further assert his authority, I intervene, my voice cutting through the tension.

"Do not disrespect your elders, Alpha," I assert firmly, leaving no room for argument. Roman steps back, seemingly affected by a force beyond the physical. The familiar sensation of the power coursing through me intensifies—a power that echoes the primal strength of my wolf. My eyes glow with an ethereal light as I fixate on Roman.

His knees buckle under the weight of the unseen force, and he clings to the edge of the table for support. The room falls into an uneasy silence as the alpha, momentarily subdued, grapples with the unexpected display of authority. The elders exchange knowing glances, recognizing the significance of the moment.

"Feray, let him go," Torben's deep voice resonates through the hall, a grounding force that reaches me even in the midst of my newfound power. I heed his words, gradually releasing the tenuous grip on the rage that had surged within me.

The glow in my eyes recedes, and the air in the grand banquet hall lightens as the oppressive force dissipates. Roman straightens, his composure returning as he regains control over the situation. The elders, ever watchful, continue to observe the unfolding dynamics.

"Forgive me, Alpha Roman. The urgency of the situation overwhelmed my judgment," Clem apologizes, recognizing the gravity of the exchange. Roman, though still visibly unsettled, nods in acknowledgment.

"Tomorrow, then Clem, you will accompany them," Roman declares, his tone a blend of authority and resignation. The decision is made, and the room exhales a collective breath held in anticipation.

As we prepare to leave the grand banquet hall, I exchange a glance with Torben. His steady presence grounds me in the reality of the challenges we face. I decide that at this point it would not benefit us to remain. Something about the meeting and the way all the elders were present set me on edge. Khal gathers up all of our papers and scrolls before we make our way out of the alpha house.

The moon hangs high in the night sky, casting a silvery glow over Blackmoor. The weight of the alpha's authority still lingers, but so does the promise of a new day. Tomorrow we will be venturing into the homes of families whose names hold secrets that may expose the secrets of my past.

Back in the crisp night air, I turn to my mates, each one bearing witness to the shifting dynamics within the alpha house. The journey into the heart of Blackmoor's history has only just begun, and with it comes the realization that our actions will resonate far beyond the grand log cabin. We are finally reaching into the very heart of my biggest question. *Who am I? And where am I from?*

There's a burning deep inside me and I know it's my heat. Tincture does its job, but the knowledge of it lingers. I won't lose my mind from the heat. I won't conceive a pup even if I wanted to. Glancing over my shoulder, I look at each of my mates. What are the odds that any of them would play nicely together?

"I see that look in your eye, little wolf…" Torben's nose is still twitching. He's caught my scent, and he won't leave me wanting.

"The nose never lies…" A giggle escapes my lips until it turns to an *oof* when Khal throws me over his shoulder and starts running down the street with me dangling upside down.

"Khal!" I laugh and scream at the same time as I jiggle. I can see Torben and the mystics in hot pursuit.

The door opens and I can see the interior of the den. Khal brings me into my room and tosses me onto my bed. Bouncing several times, I continue to laugh as I watch him trying to strip out of his fancy clothes. Interestingly enough, the second being to enter is Diaval, and he hisses, gaining Khal's attention.

Diaval closes the door behind him and uses his talons to shred the clothing from his body. Every inch of him is on display, and I can't help but stare. I lick my lips, watching him I don't notice Khal sliding up next to me naked.

"Let your draconic mates take care of you tonight. We may not be able to smell your need, but we are quite attentive." He smiles as he brushes my hair away from my shoulder.

Diaval turns my head in his direction and smirks. "Your wolf is showing. She appears hungry … Khal, feed her…" Diaval commands and Khal drops to his knees before me. His tongue shifts and becomes that of his basilisk. Gasping, I stare at his tongue as it snakes its way inside me. It slithers within me, hitting my g spot, making my legs buckle from the sensation.

Diaval grips me from behind, his hand going to my throat, holding me just tight enough I know who is in charge. "Be a good mate and not come until I say so," He whispers in my ear, his forked tongue teasing my ear lobe. I feel the command in his tone and my wolf bows down and presents to him in my mind.

Khal's tongue snakes its way inside me, hitting every tiny sensitive spot. His thumb rubs my clit and I almost tip over the edge. "Not yet…" Diaval whispers again. His grip on my throat tightens.

Khal withdraws his tongue and turns me to face Diaval. Without warning, he reaches down and grips the back of my thighs and lifts me, spreading me wide. Diaval steps forward and slips his length into me. Gasping, I arch my back, putting my hands on his shoulders. Diaval moves slowly, taking his time, dragging his length through my core.

Khal bites my shoulder as he grids his length between my ass cheeks. His pre-cum coats his length as he carefully tests my backdoor. Each nudge he gets a little further in. Diaval sees what he's trying to do and takes me from him to hold me still. Khal slips in slowly, making me feel so very full. "Move … please move… I'm so close." I whine into Diaval's shoulder, and they listen.

Diaval has a firm grip on my thighs as he picks up the pace, slamming his length deep within me. Khal grips my hips, adjusting his angle to thrust in the minute Diaval pulls out. Be it their draconic nature or it's a cultural thing with their people, they truly know how to work together. Every inch of me feels alive. My flesh is sensitive to their touch. Nuzzling Diaval, I whine as I feel the first flutters of my impending orgasm.

"Shhh my eternal … a few more moments…" He pants out as he increases the strength of his thrusts. Khal comes long before I'm allowed to. He grunts into my shoulder, gripping me tightly. I feel the pulsing of his cock in my ass and I whine louder, trying to resist the urge to come.

Diaval's movements falter as Khal pulls out. He spins us quickly, slamming my back into the wall. His hand takes both of mine off of him and holds them above my head against the wall. "Come for me, my eternal…" His voice hits that hypnotic resonance. Every fiber in my body obeys him without question and I come harder than the last time I was with him. My wolf lends her tone to my voice as I cry out, tilting my head back. One last thrust and Diaval buries himself deep within me. His cock thickens and pulses deep in my core, his hot seed filling me.

A soft knock can be heard, and I glance over Diaval's shoulder. Khal goes to the door and answers it. Torben is standing there. Slowly, Diaval releases my arms and I wrap them around him, holding on tight.

"If you would allow it, I would like to bathe our mate before bed. It's been a long few days." Torben offers remaining outside of my room.

Diaval nuzzles me and I feel him slip free. He lowers me to the ground, and I feel like a newborn fawn. My legs wobble beneath me and a giggle escapes my lips. He walks me over to Torben, steadying me as he guides me into his arms. "Sleep well, my eternal." Diaval kisses my temple before Torben scoops me up and carries me off.

CHAPTER 26
TORBEN

THE FIRST GENTLE RAYS OF MORNING LIGHT PIERCE THROUGH THE window, casting a warm glow upon Feray's fiery red hair. She lies beside me, immersed in a tranquil slumber, her features softened by the serenity of dreams. A pang of jealousy courses through me as I observe the peaceful repose she has found. Wrapped in my protective embrace, my larger frame envelops her, the bear within me stirred by a possessiveness that intensifies beyond the boundaries of our familiar forest.

Gazing at her, I run my fingers through the strands of her hair, the silky texture a testament to the delicate beauty that rests in my arms. The play of light flickers over her features, casting a gentle glow on her smooth, peaceful face. In this moment, as the world outside stirs, she is an oasis of calm, blissfully unaware of the uncertainties that the day holds.

Today is a pivotal day. We journey further into the unknown alongside the elder, seeking answers from families whose names remain shrouded in mystery. Feray's quest to uncover the truth about her birth family propels us forward. I can only hope these families have the answers that she so desperately seeks.

The weight of responsibility, both as an alpha and as the one who holds Feray close, bears down on me. I watch over her, my gaze unwavering, guarding her dreams and offering silent reassurance in the face of the challenges that await us. The love I feel for her, intertwined with the primal instincts of my bear, fuels a determination to navigate the uncertainties that lie ahead.

As the morning unfolds, the sunlight gradually illuminates the room, and I find solace in the rhythmic rise and fall of Feray's chest. The essence of her presence is a balm to the uncertainties that linger in the air. In this intimate moment, my connection to her transcends the physical, tapping into the emotional currents that bind us as mates.

The softness of her features, accentuated by the play of light, evokes a tenderness within me—a recognition of the vulnerability and innocence I see in her. Unfortunately, being as sheltered as she was, she is unaware of the dangers that lurk out in the world.

As we prepare to embark on the day's journey, the significance of the unknown weighs on my shoulders. The elders have told us to protect Feray at all costs. My precious mate is apparently more than she seems. The secret is so very buried that even my mate is unaware of her true potential.

The soft click of the doorknob turning, and the latch opening catches my attention. Lifting my head slowly, I look down the bed towards the door. Easton enters carrying a tray with breakfast foods on the plates. No sooner does he enter with the food than I see Feray's nose twitch.

"Bacon..." Feray says as she stretches. "Morning." Her gentle tone makes me smile just before she kisses my lips.

"Morning." I kiss her temple, and Easton clears his throat, getting her attention.

"The elder will be here soon. You should probably eat something. We don't need you cranky when you go to meet potential family members." He comes to the side of the bed where the small table sits near the window and sets the tray down.

Feray looks at the tray, then walks over and kisses Easton on the cheek before going to sit down and start eating. He tilts his head towards the door and I follow.

"What's up?" I whisper as we move down the hall.

"We were talking while you slept. We are going to stay behind, so the wolves aren't uneasy." His tone of voice betrays his feelings. He's not happy with the idea but knows it's for the best. "You go with her and don't leave her side."

Nodding, I look back towards the bedroom. "I wouldn't dream of it." There's a knock at the front of the den, and Easton rolls his eyes. "I'll stall the elder, get dressed, and get ready to leave. I doubt he would want to linger long." Easton turns on his heels and I hear Diaval greeting Clem at the door.

Before I have the chance to turn, Feray has her hands on my hips. "Go get dressed. We're going on an adventure." She bounces up and kisses my cheek before scooting past me.

I throw the first presentable outfit on and walk down the hallway. Clem is hanging over the tabletop with Feray as they point at different names. "Your parent's names are missing, child." Clem points at the pulsing black mass on the parchment.

Feray bites her bottom lip, then gets a wicked look in her eyes as she glances from me, then back to the elder. "That's on a need-to-know basis. Outside of my bond, it is not needed to be known." I watch her face take on some wolven features for several seconds then recede.

Khal puffs up when she makes her statement and I know she got that stance from him. Diaval notices the change in how Khal is standing and gives him an approving nod. "I'm going to go finish up in the back. I'll see you when you return, Precious." Khal kisses her gently and heads to the back of the den to sleep.

"See you soon, Khal. Love you guys…" Feray kisses Easton and Diaval before she runs down the hallway after Khal. She's gone for several seconds, then returns giggling. "Let's get the show on the road." She grips my hand and waits for the elder to go out the front door.

"We will go to the Torstens first. They are the closest to here." Clem turns right out of the door and starts walking down the cobblestone road.

"What can you tell us about them?" I tuck Feray under my arm, holding her close to me.

"They originate from Silver Falls, the town that guards the passage to Dunnum. Their shifted form has more white to it than the rest of us. The Havardr moved from Dunnum to Silver Falls, then here about twenty or so years ago before the war broke out." He lowers his head and draws in a deep breath. "It was a dark time for the packs. Two of our strongholds were at war for control of the north. We were all afraid it would spill over into Blackmoor."

His mention of the war made Feray tilt her head. Apparently, she knows something I don't. "Why did the war break out?"

Her question made Clem stop, and he looks down at his feet. "An alpha and luna went missing. Everyone blamed everyone else and boom, there you have it. All-out war for control of the north."

A shudder moves through Feray, and she stares up at me and gives me a subtle nod. "War is never a good thing. Can I safely assume that they resolved their issues?" she asks softly. I see what she's doing. She wants to know who's running the show.

"Unfortunately, the alpha in charge of the Crescent Valley is a tyrant." A soft growl escapes his lips and Feray cocks her head to the side before reaching out and touches him. I watch as relief floods his system, and he stares at her in awe. "You're more than what you seem," He whispers before he starts walking again.

Halfway down the block, we stop before a two-story stone and wood building. The house number is carved into the stone by the door. Clem steps forward and knocks at the door. Several minutes pass before an older woman opens the door. She smiles as she goes to greet Clem. Before the words leave her lips, she stops and stares at Feray like she had seen a ghost. She goes to close the door, but Clem stops her.

"By your reaction, you've already answered my most pressing question. I need to ask you several questions, and then we will be on our way." The older woman relents and welcomes us into her home.

"It's obvious you recognize my friend here. I can only assume you knew her parents." Clem states matter-of-factly.

"I believe her to be Ivan and Anastasia's child. She has her mother's red hair." The woman says as she looks Feray over.

"Torben, Feray, this is Dorothea Torsten." Clem mentions and Dorothea bows her head slightly.

"Ana's daughter's name was Thyra, she was born during a thunderstorm. You can't be her daughter." Dorothea smiles sweetly. "The little one had a birthmark just above her tailbone. It looked like a pink crescent moon." Her smile broadens as she mentions it.

"If you couldn't tell, I was Ana's midwife. I helped deliver the little bundle of joy. I moved shortly after because I found my mate and he lived here." She laughs a little. "I would love to know what happened to that little one. They disappeared sometime over the winter. When I went to visit them in the spring, their house was burned to the ground."

Her mentioning of the birthmark made me arch a brow. I don't remember a birthmark, but that doesn't mean it's not there. "Thank you for your time, Dorothea." I smile and help Feray stand.

"You two are such a beautiful couple. Hopefully, one day, I'll deliver your children." She reaches out and pats Feray's hand before Clem leads us out.

"Did that help any?" He asks as he turns us in a different direction.

"I know what my parent's names are and that wasn't it." Her eyes lower and I want to tell her what I figured out, but I also don't want to tip off the elder or the alpha.

"Maybe we should just go back to the den and have lunch with everyone and figure out what we want to do next." I offer and give Feray a slight squeeze, letting her know I'm on to something.

"Are you sure? The next family isn't all that far from here." Clem offers, motioning down the road.

"Yeah..." Feray answers, staring into my eyes. "The tonic to stop my heat makes me feel ill. My attentive mate knows when I'm hiding that I'm not feeling well. I wish to rest and maybe sleep." She forces a smile and acts like her stomach is giving her trouble.

Bending down quickly, I scoop her up, holding her in my arms bridal style. "Thank you for your help, Clem. Unfortunately, I don't believe we're going to find answers here." I turn and start walking towards the den.

"I'll let the alpha know you were unsuccessful. Are you heading back to Briarvale?" He smiles and I know we didn't mention where we were from.

"Yes, probably tomorrow night." I kiss Feray to keep her from talking as I turn us to leave. "Don't say a word." Something has my bear on edge and I don't want to find out the hard way what it is..

I hurry down the cobblestone path, cradling Feray in my arms, the urgency of the moment propelling me forward. The den where we reside with her other mates comes into view, and the weight of responsibility presses heavily on my shoulders. We need to confirm a crucial detail—whether Feray bears the crescent birthmark above her tailbone, the key to unlocking the mysteries of her lineage.

As we traverse the town, the curious gaze of its inhabitants follows us, their eyes peeking out from behind blinds and doorways. The sensation of being watched sets my bear on edge, a primal instinct to protect coursing through me. Feray, sensing my unease, attempts to soothe me with her touch, but my focus remains unwavering. I have to get her back to the den as fast as possible.

Upon our return to the den, I kick the door closed behind us, shutting out the prying eyes of the town. The urgency lingers in the air, and I address Diaval, whose dragon eyes flare to the surface, attuned to the heightened tension in the room. "We need to leave as soon as possible," I declare, the urgency in my voice cutting through the stillness. Easton, drawn from the kitchen by our abrupt entrance, looks on with curiosity.

"Why? What happened?" Diaval's inquiry hangs in the air, prompting me to take action.

"The old woman Dorothea we went to see mentioned that the baby she delivered for a couple had a crescent moon birthmark." Setting Feray gently on the ground, I barely have time to speak before she deftly removes her dress and spins around, exposing her back to me.

There, above her tailbone, a reddish crescent moon rests—a mark that holds the key to the revelation we seek. My heart seizes in my chest as the truth unfolds before me. The couple I can only believe are the missing Alpha and Luna gave birth to Feray in secret in Silver Falls and named her Thyra.

Emotions surge within me—joy, relief, and an undeniable sense of purpose. The pieces of Feray's identity, once scattered and enigmatic, now fall into place. I meet her eyes, and in that shared gaze, a connection deepens—a recognition of the significance of this moment in shaping not just Feray's destiny, but the destiny of our family.

The air in the den, charged with the weight of revelation, seems to pulse with the rhythm of our collective heartbeat. Feray, standing exposed yet empowered, embodies the strength that comes with self-discovery. In the quiet aftermath, the realization of her true lineage gives us a direction.

"Is it there? The mark? Am I Thyra?" Feray's hands tremble as she pulls her dress back up and turns to face me. Lowering my eyes, I nod. Before I can say anything, she rushes into my arms, resting her head over my heart. I do the only thing I can think of.

As I band my arms around her, I look at the others. "Diaval you need to get her out of here as fast as possible. I don't like the feeling within the town. Everyone I believe suspects who she is."

Diaval nods and looks at Feray. "Eat something my eternal and I'll fly us out of here posthaste." Diaval moves over to the map and I follow behind him. "This is where the hidden pass is to get to Silver Falls." He pulls a gold doubloon out of his pocket and holds it out to me. It has a long claw mark down the face of the coin like the one he gave Feray. "Whoever is at the gate, show them this coin they will let you pass."

The light glints off of the coin and without touching it, I know the weight it carries. It's the promise of protection from a dragon, the most fearsome shifter besides a basilisk. Reaching out, I take the coin from him and place it in my pocket. "Thank you. We'll meet you in Silver Falls." Feray stands there staring at me Diaval and I then nods resigned to being spirited away swiftly.

With the plans changing on the fly like they did, I can understand her being upset. Deep down, I have to believe she understands her safety comes first. Feray disappears into the back, then returns with her backpack on her back. She's changed out of her dress and into leather riding pants with a sensible shirt and jacket. Her boots look like they belong in an equestrian event instead of for riding a dragon.

"Ready to go my Eternal?" Diaval offers her his hand, and she readily accepts it. "Don't look so sad. Without you in the SUV no one has a reason to attack it. They will be safe. Besides, they'll have Sparky with them. He can torch anything that moves." I arch a brow, looking at Diaval after he called Easton Sparky.

"See you soon." Feray kisses me and then Easton and Khal before allowing Diaval to walk her out of the den. We're leaving in broad daylight to escape a possible threat we're not even sure exists. There's never a dull moment.

CHAPTER 27

FERAY

Diaval guides me swiftly out of the den, the urgency of our mission palpable in the air. We traverse the cobblestone street, keeping to the shadows like characters in a real-life spy movie, trying to elude the watchful eyes of an unseen adversary. The town, with its prying inhabitants, feels like a maze. Every step we take is a calculated move, a dance on the edge of discovery of my past.

As we navigate through the labyrinth of narrow alleys and hidden corners, there are several close calls that sets my heart pounding. Each fleeting moment when we come perilously close to being spotted intensifies the suspense, making our escape feel like a high-stakes endeavor. The adrenaline courses through my veins, and I can't help but marvel at the synchronicity between us in a seamless collaboration during this impromptu escape.

Finally, we break free from the confines of the town limits. The cool mountain air washes over us, rejuvenating us. Diaval, drawing in a deep breath, pauses for a moment, his gaze scanning the horizon. It's a brief respite, a stolen moment before we plunge into the next phase of our journey.

With a determined resolve, Diaval leads me down a hill, and as we descend, a vast meadow comes into view. The grass sways gently in the cool breeze. It's a serene contrast to the tension that has accompanied us through the town, a momentary reprieve in the heart of nature.

"I can shift down there," Diaval suggests, his voice low. The pressure of keeping us safe must be weighing heavily on him. As we reach the center of the meadow, Diaval turns to me, his eyes reflecting a mixture of concern and determination. "We'll head north to Silver Falls and wait for the others there," he decides, the plan taking shape in the afternoon's quietude. The meadow, bathed in the golden rays of the sun, becomes a staging ground for the next leg of our journey.

In the meadow's stillness, the bond between us strengthens. Our breath mingles with the cool air, and I can sense the unspoken understanding that we share. Diaval steps away from me and shifts to that of his wyrm skull dragon. His onyx scales are so black they almost don't seem real. As I approach, his head whips up and I watch his muscles tense, staring back towards the town.

I freeze in the middle of the field and get low to the ground, hoping the tall grass hides me. His dragon's head turns back towards me. The look he's giving me screams urgency. I stand as fast as I can and run to him and climb onto his wing tip like before. He lifts me up and places me on his neck. Shifting my hands, I use my claws to climb his neck as he raises his head higher.

My heart thunders in my chest as I reach the space behind his head between his horns. "Go!" I scream at the top of my lungs as I brace for him to launch into the sky. The sheer force of takeoff almost knocks me loose from my place.

The wind roars in my ears as Diaval's powerful wings beat rhythmically against the air. The force threatens to rip me away, but I cling desperately to his scales, my claws digging into the rough surface. Below us, the world shrinks into miniature, and the ground becomes a distant blur.

My heart pounds in my chest, a mix of exhilaration and fear coursing through my veins. I steal a glance down, and the landscape looks like a patchwork quilt of greens and browns. My gaze quickly returns to Diaval's massive form as he continues to ascend, the wind tousling my hair wildly.

I wonder what could have triggered this sudden flight, but the urgency of our ascent banishes such thoughts. The realization hits me that the others might face whatever danger spurred Diaval into action. My stomach churns with worry.

"Diaval!" I shout, my voice swallowed by the wind. I tighten my grip on his scales, leaning forward to reach his horned head. "Can we check on the others?" The rushing air snatches away the words, but I hope my plea reaches him. Diaval's body ripples with the effort of his flight, scales glinting in the sunlight.

His response is a powerful roar, a sound that vibrates through the air and resonates in my chest. It's a reassurance, a signal that he understands. With a subtle shift in his trajectory, we change course, and relief washes over me. I strain my eyes, searching for any sign of our pack below.

The landscape gradually comes into focus, and I spot the SUV just clearing the mountain pass. Relief floods my system, and I am grateful for the detour. I can tell that the SUV is moving quickly as Diaval glides on the thermals heading north towards Silver Falls.

From our elevated vantage point, the world unfurls beneath me like a sprawling tapestry. The distant, ethereal peaks of the white mountains pierce the horizon, their ghostly outlines captivating my gaze. Between those majestic summits and here lies the town of Silver Falls, a mere speck from this great height. Diaval's dragon, sensing a different thermal, adjusts its course, and we surge forward with renewed speed.

As we soar, I steal a glance backward, my eyes tracing the undulating length of Diaval's dragon. The sheer enormity of the creature never fails to amaze me. With each beat of its colossal wings, the dragon propels us higher, and I can feel the rush of wind against my face. The scales, a sea of obsidian, extend as far as my eyes can see, absorbing every ray of light that graces them.

I find myself captivated by the intricacies of those scales, each one a testament to the battles Diaval's dragon has weathered. Battle scars crisscross the dark expanse, a silent narrative etched into the very fabric of his being.

Lost in thought, I can't help but wonder about the stories behind those scars. Will Diaval ever choose to share them with me? I know him as my grumpy but fiercely loyal mate, yet the mysteries of his past linger like shadows.

The outline of the town becomes clearer the closer we get to Silver Falls. I watch Diaval tilt his head left, then right as he scans the ground below us. Eventually, he turns his head and his whole body turns, heading towards a field. Remembering from the last time I leaned forward, holding onto the ridge of bone in front of me. He lands carefully and then slowly lowers his head to the ground. His wing comes forward, and I step onto the tip like the last time and am lowered to the ground.

Diaval shifts back and closes the distance between us, pulling me to his firm chest. "The abrupt departure was not planned." He looks down at me and I see his dragon still in his eyes.

"What happened?" Furrowing my brows, I stare at him, worry building in the pit of my stomach.

His arms band tighter around me, and I hear the rumble of his dragon in his chest. "I wasn't sure what I was seeing. It looked like the town was coming out either to watch or attack. I can never tell with wolves." He winces as he says it.

"We are rather instinctual. Fight or flight seems to be ingrained in our DNA." He nods, grateful for my understanding.

Diaval motions behind us. "Just over that ridge is the town of Silver Falls." His serpentine tongue flicks out, and he tastes the air. "By what little I can taste, I believe the town is abandoned." Tilting his head to the left, I can tell he's studying me.

Turning my nose to the wind, I close my eyes and breathe in deeply. The crisp scent of snow is in the air. The impending snowstorm isn't far off. A rabbit is digging into the fallen leaves in the underbrush. Deer are some distance away, but upwind from me. I don't scent any other wolves or humans. We are the only bi-pedal beings in the area. Opening my eyes, I turn to face Diaval.

"It's just us here." There's a building tightness in my chest, and I watch Diaval rubbing his sternum. Reaching out, I place my hand over his, stopping his movement. "Sorry, I'm not good at keeping my feelings to myself." He nods stiffly as he leads me towards where the road should be.

"It's a new feeling." Narrowing his eyes, he examines me. "It's not unpleasant, just different."

Watching him, I can tell he's examining the feeling in his chest. "Do dragon bonds do the same?" I reach up and touch his scale, giving it a stroke, feeling its rough edge under my fingertip. "What do I feel like to you?" I look up into his eyes and stroke his cheek, watching him.

"A warmth, like my favorite duvet. Wrapping me up in your heat and kindness. It makes me feel less cranky, less angry, until someone pisses me off again." A myriad of emotions flicker over his normally unflappable expression.

I take a hold of his hand and start guiding us towards the road. "Each of you feels different."

Diaval gives my hand a squeeze. "How so?"

"Torben is strong, silent. He's a constant stream of love and reassurance. An almost possessiveness to his tether." Drawing in a breath, I examine the next threads. "Khal is playful and so is his bond. It's a lighthearted, almost constant stream of joy." Smirking, I can't help but chuckle. "Easton is almost unsure of what he feels. There're moments of jealousy from him, then possessiveness. He definitely loves me. He just doesn't know how to handle it. I think he scares himself."

"Scares himself?" Diaval stops us and moves me to stand before him.

"He will always resurrect. Me? If I die ... He dies with me." I search Diaval's features, looking for understanding. "Mortality is frighting to someone who has lived and died a thousand times. Death has not been a reality for him until me." Guilt consumes me as the reality of it all hits me. I am the reason Easton will meet his final death.

Diaval's eyes flare as he stares at me, and his hand goes flat to his chest as realization hits him. He reaches out and pulls me to him hard, crushing me to his chest. He envelopes me in his warmth and bathes me in his scent of chamomile, and it soothes something rough in me. It takes the sour edge of the pain that was rising in my chest.

"It's a rough transition for any of us. I'd rather not say how many years I've lived. But it is a damn long time." Pressing his lips to my forehead, I feel his breath washing over my scalp. "I won't die because you die, love." He whispers against my skin.

"That's good to know." I kiss his throat.

"There will never be another after you. Dragon's mate for life, like wolves do. I'll shift to my dragon never to walk the earth as a man again." His admission made my chest tighten slightly as I think about his monstrous shift looming over the world for eternity.

We turn and start walking again, leaving the heaviness of our conversation behind us. As we reach the road, I look both ways, still not hearing the tires on the road. "When do you think they will get here?" My attention turns down the road in the direction that they would come from.

"Approximately thirty minutes." His eyes flick up to the position of the sun and then down the road. "That is, if they continue driving at the speed they were when we passed over them." I can tell his dragon is doing the calculations for him. The occasional flicker of his dragon's slits in his eyes tells me he's close to the surface.

Looking around, I see an apple tree and walk over towards it. I hear the rustle of leaves behind me, hearing Diaval following behind me. Using my claws, I climb the tree and start picking apples, dropping them down to him. "Wolves don't climb trees." He chuckles, looking up at me as he catches the apples, I'm dropping down to him.

Glancing around, I realize I'm probably fifteen feet off the ground. "I've always climbed trees as a kid. Wolf or not, I know how to climb." When I finish grabbing the last of the good apples, I climb down out of the tree.

Landing on my feet, I move to sit on the ground under the tree. "Snack time while we wait for the others." I bite into one of the apples and wait to see if Diaval joins me in my makeshift picnic.

He looks around and finds a rock to sit on and he too starts eating the apples. After shifting and flying as far and fast as he did, I know he needs to refuel. Diaval always waits for me to eat first, forsaking his own hunger. This time I outthink him by eating before he tells me to. A sly smile crosses my lips as I stare at him behind my apple.

Feray one ... Diaval zero.

CHAPTER 28

EASTON

ANXIETY GRIPS ME LIKE A VICE, MY GAZE FIXED ON THE DIMINISHING figures of Feray and Diaval as they vanish out of sight, walking out of town. A sense of relief washes over me, knowing that Feray is with Diaval, the safest option among us. But the urgency of our plan propels me into action. Torben, and I move swiftly, loading the SUV with a practiced efficiency.

Torben gives me a thumbs up, and I nod in acknowledgment, my mind already racing ahead to the next steps. Leading a drowsy Khal out of the den, I guide him to the back seat while Torben takes the passenger seat. "I guess I'm driving," I mutter more to myself than to the others, a declaration that hangs in the tense air.

As the engine roars to life, the elder Clem emerges from between the houses, his smile seemingly kind, but with a forced quality. "Where are you off to?" he inquires, a glimmer of curiosity in his eyes. I summon a smile, attempting to maintain an air of superiority that might prove useful in these delicate moments. "Our mate's birthday is tomorrow, so we're running out to find her a present."

The elder's eyebrows raise, a hint of surprise crossing his features. I tilt my head back slightly, adopting a subtle pose that suggests a certain level of indifference. His smile becomes genuine this time. "On the far side of town, there are several vendors that may have something she would enjoy."

I acknowledge his advice with a nod and a smile. "Thanks for the tip. We'll look into it." With a wave, I pull away, heading toward the back side of the town. The elder's intentions remain unclear—whether he's aiding us or setting us up is a puzzle I can't decipher. Nevertheless, I steer the vehicle in the direction he indicated.

When I'm reasonably certain we're not being watched, I turn suddenly and press my foot hard on the gas. The engine roars to life as we speed down the cavern through the mountain. The tunnels echo with the sound of our escape, and a surge of adrenaline courses through me.

The urgency of our mission intensifies, and I navigate the twists and turns with a determined focus. Feray and Diaval are ahead of us by now. There's a symphony of emotions playing out beneath the surface—anticipation of not knowing what's on the other side.

Breaking free of the cavern pass feels like a weight lifting off my shoulders, and I draw in a deep relieved breath. My eyes scan the expansive horizon, an unspoken vigilance that keeps me on edge. Torben, sitting beside me, breaks the silence, his voice cutting through the quiet of the car's interior. "We should get there in about an hour," he says, glancing at the map on his phone before shifting his gaze to me. I nod in acknowledgment, my focus fixed on the road stretching out ahead. The sun is slowly lowering in the sky and I note that it's midday. I glance upward as an abrupt shadow fall upon the car. Diaval's colossal dragon glides overhead, silent and majestic.

"I bet Feray made him check on us," Torben muses, his eyes following the dragon's flight. I nod, a sense of gratitude settling within me for the unspoken connection between Feray and Diaval. Their bond, like an invisible thread, weaves through our shared existence.

"I wouldn't doubt it," I reply, a small smile tugging at my lips. "She's the perfect mate for us." The warmth of affirmation courses through me as I finally grasp onto the thread that is Feray in the bond. An intricate tapestry of emotions unfolds, revealing her anxieties and excitement for the path that lies ahead. Feray is a paradox herself. She possesses a captivating blend of qualities — wild yet controlled, strong yet soft, dominant yet submissive. The last one, in particular, spins my head with its complexity. She holds the power to command us all, yet finds solace in surrender. It's not a trait not commonly associated with a Luna.

As the road stretches before us, the anticipation of our imminent reunion with Feray fills the car. The paradox of her nature is not just a puzzle; it's a comforting enigma. The bond we share is a delicate dance of strength and vulnerability, dominance, and submission. With each passing day the threads of our connection tighten, drawing us closer to one and other.

I'm becoming more anxious by the moment, thinking about how far I am away from Feray. "I fly too..." I mutter to myself as the pang of jealousy raises its ugly head.

"You do realize your shift isn't big enough to carry her, right?" Torben offers gently.

Rolling my eyes, I glance from the road over to Torben, then back to the road before me. "I wish I was..." Shaking my head, I stare at the dirt road watching the leaves flittering past us.

"We each bring something different to the family." Torben says as he looks up from his phone. "Didn't you notice how different we all are?" He turns slightly, angling his body towards me. "You can match Feray's intellect and offer her challenges the rest of us can't." Torben hikes his thumb over his shoulder. "He's the sensitive one. He can relate to her emotionally better than any of us."

"Yet, he's the one that can turn everyone to stone or poison them." I mention as I keep my head on a swivel.

"I'm her safe place, her silent enforcer. She knows I will destroy anything in my path." Torben laughs a little. "All of us would destroy the world to get to her. Each of us to different degrees."

Shaking my head, I huff out a laugh. "Fire, acid, venom or ripped to pieces. Talk about the new riders of the Apocalypse." My own words make me ponder something. "I wonder if I can set Diaval's acid on fire and turn it into napalm?" The reality of it all has merit. Before I can get lost in thought, the silhouettes of two people standing in the middle of the road come into view.

"There they are!" Torben exclaims as he points down the road.

There's nothing more unnerving than watching a Berserker Kodiak get as giddy as a child on Christmas morning. His bouncing in his seat is making the SUV rock in time with his movements. "Before you accidentally roll us, please settle down." I turn slightly to glance over at him and it hits him how much his movement was affecting the vehicle.

"Sorry..." His tone makes him sound like a kid that got in trouble for stealing cookies.

"I'm excited, too. Except I would turn this vehicle into an exploding fireball." Biting my bottom lip, I pull off onto the side of the road close to Feray and Diaval. Before the vehicle is in park, Torben is out the door and down the road.

After parking the SUV I walk down the road slowly to where Torben is hugging the stuffing out of Feray. "We were separated for less than two hours." I say boredly as I roll my eyes. Turning to address Diaval, I am impacted by a small giggling body.

Looking down, I can't stop the smile that crosses my lips. "My beautiful flame." Carefully, I thread my fingers through her fiery tresses before pulling her in for a kiss. Feray melts in my arms and my insecurities fade away in an instant. This little wolf in my arms is more precious to me than any of the treasures in my treasury.

Feray's eyes flicker with the power of her wolf as she stares up at me. "My flame..." Reaching up, she traces my cheek, smiling, her eyes dancing over my features.

The way she's looking at me makes my bird rise to the surface. Her wolf is calling to my bird on a primal level. "My mate..." When she smiles, I see the canines of her wolf.

"What's on your mind Feray?" I've seen this before. She needs to scent mark me again, that and she probably wants sex.

Feray tilts her head left, then right, before she leaps into my arms. The sudden movement catches me off guard and we fall backwards. *Oof* ... The wind is knocked out of me when we impact the ground. Thankfully, I took the brunt of it. She climbs up my body the rest of the way and pulls my tie free and nuzzles my shoulder where she had bitten me before. Her teeth grip at my flesh and I hate to admit it. I came in my pants instantly.

She doesn't break the skin, but she holds me there for a few moments. "You are not less than any of the others." She said as she presses the tip of her nose to mine. She climbs off of me and heads towards the SUV.

"She's uneasy about heading into the town. She doesn't scent anything living in the area beyond wildlife." Diaval says without taking his eyes off of the SUV watching for Feray.

"The town is abandoned?" Torben lifts his nose to the wind. He closes his eyes, focusing on the minute scents traveling on the wind. "My nose isn't as sensitive as Feray's." He makes the statement and looks back at us. "I don't smell anything living either."

"Let's be prepared for anything, then." I state, looking between my bond mates.

Diaval looks back at the car, then between Torben and I. "Keep Feray with you." He looks into Torben's eyes and he gives a firm nod. "Easton and I will handle whatever threat comes. Shift and get her out of the area fast."

"Wouldn't you get her out faster?" I tilt my head, looking at him.

"No, I take too long to shift, and we will be vulnerable in that time. Khal is a good second option to get her out." Diaval taps his chin as he turns and looks down the road.

"Why is Khal getting me out?" Feray's voice catches us off guard and I almost jump out of my skin.

"Just in case there's danger, little wolf." Torben moves to Feray's side, stealing her from Khal, and presses his lips to her forehead.

"All I've known is danger since my amulet broke." She rubs the area over her sternum where I can only guess the missing amulet sat.

"Hopefully soon we will know why." I motion down the road. "Silver Falls is on the other side of the hill. Hopefully, we can find answers in what remains in the town." Every tiny movement of the skin around her eyes tells me she's not thrilled with what's happening.

She gives me a sharp nod, then moves back to the SUV and climbs into the backseat. Drawing in a fortifying breath, I return to the vehicle and drive down the dirt road. Rolling into town was like the start of some of the horror movies Feray and Khal watch at night. Dead and dying trees surround the outskirts and entering town limits it more of the same.

Most of the buildings are dilapidated beyond repair. It makes me wonder when was the last time someone lived here. I park the vehicle just inside the town, concerned about making too much noise with it. "We'll walk from here." My eyes find the others and they nod firmly, resolve flickering in their eyes as they come to terms with what may come.

We don't know if we are to face an army of the dead. A horde of wendigos or worse yet feral vampires that have a nest in the heart of the town. I refuse to voice my concerns, yet Diaval pops into my thoughts, expressing the same concerns I have. Mythic's and ancient wyrm dragons can communicate with each other without words in close proximity. I'm ready to burn the town to the ground to protect my mate, and now my bond mates.

Feray looks skittish yet resolved to go through with this next adventure. Her wolf is lurking under the surface, ready to rip free to protect its human counterpart. Torben's bear is feeding off the anxious energy that Feray is giving off. This, regardless of how it turns out, is going to be a major turning point for my mate. Either we are going to find the answers to her universe. Or hopefully at least a direction to find those answers.

CHAPTER 29

FERAY

I keep singing the song about it being the end of the world over and over in my head. There's only three places left to search for answers and this is the first we've come to. Silver Falls unfolds before us like a scene from a horror movie, a haunting tableau of decay. The buildings, once proud structures, now stand in various stages of disrepair, their skeletal frames echoing a bygone era. The air carries the scent of dampness and decay, a tangible reminder of the town's gradual surrender to time. As we step onto the cobblestone road, the crunching of fallen leaves beneath our feet adds an eerie soundtrack to our exploration.

The trees, their twisted limbs frozen in haunting contortions, loom over us with an otherworldly presence. It's as if a blight has swept through the forest, freezing life in a macabre dance of decay. The strong breeze stirs the air, carrying with it a chill that sinks into my bones, setting my nerves on edge.

The sun begins its descent behind the mansion at the end of the road, casting long shadows that stretch across the dilapidated structures. Once-vibrant hues of the sunset now take on a sinister tone, adding an ominous feeling to the already foreboding landscape. The sky, painted in hues of orange and red, seems to conspire with the surroundings to create an unsettling atmosphere.

My instincts scream at me to run. I want to flee from this desolate place that seems to hold secrets darker than the shadows that stretch across its cobblestone streets. Yet, my gut tells me differently—whispers of hidden answers, a puzzle waiting to be unraveled. I find myself at war with my own emotions, torn between the desire to escape and the need to confront the mysteries that surround my existence up to this point.

As my mates spread out, each drawn to a different abandoned building, Torben remains steadfastly glued to my side. His presence is a reassuring anchor, and I glance at him as we approach the first forsaken home on our right.

"There's something here. I can feel it," I murmur, my words carried away by the sigh of the wind as I motion to the town.

Torben leans over, his lips pressing a comforting kiss to my temple. "If it's here, we will find it," he assures me with a confidence that settles the unrest within me.

With renewed determination, we step into the shadows of the abandoned dwelling, ready to uncover the secrets that Silver Falls holds, regardless of the ominous specter that hangs over this desolate town.

Stepping across the threshold of the abandoned house, every floorboard groans under our collective weight, echoing through the desolate space. Each creak feels like a ghostly whisper, a testament to the years of neglect this once-homely abode has endured. The air inside is stagnant, carrying with it the musty scent of decay that lingers like a ghost of the past.

A sudden snap startles us as one floorboard finally surrenders beneath Torben's weight, a stark reminder to tread carefully in this crumbling building. As we traverse further into the shadows, the dim light filtering through cracked windows casts eerie patterns on the dusty floor, heightening my unease.

My attention is drawn to the mantle over the fireplace, where several pictures lie in silent testimony to a life once lived here. A line of bassinets, neatly arranged, catches my eye, the month of February scrawled beneath them in pen. There's no accompanying year, but a suspicion gnaws at me—it's the same month I was born. Swiftly, I pocket the picture, its edges worn and yellowed with time, a potential piece of the puzzle that is my life.

Moving on, Torben's voice calls out from another corner of the dilapidated house. I navigate through the remnants of forgotten memories, my senses on high alert. Arriving at Torben's side, I find a photograph revealing the back of a tall woman with hair the color of mine, her presence captured in a moment, frozen in time. In the background, a house undergoes renovation that looks to be separate from the main part of town.

"Could this be your mom?" Torben asks, his voice a soft murmur that pierces the stillness of the room.

Shrugging, uncertainty clouding my features. "I don't know. I'll take it with me just in case." With a sense of reverence, I accept the photograph from Torben and carefully tuck it into the bag, already cradling the earlier discovery.

The air in the room seems to carry the weight of untold stories, and the whispered echoes of the past beckon us to unravel the mysteries that linger within these decaying walls. As we press forward in our search, the anticipation of what we might discover pulses through the air, mingling with the melancholy scent of years gone by.

We scour both floors of the dilapidated house, our footsteps stirring up motes of dust that hang in the stagnant air. The creaking floorboards beneath our weight tell tales of a history long forgotten, the scent of decay lingering in every corner. Faded wallpaper peels from the walls like ancient memories unraveling, and the air is thick with the scent of mildew and disuse.

As we step back out into the fading daylight, rejoining Diaval, Khal, and Easton, the subdued atmosphere follows us. Their somber expressions mirror my own as I inquire about their findings. A collective shake of their heads answers my question, leaving us with the disheartening realization that these crumbling houses don't hold the key to the mysteries we seek.

In my hands, I cradle the two pictures—fragile artifacts that seem to carry the weight of untold stories possibly linked to my past. I share them with the others, and a silent understanding passes between us. Easton studies the image of the red-haired woman, a thoughtful expression on his face. "This is a positive," he declares, his words carrying a hint of optimism. He hands the picture back, and Diaval takes his turn, scrutinizing the captured moment frozen in time.

"The mansion at the end of the road should be the pack house. In theory, we should find more answers there. After that, we look for the house in the image," Diaval asserts, his words resonating with a sense of finality. I find myself nodding in agreement; it's a logical plan. The prospect of finding answers at the pack house holds the greatest odds for determining our next move.

The setting sun casts long shadows across the landscape, the cobblestone road leading us toward the imposing mansion. The air, heavy with anticipation, carries the scent of earth and old rotting wood. As we embark on the next leg of our journey, the promise of uncovering the truths hidden within the pack house and the elusive house in the photograph lingers in the air, mingling with the fading sunlight.

Stepping into the rotting pack house to search what looks like hundreds of rooms is setting my nerves off. The thought of locating the house in the picture makes the hair on the back of my neck stand on end.

The floorboards on the first floor prove more resilient than those in the smaller house Torben and I explored earlier. Perhaps it's the added protection of an entire floor above, but the uneven creaking beneath our steps isn't as disconcerting. Yet, the air down here is dense with stagnation, carrying a dampness that clings to the senses. A subtle undertone, whether mold or mildew, taints the atmosphere, leaving a lingering trace of decay.

Room after room, I discover spaces that seem to have been systematically emptied, as if a professional mover had swept through, erasing any trace of life. The abandoned remnants of a forgotten existence create an eerie silence that amplifies the sense of desolation.

My exploration comes to a halt in front of the last door at the end of the hallway—a locked barrier that beckons my attention. "Torben, I need you," I call out to my mate, and within moments, he stands by my side. Our eyes meet, and without a word, he rams his shoulder into the door, splintering it into a hundred pieces.

What greets us beyond the shattered entrance is an unsettling tableau of death frozen in time. The skeletons of at least a dozen beings litter the floor, their remains telling a grim tale. Some skeletons are mid-shift, caught in the tragic limbo between human and wolf forms. Stains on the wallpaper bear witness to old blood spray, a chilling reminder of violence that once stained these walls.

Torben and I exchange a sobering glance, absorbing the horror of the scene. Claw marks, larger and deeper than anything a mere wolf could inflict, scar the surface of a once-sturdy desk and the north-facing wall. The sheer brutality of whatever force wreaked havoc here hangs heavy in the air. The unanswered question of what transpired here is casting a haunting shadow over the room.

"I wonder what happened here?" I murmur, my voice a hushed whisper in the eerie stillness. The echoes of a violent past cling to the walls, and as we navigate the morbid scene, the oppressive weight of unanswered questions settles upon us, like the lingering scent of decay refusing to dissipate.

Navigating through the skeletal remains with a mixture of caution and sorrow, I carefully step over the bones strewn across the floor, making my way toward the desk that stands as a silent witness to the room's grim history. The air seems heavier here, as if the room itself mourns the lives lost within its walls. My fingers brush against the icy surface of the desk, and I grip the knob on the center drawer, my anticipation building.

Despite several attempts, the drawer remains stubbornly closed, a frustrating obstacle between me and the secrets it may hold. Frustration boils within me, and with a low growl at the inanimate object that seems to defy my efforts. My gaze sweeps the room, and that's when I notice it—a skeleton lying on the floor, a key peeking out from under the tattered remains of what once were pants.

"Sorry, Alpha. I need this more than you," I murmur apologetically to the long-forgotten leader of this fallen pack. Retrieving the key, I walk back to the desk, a silent acknowledgment of the tragedies that befell this place etched in my every step. The key fits snugly into the lock, and as I turn it, a sense of trepidation courses through me.

The drawer yields to my efforts, revealing a hidden trove within the recesses of this decaying room. My eyes widen as I pull out a worn pack ledger, its pages yellowed with age but teeming with the echoes of lives long gone. The ledger, a record of births and deaths within the pack, holds the key to unraveling the mysteries that have haunted Silver Falls. Perhaps my birth was recorded here? Possibly under the name of Thyra.

As I lift the ledger, my eyes meet Khal's, a subtle smile playing on his lips. His silent understanding reflects the gravity of this discovery. The pack ledger may well be the key to unlocking the secrets of my past, a tangible link to the lost history of a pack that once thrived, now relegated to the bones that lie scattered around us.

Khal motions for me to follow him and I go without hesitation. He stops and stares at the room and the claw marks within and pulls me to his side, ushering me out of the room.

"Diaval found a room on the other side of the building that we can stay in safely tonight before we hunt for the house in the picture." Khal mentions as he guides me to the room.

My other mates are in the process of moving what's left of the furniture around the room. "What did you find?" Easton asks as he approaches.

Glancing down at the ledger in my arms, I sigh. "Possibly answers. Or just more aggravation. Who knows?" Shrugging my shoulders, I glance down at the book and take the bottle of water that Diaval is waving at me.

CHAPTER 30

DIAVAL

WATCHING MY ETERNAL SEARCH AIMLESSLY FOR HER PAST MAKES MY heart hurt. Her past is an enigma at best. The longer I'm in her presence, I can see the strength within her. Her heart is open, and she gives affection freely. Watching her sort through the decay of the town, hoping for an answer to who she is, upsets my dragon.

Fix it … my dragon screams at me in my head. He's angry.

I can't … I don't know how… That is the crux of the problem. I don't know how to fix it.

Help her search for that new name that was mentioned. Thyra, I believe it was. My dragon muses. I can almost hear his talons clicking in my head.

"May I help you?" Extending my hand out to her, I arch my eyebrows up, hoping she would let me try.

Feray's eyes dart down, looking at the book in her arms and then up at me. Quickly, she nods and passes me the book. Tears rim the edges of her eyes. "I'm scared Diaval … What if I'm not in there?

Then what?" Her bottom lips quivers as she stares up at me and then sniffles.

My dragon propels my body forward, and I crush her against my chest. Wrapping my arms around her, I hold her tightly, willing myself to absorb all of her pain. Unfortunately, it is not a power that I possess. "Then we keep trying. We have all eternity." I press my lips to her forehead, trying to imbue all of my strength into her. I would smite an entire continent just to see her smile.

Walking forward, I pass our mate off to Torben and motion down the hall. "The last room on the right is the cleanest. I set it up for us to sleep there." Glancing over at Khal as he joins us in the alpha house, I motion back in the direction he came from. "Can you hunt for our girl? She hasn't eaten since we left Blackmoor."

Khal looks in the direction he just came from and nods. "Anything specific?" He tilts his head to the side, watching me, then down the hall where Feray is.

"No, we'll get her to shift so that she can eat as her wolf." Especially since we don't want to start a fire and alert anything that may be lurking.

"I'll see what I can find. I may have to go further away from here to find life." Khal mentions absently as he glances from the hall, then back to me.

"Do what you have to. The worst-case Easton will burn the town to the ground to protect her." I mention honestly.

"I'll be back as fast as possible." Khal nods to himself and turns on his heels before leaving the building. Watching him walk away, my eyes return to the journal in my hands.

I head to the office close to the room that Feray and Torben obviously are mating in. The soft sounds of her moans and the slaps of flesh on flesh distract me from the book I need to be reading. Easton watches me as I open the book on the tabletop and start flipping through the pages.

Feray is somewhere in the twenty-four to twenty-six-year-old range, so I find the years that match that assumption. Hundreds of names listed, births and deaths all in their collum. The mention of Anastasia being pregnant caught my attention. "What was the name Feray's mom had used? Was it Anastasia?" I pause, looking up at Easton.

"Yeah, that was the name mentioned with an Ivan as the mate. Is he mentioned?" Easton moved closer and my finger slid across the page to the mate's name. There it is, Ivan. "Yes, both names are mentioned."

"So, we're on the right track, then." Easton says as he looks at the book upside down, staring at the two names we were hoping to find.

"Appears so..." I pause, looking at the names, then flip through the pages further. "But look here..." I point to a notation that the child was lost.

"Do you think that was staged?" Easton pauses and starts pacing, pondering what we just saw.

"Maybe, especially if they were trying to hide who they were. Could have been a survival thing." Shrugging my shoulders, I stare at the ledger and wonder what actually happened.

"But if they were trying to hide who they were, why did they go join a pack? If it was me, I would have gone to a place like Briarvale, where it's a mixed species and not just my species." Easton makes a valid point, and it offers more questions than answers.

Shaking my head, I look through the lists further. "There were several losses that year." I point at least six other losses the same year. The other losses caused me to search my memories. "The water could have been contaminated. Perhaps the council did it." Cursing under my breath, the thought crosses my mind. "What if Blackmoor experienced the same loss?" Looking up, Easton's eyes ignite at the question.

"There's no way to find out without raising suspicion." He rubs his hands through his hair roughly. "I'll have one of the first years at the hospital inquire." Easton types furiously on his cellphone sending out a Hail Mary text. "If she can find anything out, she'll text me." He draws in a deep breath, seeming more frustrated than usual.

Running my hands down my face, this book is making my head hurt. All the needless deaths if the council had a kill order on babies the year she was born. "I swear, if I find out they killed those babies to find her..." A deep rumbling growl escapes my lips, and it rumbles the interior of the house. My dragon wants to torch the council, burning the building to the ground. Scales and bone plates shift and move under my skin. My dragon is fighting me for control. He wants out and is in a murderous rage.

I'm seeing red, my pulse thrums in my ears and all I can feel is the desire to destroy. Stepping away from the table, I feel as if my dragon is going to rip me apart. Babies, hatchlings, it doesn't matter what you call the innocent ones that had died. They are the most precious ones to dragons. Hatchlings are worth more than all the treasures in the horde.

Just as I reach for the doorknob pushed by my dragon to seek vengeance for the lost children, lithe hands stop me. Turning slowly, trying to keep myself from shifting, I see Feray looking up at me. Her eyes are wide, finally seeing my dragon's fury. Her eyes pulse with the power of her wolf. "Diaval..." Her voice resonates, sending ripples over my skin, getting my dragon's attention. A warmth moves over my flesh slowly and my drake settles down. The rage that was simmering under the surface melted away with the smooth circles her thumb made on the back of my hand.

"How?" Arching a brow, I look down at my beautiful mate.

"Because I love you..." Smiling, she stands on her tippy toes and presses her pillowy lips against mine. Her kiss was like a sirens' song and it settled something in my drake.

She's perfect ... My dragon says haughtily, and I can imagine him arching an eye ridge and raising his head in defiance.

I return Feray's passionate kiss and run my fingers through her fiery tresses. She is my kryptonite, my greatest treasure, and my life for eternity. Until now, I didn't know what love was. Love is this little wolf in my arms. Pressing my lips to her forehead, I remain there for several moments. The longer I remain in contact with her, my temper subsides.

"We have something to talk about my eternal." I lead her over to the table and where the book is. Using my index finger, I draw Feray's attention to the names on the table.

Feray's gasp, and the shiver that moved through her, made me draw her closer to me. "It says the baby died..." Her bottom lip quivers as she looks up at me. Easton moves to her other side and places his hand on her lower back.

"We believe they faked your death to hide you, since there were other baby deaths around the same time." Easton offers. "We also suspect that the council may have been involved. I've made a call to the hospital to find out if Blackmoor had the same issue around the same time." Easton pulls his phone out and looks at the screen as it pings in his hand. "Blackmoor also had a mysterious die off of pups at the same time." His first-year med student gave us the answer that confirms to me that the council was involved.

"Why kill pups? Why? It's so hard for wolves to have babies ... It doesn't make sense..." Her bottom lip trembles harder as she tries restrain the urge to cry.

"I will burn the world to ash if I have to. No one will lay a finger on you ever..." Easton turns Feray to look him in the eyes. His eyes orbs of pure fire as he stares at Feray. In the centuries I've known the man, I've never seen him get this angry. He's borderline nuclear and suddenly the fire dies.

"Easton..." Feray's voice resonates again, and I watch the fire die in his eyes. She effectively extinguished the rage simmering in him like she did with me. Watching it happen was more impressive than having it happen to me. Torben moves closer as he watches us interact.

"She's gotten good at doing that ... It's a luna gift similar to what a mother sow does with her sleuth. Just remember, still waters run deep." We will heed Torben's warning. A mother sow is nothing to be fucked with. A female wolf, especially with pups, is the most dangerous creature on earth.

While Feray had calmed both me and Easton down was amazing. Khal walks through the front door dragging a deer behind him. Feray pauses and goes deadly still. Her nose twitches, and then her head whips towards the door, seeing the deer behind Khal. Without warning, Feray shifts and her wolf tears into the deer, sending fur and skin flying everywhere.

My eyes widen watching her not having seen this level of ferocity from her. Arching a brow, I look over at Torben, who also wears the same look of shock as I do. Easton had moved Khal over to the book and caught him up on what we discovered. The rage in

Khal's eyes concerned me. Basilisks are not known to keep their rage under control.

"Is this normal?" I motion at Feray as I glance at the savage display my mate putting on.

"She doesn't feel safe," Torben muses as he watches her feed.

"Do you need to eat?" I motion to the deer.

"I will when she's done. My shift can and will eat the bones for the marrow." Torben's tone softens as we watch her eat.

I did not know that Kodiaks ate bones. That was a new piece of information as I stare at Feray eating. A good chunk of the deer is gone and Feray comes trotting over. The gentle clicking of her claws on the wood adds to the fixation of watching her. Feray's shift is seamless and she managed to not destroy her clothing like the mythics can do.

Torben kisses Feray's temple before he continues past us and shifts. Feray smiles, watching Torben move past her as he seamlessly shifts to his bear to eat. She closes the distance between them, her fingers threading through his fur while he eats. No one in their right mind would think to mess with Torben while he eats.

"So, what do we do now?" Khal says looking from the scene before us, then back over to the book.

"We look for the house in the picture." I pull the picture out and show him the image in question.

Khal picks up the picture and stares at it. "If I didn't know any better, I would have thought this was Feray." Sighing, he looks at the book flipping pages. In the far back of the book, a rough sketch of the town sits. A single house south of the graveyard was off the beaten path. It's to the west of the town and what looks like a small road leads to it across from the windmill. "We start here. Let's find that road and follow it."

With as simple as Khal made it seem it hopefully we can find what Feray is looking for. We wait for Torben to finish eating and head off toward the windmill, using that as our reference point.

CHAPTER 31

FERAY

The rhythmic crunching of leaves underfoot mingles with the thudding of my heart, creating a disconcerting symphony that accompanies our approach to the mysterious house. The wind, a capricious conductor shifts, and the musky scent of rotting leaves wafts through the air, sending a shiver up my spine. A crisp autumn breeze carries the earthy decay, a scent that lingers like a spectral presence.

Khal strides confidently at the forefront, having deciphered the clues that lead us to the house in question. His assuredness, however, cannot quell the unease that coils within me. I steal a glance at Torben, his bear's form walking beside me. He remains staunchly in his animal state, an obvious manifestation of his discomfort in this haunted place. The tension radiates from him its a palpable force in the air, and I can't help but share in his unease.

As we draw nearer, the silhouette of a half-rotted windmill looms on the horizon, a stark symbol of the passage of time and the decay that has befallen this forsaken town. Each step closer to the looming structure amplifies the anxiety that has settled in the pit of my stomach. The windmill, once a symbol of industry and life, now stands as a somber sentinel, witnessing the slow unraveling of Silver Falls.

Shadows cast by the skeletal branches of trees add an ominous touch to the landscape. The air becomes heavy with anticipation, and the distant echoes of our footsteps seem to bounce off the decaying structures that surround us. The closer we get to our destination, the more the atmosphere becomes charged with an indescribable tension, a spectral presence that clings to the very fabric of this forsaken place.

We stand frozen at the fork in the road, uncertainty casting a shadow over our group. My gaze is drawn to the left, an unseen force tugging at me, beckoning me to look in that direction. "Something doesn't feel right," I murmur, my eyes fixed on the path we need to take, dread pooling in my stomach. Torben's bear lets out a thunderous roar, an instinctive response to an impending threat. He pushes me backward, a silent warning etched in the intensity of his actions.

My senses heighten, attuned to the ominous atmosphere that surrounds us. I scan the woods, and in the shadows, red eyes ignite one by one. The realization hits us like a chilling gust of wind—we've found what happened to the pack. The scent of death and old blood, also the scent of a dank crypt.

"Vampires..." Diaval's voice cuts through the tension, and he extends an arm to shove me protectively behind him.

A soft, almost unhinged laugh escapes my lips, a grim acceptance of the impending confrontation. "Perfect..."

Easton's incredulous gaze fixes on me. "Perfect? What do you mean, perfect?" His tone carries a hint of desperation.

I meet Easton's gaze, a wicked smile playing on my lips, my wolf's canines extending ever so slightly. "They're allergic to me."

In an instant, the transformation begins. My show-white wolf erupts from my human form, and I pad forward, taking a position closer to Torben's roaring bear. The air crackles with tension as our group braces for the impending clash. The forest seems to hold its breath; shadows concealing the approaching threat. As the first vampire emerges, my presence disrupts the unnatural calm, and all hell breaks loose.

The charge of the vampires echoes through the air, the swift rustle of leaves and the soft patter of their footsteps creating a disconcerting cadence. But as suddenly as they moved, they come to an abrupt halt, their predatory instincts frozen in place. The forest seems to hold its breath in anticipation, a palpable stillness settling over the battleground.

The vampires, a sinister congregation with eyes that burn like crimson embers in the shadows, fixate on me. Every gaze is a needle-like prick against my skin, a collective focus that sends a shiver down my spine. A charged silence hangs in the air, broken only by the distant howl of the wind through the trees.

"Get the white wolf!" One vampire screeches, a guttural command that cuts through the eerie quiet. A gnarled finger points accusingly in my direction, the gesture unleashing a cascade of movement. The vampires, fueled by a frenzied determination, surge forward once more, a predatory wave eager to consume its prey.

As they close in, the scent of damp earth and decaying leaves mingle with the acrid tang of vampire presence. Before we can charge into battle, Easton moves forward and ignites every vampire he can see. The world seems to move in slow motion. I turn to watch him control the fire like a conductor in front of the orchestra.

Movement behind him catches my attention. My body seems sluggish as my muscles bunch, preparing to launch over Torben's back. Everything is moving so slowly and the fear builds in me as the vampire gets closer to Easton. I scream, but as my wolf it comes out as a howl. The vampire reaches out long gnarled fingers extending out, reaching for Easton.

Diaval turns just as my wolf uses Torben's back to launch off of. Time seems to return to normal just as the vampire's claws reach Easton's throat. My paws impact the vampire's chest. Instinct drives me and my muzzle lowers, sinking into his throat. The taste of ash and bitter, rotted blood coats my tongue, but it doesn't stop me from thrashing. The snapping of tendons and cartilage is music to my ears. A deep growl escapes my muzzle, one that I have never heard from me.

The minute the vampire's head is severed from his shoulder, I stand triumphant over what's left of the corpse as it turns to ash. "No no no..." Turning, I look back at Khal holding Easton in his lap. His hand pressed to his throat, covered in crimson.

My wolf gives me back my body as I rush over to Easton's side. "I wasn't fast enough. I'm so sorry..." My hand shakes as I extend out to touch him. Easton forces a smile looking at me. Tears well and fall freely from my eyes. I feel his immense love flood the bond from him. A peace I didn't know before in my life washes over me, and I know it's coming from him.

Gently, I take his hand and hold it tightly. He gives my hand a squeeze and closes his eyes. "No, Easton, please don't die..." I scream, watching his body go lax.

Torben pulls me back against him and crushes me against his chest. Diaval helps Khal to stand and then they move to frame me and support me emotionally. "My eternal, remember..." Diaval presses a kiss to my temple. "He's a phoenix. He will resurrect."

Sniffling, I glance from the guys over to where Easton lay far too still. "When will he?" *Return to me ...* Is the question I dare not voice.

"Soon..." Diaval says reaching out running his fingers through my hair. He pulls the feather in my hair forward and it's pulsing rhythmically. "When this ignites, so will he, and the process will begin. I've watched it now three times. It's stressful, but comforting to know that it's only temporary."

"You've watched it before?" I spin in Torben's arms to fully face Diaval.

"Yes, usually if a phoenix knows it's going to be reborn, it chooses someone to watch over them for the first week of their new life." His statement makes my brows furrow.

"What happens in the first week?" I move from Torben into Diaval's waiting arms.

"He comes back as a hatchling. The better he eats, the faster he'll grow." Diaval turns me just as Easton's body ignites.

I want to run to him, instinct driving me to extinguish the flame. The flames flicker in a myriad of colors, hypnotizing me. A whine escapes my lips as my wolf's claws at me, wanting to set its self free to save its mate. *He's coming back ...* I say to myself, or more accurately, to my wolf.

He's burning ... My wolf howls in my head, urging me to save him. My anxiety crushes my chest as I watch the flames lick over Easton's prone corpse. I feel like I am burning with him. He is a flicker in the bond as I watch him burn.

Anxiously, I bounce from foot to foot as I resist the urge to move to Easton's side. "He'll be back soon, Precious. We just have to wait and watch." Khal moves to my side and cups my cheek. I stare into his eyes, and I see his basilisks slits in his eyes.

Sniffling, I nod and look over at Easton again. I can't draw my eyes away from the ball of fire that is my mate for too long. Deep down, I blame myself for his death. I couldn't move fast enough. "Why did I move so slow? I don't understand. My wolf is fast, but I felt like I was held down with chains."

"One of the vampires had an ability. Some of them can manipulate time to a point. This one..." He motions to the ash pile. "Apparently could slow down time. Trust me, he would never blame you. You tried to get to him, putting yourself in danger to save him." Diaval mentions.

I glance away from Easton for a moment, then back to the flames as they die out. The pile of ash drew me to it like a moth to a flame. I break loose from my mates and go to kneel next to Easton's side. Something moved to my side and a guttural growl escapes my lips reflexively. Then I notice it's Torben sitting next to me.

"It takes time." Torben says gently.

In the center of the ash, I watch it start to ignite and pulse like a heartbeat. Slowly, the ash draws towards the center as if gravity is pulling it. The ball of fire grows slowly, still pulsing in time with my heartbeat. "This is different." Diaval says as he kneels next to me. When I glance up, I notice Khal is shifted and his basilisk seems to have grown in size. He coils his impressive form around us, shielding us from the outside world.

"What's different?" Tilting my head to the side, I look up at Diaval.

He touches his fingertips to my throat. "His flames are pulsing in time with your heart. Your bond is strengthening his return."

Nodding, I watch the flames as they grow. As much as the fire scares my wolf on a primal level. We know it's my mate returning. After what feels like forever, the fire finally dies and a small pile of ash remains. Movement under the ash draws my attention, and I reach out tentatively. My fingers search the ash until I find a small, warm body within it.

Carefully I lift the body from the ash and the baby phoenix looks like a macaw and a peacock had a hatchling. The tiny butterball of a chick looks up at me with an unexplained affection. It has the soft fluff of a hatchling covering its body. Tiny talon's grip at my finger as I draw him to my chest.

I stuff Easton's chick in my hoodie and then down into the top of my shirt and zip it up. Khal's basilisk turns to face me and I smile. "Hunt for us. Diaval and Torben can keep us safe. I need to feed him so he grows." Khal lowers his giant head and boops me with his nose before he takes off slithering into the woods to hunt.

"Let's go back to the alpha house. It's not safe to be out in the open until Easton is back in his adult form." I don't bother to wait for the guys to follow. I just turn on my heels and head back down the road. We have about a week before Easton is back in his adult form.

My hands frame the moving chick inside of my hoodie, knowing my mate needs time. The steps leading to the alpha house make my feet feel like lead. The weight of the world feels like it's resting on my chest with every move of my mate's chick. Hopefully, this week will end quickly.

CHAPTER 32

FERAY

KHAL RETURNS SEVERAL HOURS LATER AND DROPS ANOTHER DEAD DEER ON the porch of the alpha house. The scent of blood looms in the air, making my stomach growl. Torben leaves the sitting room and drags the body back where we were settled. We found a room with a functional fireplace and I was camped out in front of it, watching Easton's chick hop around.

In the bond I can feel Easton's love for me and he worries about if I am alright with what had happened. "I'm sorry I didn't move faster. The vampire, he had a power ... He slowed time." My bottom lip quivers as I fight the tears still blaming myself for his death. The only other vampire I have ever interacted with is Dezi. I've seen the blood lust in his eyes when I cut myself. Even when the hunger rose, he had control. These vampires, they were feral, lost to their hunger. I stare at my mate's chick, feeling inadequate and guilty. I couldn't get to him and I'm supposed to be some great luna.

"Little wolf, he wouldn't want you blaming yourself. He's alive and now you get to protect him for a while." Torben shifts a finger to a claw and slices off some meat from the hindquarter. "Make sure you eat, too." He presses a kiss to my temple then sits back, cutting a piece for himself and eats watching over us.

"Where's Diaval and Khal?" I glance over my shoulder, looking at him, and he smiles.

"Diaval went hunting for himself. Khal ate and is watching over the house." Torben states plainly, going back to his meal.

Reaching into my bag, I pull out a knife and cut ribbons of meat free from the roast to feed Easton. Raising a slice up, I offer it to Easton's chick. He chirps excitedly and snaps his beak, gobbling down the offered food. Feeding Easton's chick is a comedy in errors as he almost bites my fingers over eager to eat.

Giggles escape my lips as I watch him bounce and try to snatch the next ribbon from me. "Silly chick!" I waggle my finger in his direction. He stops and tilts his little fluffy head, then squawks at me in protest.

I keep feeding Easton until I see his crop is full and distended. He hops over to my sweatshirt that's on the floor and climbs in, then goes to sleep. My eyes move over his little body, and I use the sleeve of my sweatshirt to cover him.

"You're going to make a wonderful mom when you're ready." Torben says with an easy smile on his face.

"Fi's mom was great. She never made me feel as though I wasn't hers." Shaking my head, I swipe the rogue tear from my eye. "Do you know our birthdays are two days apart?" Smiling fondly, I think about the joint birthday parties we would have on the day between us. On the actual day we were born, Fi's mom would make our favorite meal for dinner.

"I didn't know that." Torben says as he scoots closer and pulls me to him. His thick arms wrap around me, and I feel his heart thudding in his chest.

"Yeah, I'm the eighteenth and she's the twentieth." Smiling, I lean back and close my eyes. Reaching out through the bond, I feel Diaval's dragon roaming the edge of the mountains that separate us from the tundra beyond. Khal's basilisk is slithering around the outside of the alpha house, keeping watch. "The warnings call us the children of the moon. I have yet to figure out what that means." Shrugging, I can't help but smile.

"You'll figure it out. You're the smartest woman I know." He kisses my temple and I melt into his arms. If I wasn't so concerned about another attack, this would be kind of romantic. A deep rumble escapes Torben's lips, and I know he feels the same.

"I don't feel so smart." I look at my hands and flex them as I snuggle in closer to him, resting my head on his chest. "Supposedly I'm going to be a powerful Luna, and I couldn't even save my mate." I motion in Easton's chick's direction.

"That was no one's fault." Torben spins me to face him and holds my chin in his hand, not allowing me to look away. His eyes glow with the power of his bear as he stares at me, trying to get me to see reason. "It could have been any of us. Unlike Easton, we cannot resurrect. You would be kneeling by a grave instead of watching over a chick."

Just before the tears break as I realize how much worse the day could have gone. Diaval enters the room and scoops me up out of Torben's grip. "My eternal, please understand we did all that we could. We were outnumbered thirty to one. He wiped out the bulk of the vampires, probably saved all of us." Diaval searches my features, hoping I understand what he is saying. Easton's sacrifice saved the family.

"I was almost there. Whatever that vampire did to time slowed me down. I couldn't get to him fast enough." Gripping his lapels, I try to get him to understand what was bothering me.

"Wait … You could move?" He looks at me puzzled, then over at Torben. "Were you able to move?"

"Not even an inch. I felt Feray's wolf use me to launch off of. Out of the corner of my eye, I saw her fly through the air in slow motion. It was like her wolf was floating in the air for a moment until she hit the vampire. Then I could move." Torben pauses and his eyebrows raised. "How did you manage to move?" He tilts his head to the side, looking at me just as puzzled as I feel.

"I don't know." Shrugging my shoulders.

"That's part of the power of the Luna. She has to be able to protect the pack. A lot of vampires have powers. The older they are, the stronger the powers. That's why he could slow you and not stop you." Diaval gives me a knowing smile. I swear I can see pride shining in his eyes.

"Do you think it's because I'm a Luna?" I glance anxiously between my mates and then at the chick in my sweatshirt.

"You're a true Luna. Straight down your bloodline. Never forget it. We are your pack and your family." He smiles and leans down to kiss my cheek.

"We should sleep." I change the subject as I stare at my sweatshirt moving from Easton's chick. I get up and move away from the guys and strip out of my clothing. My shift is fluid and painless, which differs from how it usually goes. Once my paws hit the floor, I shake out my fur and move over to the sweatshirt and curl myself around it.

Gently, I stick my nose under the sleeve and sniff Easton. Flicking my ears, I listen intently to the flutter of his baby phoenix's heartbeat. Consciously, I have to remind myself that he is my mate and not my prey. Irrationally, I haven't eaten enough, saving the majority for him. An entire deer is far too much for a hatchling. But here I am, ignoring my needs to tend to his. He saved us, and I will never forget it.

THE NEXT MORNING comes far too quickly and my stomach is growling loudly. Using my muzzle, I move the sleeve of the sweatshirt aside and see that the chick has tripled in size. It has feathers and looks like it might be able to fly. Carefully, I unwrap myself from around the sweatshirt and walk over to what's left of the deer and start eating.

"Are you ready to go exploring Feray?" Diaval asks as he walks up alongside me and threads his fingers through my thick fur.

Turning my bloody muzzle to him, I nod my head. I decide to take several more bites before heading to where I left my clothes. Shifting back is painless as well, and it makes me arch an eyebrow, thinking about it.

"I know that look, Precious. What's puzzling you?" Khal says as he steps over what is left of the deer.

"Shifting doesn't hurt anymore." Lowering my gaze, I shift my hand back and forth watching it, waiting for the pain that never comes.

"There's always a little of pain with shifting, even for me." Diaval says as he shifts his hand to have dragon's claws, then back again.

"Same with me." Torben shifts his hand to have his bear's claws, then back again.

"Mine doesn't hurt." Mentally, I am adding another notch to the freak belt that I apparently am wearing.

"I'm sure it has something to do with being a luna and needing to shift quickly." Diaval states matter-of-factly.

"You're probably right." I shelve the conversation for now as I reach down for Easton. He pops up and runs over to the deer to feed himself. A soft laugh escapes my lips as I shake out my sweatshirt and slip it on.

I watch him eat his fill before he comes to stand before me. Reaching down, I scoop him up and stuff him inside my hoodie. Time to find the house in the picture. Khal leads the way out of the house and down the main street.

Cradling the baby phoenix inside my hoodie, the surrealness of the situation settles over me like a thin veil. It's astounding how quickly he's grown. He's transformed from a vulnerable hatchling to a young bird adorned with feathers, already a quarter of the way to adulthood.

The cobblestone beneath our feet seems to absorb the gloom of the abandoned town, mirroring the overcast sky overhead. As we traverse the desolate streets, my eyes catch on details that I had previously overlooked—the broken windows, the claw marks etched on doors. The revelation of these signs of struggle leaves me with a disquieting sense of realization.

Why didn't I notice them before? I question myself, the subtle clues woven into the fabric of this forsaken place becoming more apparent with each step. The vampires wiped out an entire town, probably overnight.

Dried leaves, remnants of a long-forgotten season, skitter across the cobblestone when the wind blows, adding an eerie symphony to the atmosphere. The sound, coupled with the occasional creaking of a rusted sign swinging lazily, intensifies the ghostly aura that hangs over the abandoned town. The windmill, a skeletal silhouette on the horizon, marks the intersection leading to the road we seek.

"Are you okay, Feray?" Torben's voice cuts through the ominous quiet, and I realize how tense I've become.

The intersection looms ahead, a place stained with the memory of Easton's death and rebirth. "Yeah, just afraid of being attacked again. That and finding the house and there's nothing left, or there are no clues to who I am," I confess, my words laced with a mixture of anxiety and determination.

Inside my hoodie, Easton stirs, his little phoenix head popping out of the top. I bite my bottom lip, the weight of our quest pressing down on me like a heavy fog. The baby phoenix, with his radiant plumage, seems to sense my unease, offering a comforting warmth against the uncertainty that hangs in the air.

His shift nuzzles against my jaw and makes a cooing sound that seems to settle something deep within me. We reach the intersection and what remains of the battle has been blown away on the wind. Well, everything except for the stains of Easton's blood on the cobblestone.

"Don't dwell Precious." Khal blocks my line of sight and tips my head up to look at him. "He's alive and well in your hoodie." Khal's lopsided smile makes me laugh half-heartedly. He's right, I have Easton in my arms, and I didn't permanently lose him. Perhaps I am displacing my fear of being alone again on this minor bump in the road. Between the death of Fi's birth parents and now who knows what happened to mine? The fear of loss is at the forefront of my mind.

"He is, and I'm thankful." I kiss the top of his little bird's head, again ignoring the predatory instinct to bite his head off.

"We all owe him a debt that we can never repay." Diaval says and bows his head lower than Easton's. For a dragon to lower itself like that speaks volumes about the respect that is given. I watch Diaval take point and head down the path before us. This small exchange feels big and I feel like the dynamics in our family just shifted.

CHAPTER 33
KHAL

Torben and I decided last night that Feray would always have two of us with her. One dragon kin and one other mate. In theory, Easton is the one I should be paired with. Unfortunately, given his present situation, Torben is on double guard duty.

Dried leaves, brittle echoes of seasons long gone, skitter across the cobblestone underfoot. The haunting sound if their movement adds to the eerie ambiance. The atmosphere hangs heavy with a palpable tension. Add in the bare trees overhead, with their gnarled limbs, swaying in the wind. Their branches rub against each other, producing bone-chilling creaks and unsettling whispers that seem to echo through the desolate town. It's a symphony of eerie noises that sends shivers down Feray's spine, making her visibly jumpy.

The skeletal trees, devoid of leaves and adorned only with twisted limbs, cast elongated shadows on the cobblestone streets below. The wind, carrying with it the scent of decay and memories of battles past, ruffles the feathers of the baby phoenix nestled in the safety of Feray's hoodie. If not for her proclamation as Easton's sole guardian, I can't help but imagine her transforming into her wolf form. I can clearly picture it in my mind. Her hackles raised, growling at every ominous sound that pierces the unnerving quiet.

Passing by some of the trees, scars of past battles are visible. Claw marks mar their trunks, testaments to the struggles endured by the long dead inhabitants of this once-thriving town. Two trees, their bark entwined with remnants of weapons, stand as silent witnesses to the violent history etched into the very fabric of Silver Falls. The aspen trees, marked with the indelible traces of conflict, seem to echo the very essence of Feray's unease.

Her head remains on a swivel, vigilant and wary, scanning the surroundings for any potential threat. It's a heartbreaking sight— the transformation of my once-bold and fearless mate into someone who now fears the unknown more than ever. All because she feels she couldn't protect Easton.

Determination wells up within me, and I silently vow that, as long as I draw breath, Feray will not know fear. My heart beats with an unyielding resolve to shield her from the shadows that seek to consume her. I make a silent vow to myself to stand beside her as we confront the mysteries that linger in the shadows of Silver Falls.

Through the narrow gap in the trees, a skeletal framework emerges—a haunting reminder of what once stood as a house. The tall stone fireplace, defiant in its solitude, stands on one side. It's like a sentinel marking the ruins of what appears to be a collapsed farmhouse. The air here carries the scent of aged wood and earth, a subtle reminder of the passage of time that has weathered this once-homely abode.

Feray, guided by some innate sense, comes to an abrupt stop in her tracks. Torben and I move alongside her, hands gently placed on her lower back in a reassuring gesture. "My wolf knows this place," she whispers, her voice barely audible above the rustling leaves and the distant murmurs of the wind. The revelation hangs in the air, heavy with the weight of blood born memories she may not yet fully grasp.

Diaval, having overheard her, turns to face the skeletal remnants of the farmhouse, a sadness shading his usually stoic visage. "Like dragons, wolves know where they were born. This was your home, I assume," he says, stepping forward with a quiet understanding. He carefully pulls Feray into his embrace, mindful not to crush Easton nestled in her hoodie. "We will face this as a family," Diaval says. His words are a firm declaration that the family will stand as one.

Pressing a tender kiss to the crown of Feray's head, Diaval imparts a silent promise. A reassurance that whatever lies within the shattered walls of this once-hallowed home that we will confront it together. The air grows thick with the scent of anticipation and unspoken emotions as we stand on the threshold of Feray's past, ready to unravel the mysteries that lie within the ruins of her ancestral home.

Feray nods in response to Diaval's words, finding solace in the embrace of her dragon mate. A subtle nuzzle against the underside of Diaval's jaw speaks volumes, a silent exchange of comfort that transcends words. Stepping away, she shifts her gaze towards the tree line, her expression a mixture of anticipation and trepidation. The air, heavy with the scent of damp earth and the distant echoes of forgotten whispers. My senses bristle at the feeling that surrounds us as we prepare to confront the secrets hidden within the skeletal remains of her childhood home.

"Let's go take a look and see what we can find," I suggest gently, moving to stand alongside her. Feray turns her haunted gaze upon me, her eyes revealing the depths of emotions swirling within. I've come to understand that when faced with something significant, Feray retreats into a contemplative silence. She tends to process the complexities of her thoughts in her own time. It's a learned defense mechanism, perhaps forged during her upbringing by witches. Her survival meant navigating a world of magic she couldn't access.

As we approach the remnants of the farmhouse, the atmosphere thickens with the weight of anticipation. The ground beneath our feet, scattered with dry leaves and stray twigs, seems to echo with the whispers of the past.

Feray stops dead, staring at the structure and then around the entire property. Remnants of a silo leans against what's left of a barn whose roof has long caved in. The barn itself has hints of the red color that it used to be. Boards that made up the walls have started falling off. There's a wagon standing just outside of the barn as if it was set to leave. Looking closer at the wagon, I notice several steamer trunks resting in the back packed ready to go.

Glancing around, I notice the nose of a car sticking out of a small shed that's close to the house. It makes me wonder why they would choose the wagon and probably horses over a car that can move faster? "What's that look for?" Diaval moves closer to me as Torben takes Feray in his arms, moving towards a storage shed.

"Why the wagon?" I motion to the item in question and the trunks in the back. "They have a car over there." I point toward the nose of the car sticking out from under a weathered tarp and the collapsed roof.

"Maybe the car stopped working? Or it's because horses, being a prey animal seem to sense predators faster than another predator." Diaval muses as he looks between the two objects. "Did you look in the trunks yet?" He reaches out, grabbing one and takes it off the wagon and sits it on the ground in front of us.

"No. I'm not sure if we should be the ones to do it." I meet his questioning gaze and he nods.

"My eternal, we found steamer trunks that are locked and undamaged. Let's see if there're any clues in them." Diaval's tone catches Feray's attention, and she stops in her tracks and changes course to head over to us.

"I'm not sure how I feel about this." Feray bites her bottom lip as she gets closer to where we are.

"Do you want me to open it?" Torben offers. He shifts his hands to have claws and he motions to the trunk closest to him. With a slight nod given from Feray, Torben rips the top off the trunk.

Within the trunk, women's clothing is neatly folded. Feray leans closer to the trunk and sniffs, trying to catch a scent. The only thing we can smell is the eucalyptus leaves that rest on the right side of the trunk.

"They're used to mask the scent of a shifter. It distracts you enough with its pleasant scent to not search further." Torben offers as he takes a protective stance, watching over Feray.

With a shaky hand, she reaches out and pulls several tops out. Under the one top, a single red braid of hair rests. It's the same color as Feray's and I can only assume it's her mothers. "I wish Fi were here. I'd ask her to do a locator spell for me to find my parents." Feray lifts the braid to her nose and sniffs and pouts. I can only assume there is no scent left for her to smell.

"If they are out there, we'll find them." Diaval says with confidence. Easton's chick squawks, chiming in the best he can. "I'm guessing my compatriot agrees." Diaval says, motioning to Easton.

Feray keeps digging and pauses halfway down inside the trunk. There's a blanket in a sealed plastic bag. Someone went through a lot of trouble to protect it. Opening it carefully, Feray's hands tremble and I move to stand behind her, lending her my strength. The minute the bag is open, she shoves her face in it. The action catches me off guard, and I look at Torben.

"She's hoping for a scent. Then she can recognize the owner." He smiles, waiting and watching her.

When Feray lifts her head, tears rim her eyes. Her cheeks are turning pink as she strains to hold back the emotions threatening to escape. "It's mine..." She offers me the bag and dives into Torben's arms, causing Easton to squawk, reminding her he is still in her hoodie between them.

Gently, I pull the material out of the bag, and it's revealed to be her baby blanket. Hand sewn in the blanket's corner is Feray's birth name. Thyra Feray Jökull with her birthdate and weight. At least now we know who she is. But her parents remain a mystery. I pass the blanket off to Diaval and he makes a clicking in the back of his throat.

"You know something..." I stare at him as he tugs me away from the others.

"Her parents are the missing alpha and luna from Crescent Valley." He looks over at Torben as he leads Feray to go sit closer to the small stream on the property.

"Are you sure?" I glance over at Feray for a moment, then back to Diaval.

"She bears the mark of her mother's bloodline. The male came from Dunnum to meet the Luna in the Crescent Valley, how it's always been done." He stares at Feray, then back at me. "Her disappearance caused a rift in the process. No Luna, no succession of power."

"How does the succession happen?" We walk further away and keep an eye on where Feray is.

"The present Luna gifts the next Luna her powers and memories. From what I can tell, Feray has the power, but not the memories and knowledge of how to use it." He arches a brow, staring at me.

"So, what does that mean?" Clearly, I have no knowledge of wolf politics or traditions.

"It means her mother is dead and upon her death, she inherited the power. As for her dad, without a new alpha to pass the power onto, it's lost to the void." Diaval's dragon rises in his eyes, and I know he will destroy the world to protect what is his.

"Do we tell her what we suspect?" I keep an eye on Feray, playing with Easton's chick on her lap.

"No. I have a bad feeling we will find all the evidence we need for her to piece it together herself. Our job is to protect and support her however she needs us," Diaval says as he removes the next trunk and rips the top off. More clothing. This time it belongs to a man. Sharing a glance, we assume it must be her father's. There's one last trunk, a smaller one. Nodding again at Diaval, he takes it down and rips the top off using his talons. Baby clothing and a picture on top. The woman whose picture we found earlier, a man with broad shoulders, and a baby in a blanket.

Diaval hands me the photo and I stare at it. It's definitely the woman from the other picture with the same house in the background. "I'm eighty percent sure that's the missing alpha and luna." Diaval whispers. "We won't know for sure until we get to the Crescent Valley."

"What do we tell Feray?" I hate keeping secrets. Given my family background, some secrets are kept to keep others safe.

"We show her the picture." Diaval stops and just stares at me.

The silence speaks volumes. We show her what her parents looked like, but not who we suspect they are until we have concrete proof. "Agreed. Do we tell Torben?" Arching a brow, I stare at Diaval.

"We have to. Then we make him swear to keep it a secret until we know for sure. I'll tell Easton as soon as I can mentally link to him again." Diaval states speaking softly so our voices don't carry.

We decide to sit back and watch Feray explore the wreckage of what was the home of her birth. Torben urged her to search the house last so that we can do that as a family. Whatever the bear saw that made him say that can't be good.

CHAPTER 34

TORBEN

THE DESOLATE LANDSCAPE OF WHAT WAS ONCE THE BIRTHPLACE OF MY mate sends a chill down my spine. Merely being here is making the hairs on my arms stand on edge. This isolated farm, long forgotten like the main village, carries an air of abandonment. Beneath the surface of this collapsed farmhouse, something more sinister lingers.

Large claw marks, etched into what remains of the standing structures, tell a tale of violence and chaos. Deep gouges speak of a creature unleashed on a rampage, hunting with a ferocity that left its mark on every surface. I keep a running tally of the damage, each scar a testament to the strength of the entity that once terrorized this place. It becomes clear that the creature that attacked was formidable. It's possibly even stronger than I am when I shift. It's a realization that adds a layer of complexity and terror to the mystery we're unraveling.

Feray, grappling with the weight of her past. She discovered a blanket bearing what was intended to be her parents' chosen name for her: Thyra, meaning thunder. Perhaps my beautiful mate was born during a horrible thunderstorm, and it inspired her name. The last name, a connection to the elder gods and the lands beyond the frozen mountains of the north. It makes me wonder which of the northern packs her bloodline hails from.

The changing hues of Feray's coat, now a pure white, also captivates my attention. I recall the lessons from my past, where some animals adapt their fur color from brown to white as winter approaches, using it as a form of camouflage. I'm starting to suspect that come spring, Feray's fur may undergo a transformation, taking on the qualities of a timber wolf. The change in color will help her blend seamlessly with the changing landscape.

"Feray, come look at this." Diaval calls her back over and she looks up at me expectantly.

Smiling, I bend down and help my beautiful mate stand as she cradles Easton's growing Phoenix chick to her chest. In front of Diaval is a smaller trunk that he had ripped the top off of. It's filled with baby clothing and blankets. Feray carefully sits Easton down and pulls items out one at a time, looking at them. She sniffs each piece and sometimes a small smile crosses her lips. I can tell when she found an item with a tiny bit of scent on it. A soft rumble escapes her lips, and she sets the item aside.

"We found this." Khal offers her a picture. The same red-headed woman from the picture she found earlier is in the image. Diving into her bag, she pulls the other picture out and compares the two.

"It's her." Her voice is barely audible as her hands tremble, holding the two pictures side by side.

Her eyes become fixed on the image of the family, and I sit down and pull her into my lap. Tentatively she touches the man's face and then she looks up at Diaval. "Do you think this is my dad?"

The uncertainty in her voice gets my bear's attention. We become hyper-fixated on her micro-tells waiting to see when she needs us to shore her up.

Diaval clears his throat and draws in a deep breath. "From what the evidence points to, I can safely assume these are your parents and that's you in the image." His tone is different from when he is completely sure of something. I stare up into his eyes, almost challenging him. The minute Feray's gaze drops to the image in her hand, he double blinks at me. Khal mouths, they will tell me later.

With a quick dip of my head, I acknowledge what they are telling me. Diaval suspects something he's not ready to tell Feray. This can either be very good or very bad. Given how this town looks, I have a sinking feeling it will not be good news.

"You look a lot like your mom, little wolf." I whisper softly to her as she stares at the picture.

A soft laugh escapes her lips. "I definitely have her hair. Bright red and completely unmanageable." Another chuckle escapes her lips as she stares at it more. "My dad is handsome. I can see why mom chose him. He looks strong, like you." She leans back and nuzzles my cheek before kissing it.

"He looks like a rather powerful male. Your mom chose wisely." I smile, trying to keep her on the lighthearted side of this find. My suspicions with all the claw marks and destruction. Her parents didn't make it out alive. Which raises the question of how did she survive? I'll deal with that question later when I can talk to Diaval.

"Hey Feray, let's go hunt for Easton's next meal. If we can get a deer, we can share it with everyone." Khal offers and I know it is because Diaval needs to tell me something and he doesn't want Feray to hear.

"That's a great idea. Tor, do you mind watching Easton while we go hunting?" Feray reaches over and picks up Easton, then stuffs him inside my flannel shirt.

"Sure, go take a break. We can search more after you get back and we have lunch." Feray squeals and kisses my cheek before turning around, finding Khal shifted already. She runs to him and climbs up onto his back and rides off into the mountains on the back of a basilisk.

"Well, that went easier than I had thought it was going to happen." Diaval says as he steps closer. "Pay attention Easton. I know you'll be back to your old self sooner than later." Easton squawks at Diaval. "Don't be so sassy its unbecoming of you."

"Can we get to the point before she gets back?" I'm getting irritated at the constant back and forth between the two ancients.

"Yes, I suspect her parents are the missing alpha and luna and that they didn't survive the attack." Diaval's thought process aligns with mine and I nod. "You agree?" He arches a brow, looking at me.

"Yeah, follow me." I lead them across what's left of the compound to where the first of the large claw marks are. "Whatever it is, stands as tall as I do when I'm shifted." I splay my fingers and make a mock swipe at the tree. "It has hands with claws, not a paw. The marks are spread apart, not equidistant. Which means the digits can move independently. It's not a shifter that did this." I shake my head and move closer to what's left of the house.

Pieces of a ripped apart door lay on what should have been the front lawn. Flipping the pieces over, the same claw marks appear again. Diaval starts up the stairs and I stop him. "Let's wait for Feray. If we make a discovery without her, no matter how insignificant it is, she may get mad at us for not waiting." I may be a berserker, but I am not insane. Pissing off your mate and then having to sleep with one eye open isn't high on my list of things to do.

"The way the marks look, I hate to say it. It is a demon of some sort that made these gouges." Diaval shifts his hands and uses his claws to mimic what the attacker had done. The distance is almost correct except for the middle finger.

"Do that again. Just stop when your claws touch." Diaval does as I ask and then we see it. The middle finger is longer by a lot from the other fingers.

"So it must be a humanoid demon, or one that has taken over a human body and distorted it." Diaval shifts his hand back and looks around, studying things closer. A tuft of fur is stuck in the rail leading up to the porch. "Look…"

"Shit … Is that what I think it is?" The sinking feeling of dread fills me. It's the same fur the wendigo had that was chasing Feray's wolf.

"It is…" Diaval stares at it, then back at Easton. "Is it the same one? Besides Feray, you got the best look at it." Easton's chick wiggles its way out of my shirt and glides to the rail and hops up it, getting closer to the fur.

His small bird head flips left and right, tilting as it studies the fur. Suddenly, he picks his head up and stares at Diaval. "He says no. This fur is different and darker. The fur was from a bear, the one he torched was from a cougar." Diaval extends his arm out and Easton hops on and climbs up onto his shoulder. "Speed versus strength. Which means the one that went on the rampage here still exists."

"Shit, she's out there…" I turn to leave and Diaval wraps a hand around my wrist, stopping me. A deep growl escapes my lips as I bare my teeth at him. My bear wants its mate in his line of sight now and Diaval is standing in the way.

"She's riding a thirty-foot-long basilisk with stone gaze and venom. I think she's as safe as she's going to get unless she was on my dragon's back." His irritated tone grates on my nerves. It's as if he expects me and my bear to not get overprotective of our mate.

"Let's agree on a few things here…" Diaval releases my wrist and I take a deep breath. "Feray has probably been hunted since before birth." Both ancients nod along, agreeing so far. "If we're correct, whoever is doing it has a lot of money or power."

"Or both, and don't forget connections to someone willing to work in the dark arts and necromancy." Easton squawks in response. "No, it's not my ex. The attacks, especially since this one happened long before she knew I took Feray as a mate."

"To what end would someone hunt a Luna and Alpha to this point?" Shrugging my shoulders, I don't understand what there is to gain by their deaths.

"They weren't ordinary. If they are who we suspect, Feray is the last true Luna. The last that can unite all the packs as one." Diaval says and lowers his head. "The alpha's gift is lost because he didn't have anyone to pass it to before his death."

"You think they're dead?" I look at the state the house is in, then back at Diaval.

He reaches out and tugs me closer to the stairs and angles me to see inside what's left of the house. At the foot of the stairs, the white of a skull can be seen sticking out from under a burned board. The fire didn't burn anything apparently. "What it looks like is that someone burned this place, probably to hide the bodies. Or it was done to bury them. Running on the assumption that maybe Fi's parents knew Feray's and…"

"That's how they ended up with a wolf being raised as a witch." I bit my bottom lip, swallowing that revelation.

"It's possible. But we don't know. We don't want to deliver a false narrative to our mate. It is only a theory—one with a sound basis—but conjecture nonetheless." Diaval says as he walks away from the house. "They should be back soon. We will do whatever Feray wants. Whatever she needs us to be, we will be it." Diaval says before walking off with Easton on his shoulder.

For being a grumpy bastard, this is the most selfless thing I have seen the ancient do. I stare back at the skull and wonder which of her parent's skull it is. Shaking my head, I walk back towards where we had set up camp for the investigation. My stomach is in knots thinking about what this discovery is going to do to our mate.

I ponder what I can do to lessen the impact of finding at least one skeleton. There's no right answer for this in any of the scenarios I've run through my head. They all end with my mate in tears and either a mess or on a rampage. Neither will be pleasant to deal with, one will be more manageable than the alternative.

CHAPTER 35
FERAY

Riding on the back of my mate's basilisk is an exhilarating experience. The rush of wind against my face and the rhythmic sound of his scales moving through the leaves is soothing. His giant creature navigates effortlessly through the dense forest, using its colossal tail to push off trees. The brush of scales against the foliage is a much-needed distraction. Yet, beneath the surface of this momentary liberation, a disquieting undercurrent tugs at my senses.

Deep in the pit of my stomach, a persistent unease lingers, fueled by the sense that something is amiss with Torben. His usually steadfast demeanor is marred by a subtle tension, a silent burden that he carries. The unspoken weight of his emotions hangs in the bond, and my mind races to decipher the cause. It's clear he's grappling with something, and the ominous possibilities play out in my mind. It sends a chill up my spine, wondering what could have caused such a shift with my usually unflappable mate.

As Khal glides through the forest, my thoughts spiral into the worst-case scenario. Maybe they stumbled upon something unsettling while I was away. Fear creeps in, and I can't help but entertain the darkest possibility—that my parents for reasons unknown simply didn't want me. The prospect lingers like a shadow, casting a dark cloud over the otherwise liberating ride. If they gave me away, why not to another wolf family? Giving me to Fi's family doesn't make sense, unless the needing to hide me angle is true. Maybe it's not that they didn't want me, maybe it was for my safety?

Lost in my thoughts, I become a passive observer during the hunt. Khal's efficient strike, using his tail spike to kill a deer, goes barely by me. The emotional turbulence within me has momentarily eclipsed the primal instincts required for the hunt. Our time in the forest is usually more enjoyable, but this time it didn't distract me the way it usually does. Torben is a maelstrom of emotions distracting me. Diaval has almost shut the bond down to the point I barely feel him. Easton is focused on being hungry, not letting anything else infiltrate his thoughts. They definitely found something, and they don't know how to tell me they did. It was probably an accident.

The hunt that was supposed to be as freeing as it is productive has taken a dark turn. I feel Torben's concern is growing, and other warring emotions within in. Unlike Easton and Diaval, he is not practiced in shutting down his emotions. It feels like a massive storm is churning in his chest. Almost like he is one step away from losing it all.

"We need to go back Khal ... Something's happened." Before his basilisk can turn, I leap off and shift midair. My paws hit the soft soil and I take off running. I feel like the world around me is turning into a blur. Every fiber of my being is burning from exertion as I fly over the earth. Each step feels charged, propelling me forward like a white comet streaking towards its destination.

All I can think of is that my mate needs me. The weight of their discovery feels like a fallen tree resting over his heart. I blow past Diaval, and he whips around to watch me. It looks like he was moving in slow motion to me. Torben turns slowly just in time to catch me as I leap into his arms. I shift as his arms band around me, and we fall to the ground further away from where we impacted.

We roll for several moments, coming to a stop only because of a tree stopping us. "Little wolf, are you okay?" He searches me even though he took the brunt of the impact.

"I'm fine Tor, I was worried about you, so I got back here as fast as my paws could carry me." I smile, looking down at him, proud of myself and how fast I moved.

"Do you realize how much ground you covered and how fast you were moving?" Diaval states as he offers me a hand to help me stand up.

"No?" I look around and see the disturbed ground from the path I took.

"Feray, you moved as fast as a car driving at about sixty miles an hour. It took you less than five minutes to get from where Khal took you to back here." Diaval strokes his chin and raises his brow. "The bond worked as navigation for you. Guiding you back here in an instant when you let your instincts take over." He looks around the forest, then back at me again. "All I saw was a white blur going past me. You barely disturbed the soil under your feet." He nods as if having a conversation with himself.

"Torben's upset. I had to come back." I look over at my bear mate as he rubs the back of his neck, looking away.

"As much as I was against the idea, you need to see what we found by accident." Diaval says before leading the way back towards the remains of the house.

Torben pulls me against his side and tucks me under his arm. The heat radiating from his body soaks into me, and I slowly relax. "What we are about to show you will change everything." He presses his lips to the crown of my head and lingers there.

I brace myself for whatever it is. I know it's going to be really bad by the way he's acting. Diaval steps up what's left of the staircase leading into the house. Each board protesting under his weight. Looking around, I notice that most of the house has been destroyed by fire and time, but there're sections still left standing.

A small ornate box catches my attention by what looks to be the fireplace, and I move away from Torben. Within the box on top of crushed blue velvet, two amulets like the one I had worn sit. Hesitantly, I reach out and touch them. My hand trembles, recognizing the power in the gem. "Mine was like this … The exact same one, just smaller." Staring at them side by side, a great weight falls over my heart. My parents were being hunted and hid their wolves to not be found. If that's true … Why did they take their amulets off?

"Yours?" Diaval steps closer, looking at the amulets.

"Yes, until the night of the ascension, I wore one exactly like this. Before the ascension, I didn't have a wolf, or so I thought." A soft, bittersweet laugh escapes my lips. "Torben taught me how to shift and hunt." I turn my gaze to him fondly, grateful he was there for me when I needed him most.

"So a witch bound your wolf, then?" He glances from the amulets, then back to me.

"I can only guess seeing these my parents needed to hide. Can't hunt a wolf, you can't find it or sense it." I stroke my finger over the stone and my wolf growls in my head. "I can only imagine the hell my parents' wolves gave them. Mine doesn't like me touching the stone." Closing the box for now, I hand it off to Torben as I walk around the room, looking at what's left of the little trinkets.

I turn towards the stairs, and that's when I see it. The white of a skull sticking out from under boards. A deep growl escapes my lips as my hands shift. Using my claws, I rip at the wood until I uncover the skeleton. Deep grooves are cut across the skull where the face should be. The finger bones all bear the same deep groves, as if held up in defense.

"By looking at the hip bones, Easton says this body is male." Diaval says, looking at the phoenix on his shoulder.

Nodding, I keep examining the area. A pocket watch is all that is left near the bones. *Claridon Jökull.* Is inscribed on the lid of the pocket watch. "This is my dad..." I say with certainty. All the records point to him. Here he is years dead, and I still don't know why.

"Why did they have so many different names for you?" Diaval muses as he looks around.

"Thyra they put down as dead on the records here. Maybe Feray was the next name for her to assume for their next move. That is, if we base it off of the trunks being packed." Torben offers as he watches me gathering up my father's bones on a cloth. "What are you doing, little wolf?" He crouches down and hands me several bones.

"I'm going to ask Easton to cremate him. If we find my mom too, then I'll add her bones to the pile so we can lay them to rest." I'm numb, if I'm being honest with myself. I want to cry and rage, but at what or who?

"What did I miss?" I hear Khal's voice behind me and see Diaval move quickly to catch him up.

Easton glides over and stands close by, watching me work. "I want to finish searching the house, then leave. We'll cremate my parents before we hit the tundra." When I have all the bones stacked, I tie the cloth shut and stand up with it.

I offer my forearm to Easton, and he flies up and lands on it. Torben takes the bones from me as I wander around what's left of the downstairs. Pots and pans remain on the stove as if making dinner. Bowls and utensils are in the sink, I'm guessing, waiting to be washed. The guys remain silent as I explore the downstairs.

I'm starting to piece together the final hours of my parents' lives. It appears they were preparing a meal, maybe their last one, before departure. Turning my head quickly, I look back towards the front door and I can almost imagine a dark being ripping the door to pieces before it entered the house.

"Where would I send my mate with a baby to be safe?" I say out loud as I move to stand where we found my father's bones.

"What are you doing, precious?" Khal moves towards me, and I can imagine him as the beast approaching.

"She's working through the scene. We found what we can only assume to be her father's bones at the foot of the stairs." Diaval informs Khal.

Where would I send my mate and baby? I say to myself and look up the stairs. "Dad sent mom up the stairs. He stayed behind to hold the beast off. He made his last stand here." I point to the floor beneath my feet. Turning slowly, I go to head up the stairs and Torben stops me.

"I'm not stopping you." He says quickly. "Let me come with you. We don't know what we may find up there." I nod agreeing with him. To be honest, I'm almost afraid of what's at the top of the stairs.

Each step up the flight of stairs, my feet feel to be made of lead. As much as I want the answers to what happened. Or even why it happened. I know I'll never get them. Closure is all that I will get out of this leg of the trip. Dad died protecting me and mom. Did mom live? I don't know. As we near the top of the stairs to what is left of the second floor, I have a sinking feeling we are about to find out.

Torben stops me, and Easton goes flying down the hallway ahead of us. Diaval moves alongside me and gives me a gentle nod. They know something. Deep gouges from claws mar the walls as if whatever it was dragged its claws to frighten my mother.

I poke my head into each room on the way down the hallway. One room that was scorched by fire appears to have been my parents' room. A large metal bed frame sits under the missing ceiling. Leaves and other pieces of debris litter the floor. A heap of what I can guess was the bed sits in the middle of the frame. Nothing to see here.

Turning back down the hall, there's but one room left and Easton comes out squawking, using his wings to stop me. "Maybe I should go first..." Diaval offers, and I nod. Easton let him pass and I stand and wait. I can only imagine what he found that made him stop me.

CHAPTER 36

DIAVAL

Don't let her come down here ... Easton keeps yelling in my head. You need to fix it before she comes in.

I thought he was irritating before...

It's when I step into the room that I understand his panic. Her mother's skull is stuck on the end of a post of the baby's crib. The skeleton is splayed out as if crucified. "Bloody fucking hell." *A little warning would have been nice, crispy.* I fire at Easton through our mythic bond.

Doing the best that I can, I rearrange the crime scene so that it's not so horrific for her to see. I remove all evidence of her having been impaled or crucified. The room is a war zone, and you can tell the luna put up a hell of a fight and probably outlasted the alpha. A cornered mother fights her hardest when her baby is nearby.

With that thought in mind, I look around. In the closet appears to be a place where she could have hidden the baby. Maybe she did hide her? Maybe Fiadh's parents were due for a visit and found the scene. They found Thyra, renamed her similar to their daughter, and ran. That's the most palatable version I can come up with.

The big questions that linger are why would the alpha and luna run, and why were they being hunted? Who would benefit from the tundra being in chaos? There are two wolves that hold seats of power on the council or in the library. Neither of them has half the strength that my mate has. Hell, she doesn't know about half the strength she has.

The hidey hole in the closet's bottom was brilliant of her father. From what I remember of the alpha, he was a master woodworker, and he probably constructed this as a failsafe for his daughter. It's wide enough and deep enough to hide a toddler if needed.

Shaking my head, I look around, thinking about the fear that must have coursed through the luna in her final moments of life. She knew this was going to be her last battle. She died protecting her daughter. It's the greatest honor for any parent. The survival of our young is of the utmost importance.

When I am positive the room won't add any unneeded trauma to my mate, I call for everyone to enter. Feray enters first and I can watch her nose working overtime. Every twitch and sudden turn of her head makes me study where she's looking.

"It was one of those things..." she states as she stares at a dried bloody hoof print. *Fucking hell, I didn't see that.*

Splaying her hand wide, she swipes at the wall where the claw marks are then turns. There's a deadness in her gaze, as if she's looking right through me. Her fingers trace the edge of the crib. On the headboard, her name is painted. Thyra Feray Jökull. She reaches out and touches her name and runs her fingertips over the letters.

I step into her personal space and hug her from behind. "What do you need of me, my eternal? Name it, it's yours." I kiss her temple again and her frame remains rigid.

"I want them to burn." Her voice rings hollow. But her desire for retribution makes my dragon pay attention.

Moving quickly, I kneel before my mate and take her hands in mine, staring up at her. "Who? Who do you want to burn?" I give her hands a squeeze as I watch her gaze fall to her mother's skeleton.

"The ones that stole them from me." A growl escapes her lips that makes the hair on the back of my neck stand on end. Her canines are descended as she grits her teeth staring at me. The full fury of her wolf blazes in her eyes. She's on the verge of using her alpha bark and doesn't know it. Honestly, I don't know if because of our bond I can resist the command.

"My eternal, I will torch the entire valley and mountains if I thought it would help. For now, let's lay your parents to rest and salvage what we can. We can hunt for those responsible after we're done." I slowly stand and draw her into my arms. She's trembling and I'm not sure if it's from rage or pain. Either can be deadly with her right now.

"Okay…" she says against my chest just before the sobbing begins.

Torben motions for me to tighten my grip on her and hold her tighter. I adjust my grip and the sobs turn to wails and I can feel the pain bleeding out of her. She cries until there's no noise, just shudders of her body. My dragon croons to her, his rumble settling something in her.

Easton lands on the rail nearby and uses his beak under her elbow to get her attention. "Fuck, I need to feed you." She uses her sleeves and swipes at her eyes.

"That can wait. Finish what you need to here first. We'll go back to the alpha house when you're done, then plan our next move." I kiss the crown of her head and release her.

Feray moves around the room looking at everything, including the hiding place in the closet. She finds a small bear and a pacifier in the clothes in the closet. Carefully, she pulls out each piece of clothing and looks at it. "They must have tried hiding me in their clothing." She muses, and Khal kneels alongside her.

"I can only guess they used their scents to keep you calm and quiet in your hiding place." He shows her how the lid works, closing the hiding spot. Feray nods along, listening to Khal, and it's unnerving to me watching how detached she is.

"She's doing better than I anticipated," Torben mentions as he watches Feray and Khal dig through the closet.

Slowly, I turn to look at him. "She almost used her alpha bark on me to burn them to the ground." I enunciate every word so that the gravity of the situation sinks. "I think her parents unconsciously willed their daughter both of their powers."

"What if they did it on purpose? What if whatever is after them, they believe she needs the power?" It's now that I start to truly look around. The destruction, and how long the Luna must have held on.

"Worse..." I pull Torben out of the room, and Easton follows, gliding to land on his shoulder. "Hear me out. Dad wills his mate his power to help her protect their daughter." I motion to the bottom of the stairs and then to where we found the luna. "Mom, knowing deep in her soul, her daughter would be hunted forever, willed her their combined powers." Quickly, I glance over my shoulder to the room, making sure she hasn't followed us.

"Then that means she holds the alpha's and luna's powers." Torben says as he glances back at the doorway and then back at me. "We need an alpha we can trust to help train her."

Shaking my head, I look down at the floor. "The three of us will have to do it. Khal is a lover, not a fighter. For once, I would love to have his twin here to piss her off so we can safely see what she's capable of."

Torben's large hand rests on my shoulder, and he nods. "I can teach her to control the rage." He nods his head before turning back to the room our mate is in.

"We're going to be stuck with the heavy lifting on the healing and alpha bark lessons." I look at Easton as he flies over and lands on my shoulder.

I walk us back into the room, and Feray is finishing wrapping her mother's bones up. Her eyes lock with mine and they are all wolf. "We need to feed Easton and lay my parents to rest. They've waited long enough." She takes the bone filled cloth and walks past me, heading towards the stairs.

"What did I miss?"

Khal holds several items to the room in his arms. "She knows her mother died saving her. She figured out that the answers she seeks are in the tundra somewhere." He pulls out a map from the belongings. Along the margin is a history of which alpha and which luna came from what town. Hundreds of years of wolf history were written down. Her mom came from Crescent Valley, her father from Dunnum.

Looking down the list of names, I remember most of them. Some of them were righteous leaders, others were borderline mad with power. "They should match up with the names on her family tree somewhere." Khal says as he walks down the hallway following Feray out of the house.

Easton and I bring up the rear and come outside to find Feray shifted, digging in the middle of the yard. Torben's bear is using its massive paws to move the soil she's kicking out of the hole. "She's making quick work of the yard." I say more to myself than anything else.

"This isn't how we wanted her to find her parents." Khal says as he stands there holding the bags of bones. "The only bright side is that she knows what happened to them instead of never finding them." He stares down at the pile of Feray's and Torben's clothing. The box holding the amulets rests on the top as if placed there reverently.

"I want to know who made the amulets." Glancing away from the box, I see a very naked Feray walking over towards us.

"I'm going to send them to Fi. Maybe she can sense who made them." Feray gets dressed and takes the bones from Khal and walks over to the pit she made. Torben's bear is dropping pieces of the house into the pit to burn. When Feray approaches the hole, she leaps down and lays the bags how she wants them. Torben leans down, lowering his head for her to use to get out.

"Easton." Feray raises a hand, and he flies to her. "Torch them. Send them to the afterlife." He nods his head, then rises off of her and ignites. Gone are the dull plumes of his peacock-like form. Every feather burns as bright as the sun as he hovers over the pile. A cone of what looks like pure magma comes out of his beak, burning everything on contact.

Feray's dead stare concerns me. Something within her has snapped and I don't think there's a way to go back to how things were. My innocent sweet mate is forever changed, having seen how her parents died. When Easton is satisfied with how the fire is burning, he extinguishes his flames and lands on Feray's arm again. She walks away with him as if nothing has happened and starts feeding him the venison that Khal brought back.

Feray lays curled up with her head on my lap, flaming locks fanned out in all directions. If I were to suspect anyone of being a phoenix, it would have been her with her hair color. Sometime while Feray sleeps, Easton regains his human form and starts working with Khal on the items that Feray retrieved.

Easton comes over and sits down beside me, showing me the map and the filled in names on Feray's family tree. As I had suspected, she is the last true born luna. What will this mean for the sisters? Feray's place is on the throne in the Crescent Valley. The witch will end up being the Queen alongside Revelin when he ascends.

Feray slowly rouses from her sleep, and she rubs her eyes, staring at Easton. "You're back!" She turns and lunges at him, tackling him to the ground, covering him in kisses. Her wolf is making happy sounds in the back of her throat.

"Thanks to you, my flame." He kisses her back and hugs her to him.

"That was probably one of your faster resurrections. Good job, old friend." Smirking, I help him sit up.

"What do you mean?" Feray wraps her arms protectively around Easton, holding him to her ample chest.

"What he means is sometimes it takes me a month to return to normal. You and Khal kept me fed with pure protein, so it was easier to grow faster and regenerate." Easton smiles and kisses her cheek.

"Oh ok..." Feray looks over at Torben as he stands by the pit watching everything burn.

"The fire may attract unwanted attention." I mention as I stand up and watch the woods.

Feray frees herself of Easton's grasp and looks around. "Let them come. I'm done running and hiding." The steel in her voice makes my dragon perk up. He's watching and listening to her intently. "Ro, I need you." Feray calls for the pixie that looks like a throwback to the punk era of the eighties.

"Oooh, something changed..." she says as she manifests on Feray's palm.

Before Feray can make the motion, I pick up the box containing the amulets and open it for her. How did I know that's what she wanted?

Feray reaches in and takes one amulet out and offers it to Ro. "Take this directly to the prince. I want to know who made these. If they are still living, I want to know why they were made and who contracted them."

Ro takes the amulet from Feray and almost looks concerned. "You don't want me to give it to your sister?"

"No, it's safer if she's not involved. The prince has armies he can command to keep himself safe. My sister has a penchant for getting into fights or finding trouble. If she asks, tell her I said to do it." Feray keeping something from Fiadh is unusual, but her assessment of her sister is spot on. Her sister would blindly go to war if she thought it would help or save Feray.

"As you wish…" Ro looks over at me as if to help her.

"Oh no little one, I will not cross my mate. Do as she asks, seek out the Prince." Turning my gaze skyward, I study the moon phase. "The full moon is in three days' time. We will wait till then before moving on." I look back at Ro before she hugs the amulet to her chest and vanishes from sight.

"What happens on the full moon?" Feray moves to stand before me, her lithe hands slide under my suit jacket to rest over my hips.

"The hidden pass to Dunnum becomes visible at midnight to any wolf seeking to find it." Bending down, I press my lips to her forehead. We can be walking into the biggest trap in the history of traps. Or it will be a winter wonderland that Feray will find all the answers she's ever needed and then some. Hopefully, there's family left alive for her to meet that's worth having, so she's not so alone. A wolf needs its pack as much as the pack needs its luna. As much as the guys and I try, we can never do as a pack can do for her. We can't hunt like she does or move as fast as she can.

Our future rests in my arms with her head on my chest, listening to the steady beating of my heart. All the years of my existence, I have never dreaded the moon changing its phase as much as I do now. Traversing the cavern into the arctic wolf territory will not be without its perils. The tundra when we reach the Crescent Valley will render mine and Khal's shifted forms useless. It will be far too cold for us to shift if we are needed.

Torben and I have already had this discussion at great length. His and Feray's shifts are meant for the extreme weather. Though I am concerned he will want to hibernate. He says being mated to Feray has destroyed that drive, that somehow her wolf is keeping his bear awake.

There's more to our mate than meets the eye. I, for one, cannot wait to see all that she is to become.

BONUS SCENE:

-EASTON'S POV-

As much as I am not fond of the idea, Feray learning to fight is a necessary evil. Torben has shifted, and he has been going head-to-head with our mate for almost an hour. She dodges his swipes with almost a practiced ease. Now that I think about it, he telegraphs his moves before he makes them.

"Khal shift, and get into the mix. She needs a harder opponent." I yell, and Torben backs away.

"What do you mean, she needs a harder opponent?" Diaval asks as he gets closer.

"Torben is telegraphing his moves before he makes them. At least with the basilisk he can't telegraph. His scales hide his muscle movements." I explain my reasoning. Diaval turns to watch Feray lunging and striking Khal more ruthlessly than she was Torben.

"I see what you mean. With his armor, she's not afraid to attack." I'm so focused on Diaval it's not until Torben approaches that I notice it's too quiet.

Slowly we turn and see Feray in a staring contest with Khal's basilisk. Her eyes are glowing a brilliant gold and suddenly his shift releases his human form. He falls on his ass and stares at her. "How did you do that?"

"How did she do what?" We jog over and stare at him, then over at Feray's wolf as the glow recedes from her eyes.

"She forced my shift. All I heard in my head was the word *shift* and I did." He looks from our mate, then back up at me as Torben helps him to stand.

"That is an alpha power, not a luna one." It seems our theory of her inheriting both parents' powers is accurate.

"Feray? Can you force Torben to shift into his bear?" Diaval asks her, and she turns to look at Torben. The same glow we saw before illuminates her eyes as she stares at him. Within seconds, his bear rips free of his body and shakes its head.

"Shit..." I stare at Diaval, and he has the same look of shock and concern on his face as I do.

"If she can do that, what else can she do?" Khal questions as he moves to Feray's side.

Diaval and I look at each other, sharing memories of what the Alphas and Lunas of the past were capable of. "Just about anything she puts her mind to." I break eye contact with Diaval before I move to kneel before Feray's wolf.

I stare deep into my mate's eyes as the feather on her wolf's head ignites.

Did I do something wrong? I hear her voice softly question.

"No, not at all. You did everything perfectly." Her eyes flair as she stares at me and her tail wags quickly.

You can hear me?

"Of course, I can." Smiling, I touch her feather. "Our bond allows it. You making the attempt established the connection. Moving forward, you should be able to do this any time you wish." I caress her cheek, happy that she has yet another way to communicate.

Can Diaval hear me too? She turns her head expectantly, with her tail still wagging.

"Of course, I can. You have my scale." He tilts his head, looking down the bridge of his nose at her.

You know I don't like it when you do that. Come down here. It feels almost like a punch to the gut when she says it and Diaval falls to his knees before her.

"What just happened? What are we missing?" Khal says looking between Diaval and I.

"Because of our scale and feather, apparently, we can mind speak with Feray. She didn't like the look Diaval gave her and drove him to his knees." I shrug my shoulders after explaining it. I'm honestly not sure how to navigate the changes.

"So what you're saying is she used her alpha bark on Diaval and forced him to drop to his knees." Torben says as he pulls the shirt over his head.

"The short version, yes?" I'm still questioning the whole thing myself.

Can you hear me? Feray walks past Diaval to stand before Torben, waiting to see if he responds.

"What do you need, little wolf?" He smiles and bends down to run his fingers through her fur.

"He can't hear you." I say sadly as I look at Torben.

"She said something to me? What did she say?" His eyes darted from Feray to me.

"She asked if you could hear her." I shrug my shoulders.

"Oh ... No little wolf, I can't hear you." He looks genuinely sad.

"It's an ancient thing, or a mythic thing, I believe. Our shifts differ from yours, and for whatever reason, she cannot connect to yours like she does ours." I'm running on the assumption that because of the scale and feather she can mind speak like we do.

Her wolf turns expectantly and stares up at Khal and he tilts his head, looking at her. "If you're saying anything I can't hear you, Precious." Her tail lowers, and she shifts back.

Torben immediately throws his button down over her shoulders. "You did really good today." He affectionately kisses her cheek and smiles at her before walking away to grab her clothing.

"So there's a theory Diaval, and I have been kicking around and we want to share it with everyone." I glance at the others as Diaval comes to stand beside me.

"What is it?" Feray asks as Torben hands her the outfit she had on earlier.

"Okay, so think back to inside the house. We found your dad at the foot of the stairs." I try something and create the image of what we suspect happened. A wendigo enters the house and her mother is sent upstairs like she suspected. Her father, the alpha, fights the beast as long as he can. After sustaining the blow to the face, he wills his power to her mother.

The Luna, feeling the surge of power, knows her mate fell in battle. Rushing to the closet, she tucks Feray into their laundry and down into the hiding spot and closes the closet door. She battles far longer than her mate, using Alpha and Luna's powers on it. Eventually she falls as well and before she dies, wills both sets of powers to Feray.

I watch my mate's eyes flicker as she takes in the scene I had shown her. Diaval while I was showing Feray what had happened was explaining it to the others.

My flame bites her bottom lip and nods tersely. "I was right." She says as she glances over her shoulder at what's left of the house.

"You were." Reaching out, I cup her shoulder and stare deeply into her eyes. "Having both sets of powers is a gift. Unlike your mom, you have more than a few seconds to figure out how to use them effectively."

"We are going to help train you." Diaval interjects.

"As an alpha in my sleuth, I can help with the alpha powers." Torben offers.

"I can help with the mind control powers." Khal says with a shy smile. I always suspected basilisks could turn others into puppets or draw secrets out of people.

"Dominance and intimidation are my department, my eternal," Diaval says, this time not cocking his head like he usually does.

"I can teach you how to heal others." Smiling, I offer my mate my hand and she accepts it with a smile.

With a soft nod and a squeeze of my hand, she releases me and goes to hug everyone before dragging Khal over by the funeral pyre. He shifts, and she climbs up and into his coils. There's a lot for her to process. I just hope she realizes she can lean on all of us for support.

Up next Waxing Gibbous. Time for you to catch up with Fiadh and her guys.

Waxing Gibbous

LOCATION GUIDE

Beyond here you will find all of the names of the places that Feray and the guys visit including maps.

LOCATION GUIDE

Location Guide:

- **<u>Briarvale:</u>** A town with mixed species and several districts as follows.

1. Night District: Vampires, demons, ect

2. Witch District

3. Magical District: other magic users that don't fall under witch or elven.

4. Elven District

5. Shifter District

6. Dwarven District

7. Entertainment District

8. Briarvale General Hospital

9. Cocktails and Screams

- **<u>Norberg:</u>** Small deadly town to the west of Briarvale. Inhabitants are mostly basilisks, and other venomous creatures.

- **<u>Thornford:</u>** Mixed species town filled with artisans and other creatives.

- **<u>Vasserdell</u>**: The last known dragon stronghold.

- **<u>Blackmoor:</u>** Wolf stronghold primary coat colors of black, gray, timber wolf pattern.

- **<u>Silver Falls:</u>** Desolate wolven town just south of the arctic. Coat colors used to include variations of dark colors mixed with white.

- **<u>Redshale:</u>** Mixed species town primarily big cat shifters and some rare shifters.

- **<u>Moors Farm:</u>** Farm that produces a bulk of the grains, fruits and vegetables for the different restaurants and bars. (Taken over by the basilisks to grow the ingredients for their drug trade.)

- **<u>Sceleon HQ:</u>** Basilisk stronghold and corporate HQ for all of the darker dealings. Drugs, murder etc. all are controlled by the HQ.

- **<u>Dunnum:</u>** Wolf stronghold sheltered by a large mountain range. Difficult to get to for other species without a wolf with them. Secret entrance hidden until midnight on the night of a full moon can only be seen by a wolf. Primary coat color white with gray or black markings. Alpha's most of the time come from this town.

- **<u>Crescent Valley:</u>** Arctic Wolf stronghold. The wolves here do not migrate, and their coat color changes with the season. Luna's are born here, last known location for birthing what is called a true Luna. More hidden than Dunnum, one final puzzle to solve to gain entrance to the wolven.

DUNNUM
CRESCENT VA
SILVER FALLS
MOORS FARM
BLACKMOOR
THORNFORD
VASSERDELL

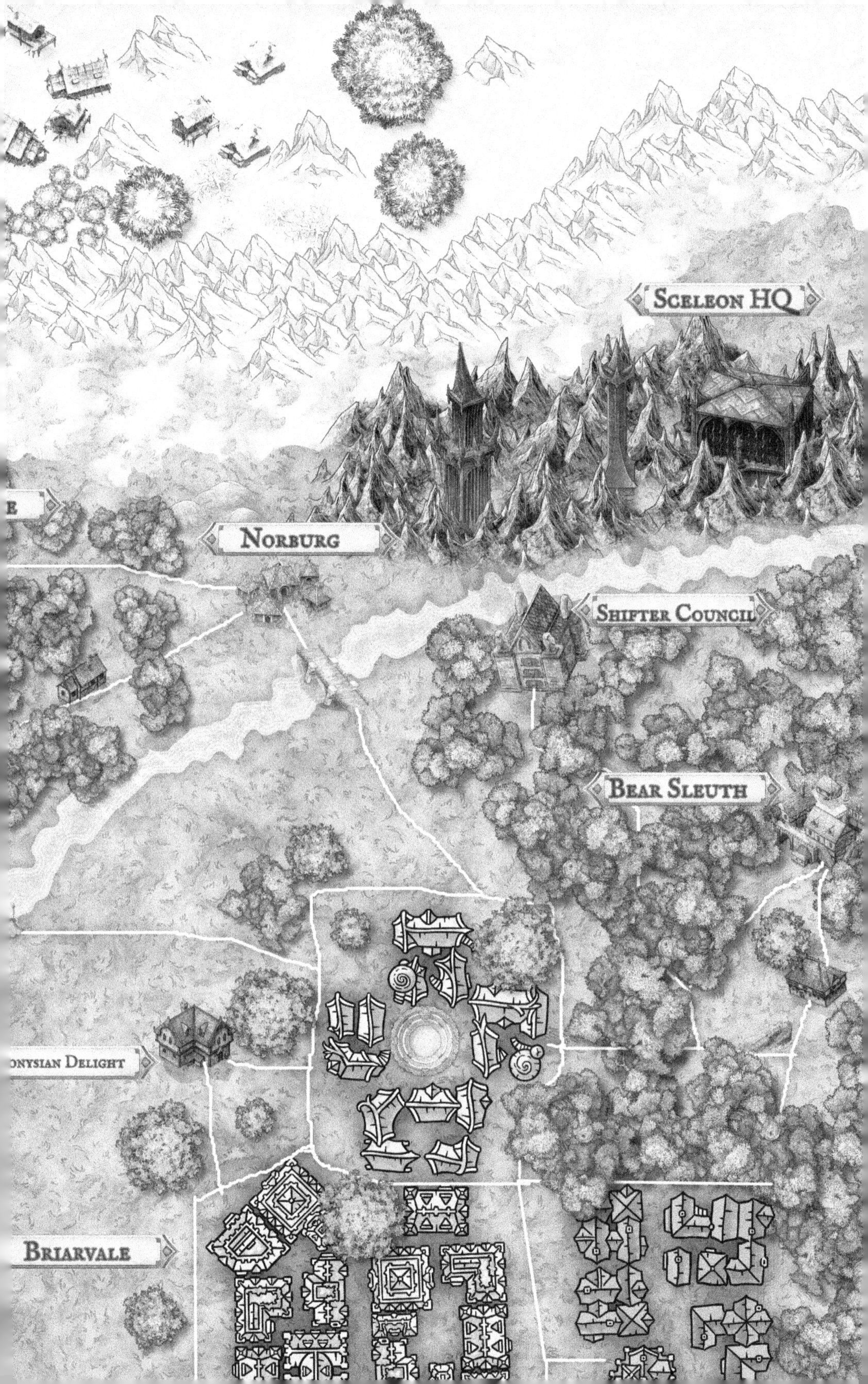

Sceleon HQ
Norburg
Shifter Council
Bear Sleuth
onysian Delight
Briarvale

Silver Falls

Dunnum
Crescent Valley

Skarde Friberg - Dunnum

Gisli Krum - Crescent Valley

Arvid Aven- Dunnum

Wren Falkenberg - Crescent Valley

Agnar Ander - Dunnum

Jora Bielke - Crescent Valley

Arnbjorn Karsten - Dunnum

Alva Helvig - Crescent Valley

Dyri Hjorth - Dunnum

Hilda Skau- Crescent Valley

Claridon Jökull- Dunnum

Lyra Sveltson- Crescent Valley

CREATURE GUIDE

Beyond here learn about the various creatures you will run across through out the Children of the Moon world.

*The guide will expand with subsequent books.

CHAPTER 1

CREATURE GUIDE

● **Wendigo:** DEMONIC CREATURE CREATED THROUGH THE USE OF DARK / forbidden magic. Typically has horns like an elk, large hulking frame, hands are humanoid with the middle finger far longer than the rest of the fingers.

1. **Bear Wendigo**: Bulk of the creature's form is created from a bear carcass. This build is for strength and destruction.

2. **Cougar Wendigo:** The build of this creature is made from a cougar carcass. This build is slightly smaller and is built for speed and agility.

● *Power source*: Each wendigo has a different possessed creature in its chest to power the creation. Remove the body from the husk and kill it and the wendigo dies.

1. **Mage:** The ultimate battery- not only does it have the mages life force it also has the mage's connection to magic to fuel the beast.

2. **Human**: Standard battery: the strength of the human adds to the strength of the wendigo. Consider it the low-end model of species.

3. <u>Shifter:</u> This gets tricky, whichever shifter is in the chest will add to the strength of the wendigo.

4. <u>Mythic:</u> This is a weapon of mass destruction and almost impossible to kill. The same mythic that is in the chest is the one that can kill the creature and be able to withstand its assault.

● **DRAGON:** Mythic class creature, high defense and ability to wield an element. Excellent eyesight, hard scale armor. Can half or partially shift when human. There's three stages of Dragon's life. *Hatchling:* Birth to fifty years old. *Adult*: fifty years old to seven hundred years. *Wyrm:* eight hundred years old +. **Male Dragon** - Drake. **Female Dragon** - Hen.

1. <u>Skull Dragon</u> (black dragon, Abyssal Dragon): Powers of intimidation and domination. One of the largest dragon species. Weapon: Acid cloud or acid breath, highly flammable.

● **PHOENIX:** Blessed and cursed with eternal life and resurrection. Can share their lifespan only with a true mate. The only two ways a phoenix can be killed permanently is during the burning stage that the fire is put out. The second way is the death of the mate. Possesses phenomenal eyesight, other senses are just above humans.

● **BEAR:** One of the largest terrestrial predators. Three subspecies exist. Can bulk their human form with the size of their shift. Excellent sense of smell, has the strength of their shift in their human form. Can quarter shift and use their beast's strength and claws. (Boar- Male) (Sow-Female)

1. <u>Black Bear:</u> Smallest of the bear shifters Black coat mostly solitary.

2. <u>Brown Bear:</u> Largest of the bear shifters, also known for producing berserkers that are unrivaled in strength and rage. Live in sleuths and it is very common for them to live in large poly families. (One female multiple males or two females multiple males)

3. <u>Polar Bear:</u> Resident of the frozen north. We have not met them yet...

● **Wolf:** One of the widest spread shifter species in the world. There are multiple subspecies of wolves. Has the strongest sense of smell out of all of the shifters. Great eye sight day and night. Can half shift.

1. <u>Timber:</u> Most common coat color consisting of browns, white, black and cream color variations. Live more in the forest areas.

2. <u>Shadow mount:</u> Live in the mountain regions or at the base of the mountains. Coat colors Black, grays and any combination of the two.

3. <u>Pre-arctic:</u> Lives just below the mountains that separates the Arctic region from the southern region. This is the region where you start seeing larger patches of white in the wolves coats.

4. <u>Subarctic:</u> First of the snowy regions where greater than half of the year is covered in snow. The wolves' coats are greater than fifty percent white and will sometimes migrate south beyond the mountains to the warmer regions depending on the conditions.

5. <u>Arctic:</u> The most difficult terrain to survive in. Double coats, pure white in the winter then changes to a lighter version of a timber wolves coat in the summer. The arctic wolves during a

blizzard will shift to their animal and all snuggle in one den for warmth.

- **<u>Basilisk:</u>** Part of the dragon family. Can grow in excess of forty feet long with impenetrable armor scales. Possesses toxic venom, stone gaze and mind control over lesser beings. Cannot control other dragon kin.

- **<u>Fox:</u>** Sneaky little self-important bastards. Two species exist: gray and red. Both usually work in different spy networks for the demons or basilisks.

- **<u>Snow Leopard:</u>** Rarely found too far south from the snowy mountains of the north. Work in security and spy work. They live a solitary life until they have a mate and family.

- **<u>Pixie:</u>** Tiny tricksters. Most times used by the fae as messengers and can be spiteful little assholes. Tend to speak in rhymes or a pattern. Can move easily between realms and have been known to poison people that offend them.

- **<u>Unicorn:</u>** Hunted almost to extinction. Can be spotted by a faint purple star on their forehead in their human form. Lifespan or cycle unknown. They were slaughtered for the healing properties in their horns. Unknown by the murders the horns don't work when the unicorn dies.

- **<u>Vampire:</u>** The undead, created by being bitten and dying with a little of its creator's blood in its mouth. A true vampire drinks the blood of its creator after it rises and then is free of the sire bond. Allergic to sunlight and can die either by beheading or removal or stake through the heart.

1. Vampire spawn: Created by being bitten and dying with a little of its creators. Fed vermin and kept feral not being fed enough. Bound to its sire unable to refuse the command of its creator. Over

time becomes mindless, incapable of independent thought. They tend to move in packs controlled like a hive mind.

- **<u>Fae:</u>** Highly intelligent magical beings. Human-like with pointy ears and otherworldly beauty. Cannot lie but can manipulate words to hide their true intention. Highly sexual and can seduce just about anyone or anything. Royalty can move between realms at will using portals. Common Fae cannot create portals. Most wield some form of elemental or earth-based magic.

SERENITY RAYNE

A little about me!

ABOUT THE AUTHOR

Serenity Rayne spends most of her time either howling at the moon or creating cheeky crafts in her lair. Since she published the first book in the bestselling Aurora Marelup series, she's released sixteen more books while surviving being a nurse during the COVID-19 pandemic.

Serenity writes strong women who find their way in the world through blood and fire, learning to love and trust the men who adore them. Her books also feature positive LGBTQ representation, loss, and all the emotions that transcend species. Though her catalog has been focused on paranormal why choose and horror, she is now branching out to write contemporary why choose as well. She lives on a farm with dogs, chickens, peacocks, a one-eyed horse, and her son, who is way more like her than he wants to admit.

SIGNED BOOKS AND MERCH

www.SerenityRayneRomance.com

This is the only place to get official Serenity Rayne Merchandise as well as book swag and signed books.

FOLLOW SERENITY EVERYWHERE:

Facebook: Serenity Rayne

Readers Group

Twitter: Author Serenity Rayne

Instagram: Author Serenity Rayne

Goodreads: Serenity Rayne

BookBub: Serenity Rayne

Amazon: Serenity Rayne

Website - https://serenityrayneromance.com/

JOIN MY PACK UPDATES!

Bi-weekly updates on new releases, snippets from works in progress and contests. Click the link and join in on the pack fun!

https://manage.kmail-lists.com/subscriptions/subscribe?a=RHsgWs&g=R9Jcnd

ALSO BY SERENITY RAYNE

Pre-orders:

Embraced By the Alpha Pack

Children of the Moon - Full Moon

The Aurora Marelup Omnibus 5 year special edition

Shifters:

Claimed by the Alpha Pack

Children of the Moon: New Moon Rising

Children of the Moon - Waxing Crescent

Her Elemental Mates

The Aurora Marelup Saga

Ascend

Hunt

Fight

Attack

Welcome Home

Klaus Christmas

Princess Lost

Destiny Found

Tiamat

The Dark Angel Chronicles:

Discovered

Innate

Balance

Destroyer

Daughters of the Destroyer - Nikita

Stand alones:

Heart Shaped Box

Blood Moon Pack

Once Upon the a Raven

www.ingramcontent.com/pod-product-compliance
Lightning Source LLC
Chambersburg PA
CBHW060632310726
48982CB00003B/753